UNDER THE EMBER STAR

Ginn Hollis was fourteen when her father's mysteri-
ous death left her alone on the planet Kelmer. She's
grown up since then; she's hardened. Kelmer is a harsh
world, an old world. Its people are ancient, its civilization long fallen and dimly dreaming under a brown
dwarf sun the natives call the Ember Star. But now,
long dormant forces are beginning to stir on Kelmer,
forces that could destroy the planet forever...or bring
it back to life.

One being stands at the center of the turmoil. His
origins are veiled. His destiny is unclear. Everyone
wants a piece of him. Alive. Or dead. Only Ginn Hollis
can protect him from both sides. If she can save herself
first.

Borgo Press Books by CHARLES ALLEN GRAMLICH

Bitter Steel: Tales and Poems of Epic Fantasy
In the Language of Scorpions: Tales of Horror from the Inner Dark
Midnight in Rosary: Tales of Vampires and Werewolves in Crimson and Black
Under the Ember Star: A Science Fantasy Novel
Write with Fire: Thoughts on the Craft of Writing
Writing in Psychology: A Guidebook (with Y. Du Bois Irvin and Elliott D. Hammer)

THE TALERA CYCLE

Swords of Talera (Book One)
Wings Over Talera (Book Two)
Witch of Talera (Book Three)

UNDER THE EMBER STAR

A SCIENCE FANTASY NOVEL

CHARLES ALLEN GRAMLICH

THE BORGO PRESS

MMXII

UNDER THE EMBER STAR

DEDICATION

To My Northshore Writing Friends:

Cheryl, Linda, D'Wanna, Laurie, Al B., Al O.,
Sandra, Eve, Mignon, Barbara, Alice, Kenny,
Jim, Paula, Michael, Mike, Isabella, Sarah;

And with Special Thanks

To Leigh Brackett and C. L. Moore,

Who wrote this stuff better than I ever could.

AUTHOR'S NOTE

I use the word "Day" with a capital "D" to refer to the four-teen-day light period on the planet Kelmer, and "Night" with a capital "N" for the fourteen-day dark period there.

CONTENTS

CHAPTER ONE

A Hot Time in Old Towne Tonight

Ginn Hollis slipped down the alley behind Red Jac's Tavern #4, her right fist folded around the butt of her blaster. Her breathing was soft; her hunt-boots made no sound.

It was the last day of Night and the world was a dim, cold place. Ginn wore a heavy jacket and insulated BDUs against the chill, and light-lenses—which resembled a pair of green wraparound sunglasses but had the opposite effect—enhanced the near darkness for her. With the lenses activated, piles of trash formed shadows against a gray background while scuttling bugs left yellow and red streaks. She stepped over a silver ribbon of spreading vomit.

Her nostrils curled. The vomit was fresh, stinking.

Sage mead. It smelled foul even when unadulterated with stomach acids. But at least whoever had heaved up a night's consumption was gone. *Back inside the bar*, she imagined.

Three rickety wooden steps took Ginn up to the rear door of Red Jac's. She paused, drawing her blaster. In the near distance she detected the ever present hum of the space port, and half the ambient light that filtered into this back alley came from the glow there. Even closer, from within the much darker settlement called Old Towne that surrounded the bar, she heard harsh laughter and someone butchering a song; she heard a scream that cut off abruptly. At the tavern's door she heard nothing. Yet the silence promised menace.

Leaning close to the door's weathered boards, she whispered.

"It's Ginn."

The menace coalesced into a sound then, a low, rumbling growl that ended in a faint huff of expelled air. Ginn's hand found the door-latch, lifted it. She eased the door back. A shadowy bulk stalked toward her; the growl repeated. A pair of slanted eyes flared green under the enhancement from her lenses. She stood very still as the dagvyre sniffed her, relaxed as it whined and licked her hand. She scratched behind its horns.

"Good dog," she murmured, though dagvyres were native to this world of Kelmer and only vaguely resembled the pets she'd known as a child on Earth.

This one was a guard beast, as many dagvyres were. Only, Ginn had taken time to get to know it, to give it something to kill the sand-fleas infesting it, to feed it over weeks as she fed it now with a chunk of dark-meat. And so, it did not consider her someone to guard against.

She strode past the animal and down a short hallway.

A locked storage room loomed on the right. A stench on the left marked the bathroom. In front of her stood the door to the main tavern area. It would be much brighter there than in this hallway, but her light-lenses would adjust automatically. She jerked open the door and stepped through.

A guard stood before her. Not a dagvyre. A man. A big one. He wasn't as ready for trouble as Ginn was. In twin, fluid movements, she thrust the barrel of her blaster into his side and with her left hand plucked *his* weapon free of its holster.

"Wha—" he started to protest, and she slashed him over the head with his own gun. He went down, and though he wasn't completely out there was no fight left in him.

The stocky bartender had some fight, some thought of it anyway. His hand streaked toward his cash register.

"Unh uh," Ginn said, jabbing the killing end of her blaster in his direction.

The man froze, then slowly placed both hands on the scarred surface of the bar where she could see them.

"Smarter than you look," Ginn said.

The bartender smiled faintly, though it didn't extend to the flat, mud-brown of his eyes.

No customers sat at the bar itself and Ginn's gaze had already taken in the tables beyond. Of the three individuals there, two were human and looked like orbit truckers long gone into their cups. Neither did more than blink at her owlishly.

The third being was an aborigine, a Kelmerian. This one was an employee of Red Jac's, a fire-gyrl as they were called. Its thorn-thin body hid behind opaque silks, with padding beneath to hint at womanly curves. A mantilla covered the hairless, oval-shaped skull, but the revealed face—except for the lack of a nose—was fine and delicate and close to human, with the lush mouth and large, thickly lashed almond eyes that many men found sexually arousing. Those eyes were glazed now. *Drugged.* Ginn looked away.

"I'm here to take delivery," Ginn said to the bartender, her voice suddenly rough.

The man frowned, as if he didn't understand, and Ginn's finger caressed lightly along the trigger of her blaster. The weapon's barrel flared red and the man jerked as a tiny pulse of heat reached out and curled around him. He knew how easily that heat could be followed by flame.

"I understand," Ginn said. "You want it to look good for your boss. But I know your boss and he's going to be pissed anyway. So you might as well save yourself some pain."

The man's lips smacked dryly as he opened them, but he didn't speak. His hand drifted again toward the register.

"Only the vial," Ginn warned. "Leave the needler you've stashed in there alone."

The man nodded, opened the register and slowly drew out a plastic sealed package about the size of a playing card. He slid it along the bar toward Ginn.

Ginn waited until the man reclosed the register, then tucked the guard's blaster behind her belt and picked up the package to slip it inside her jacket and down the front of her tight black tee.

She motioned with her own blaster for the bartender to lie on the floor beside the dazed guard. He obeyed.

"Taylesh," Ginn said, using the native word for thanks.

She then took what looked like a small button out of one pocket of her BDUs and pressed the center of it with her thumb before laying it on the bar. A faint whine grew in the air. A grid of hair-thin green lines built itself around the two men on the floor.

"This goes boom," she said for the men's benefit. "Lay there for fifteen minutes and it'll deactivate. If anyone touches it or you two get up before then, you won't have to worry about your boss being pissed."

She backed into the hallway, turned toward the exit while holstering her blaster. The dagvyre stood between her and the outside and she patted it once and started around it. It moved with a low growl to block her way. She paused. The beast looked at her, then toward the door again as if it heard a sound she could not. Dagvyres were smart; no one knew quite how smart. Was this one sending her a message? If so, it got through.

Damn!

There was no time for this. Quickly, she moved back down the hall and turned left into the single small bathroom. She almost wished her lenses didn't work quite so well. The fetor was bad enough, but to be able to see the spattered sources of the stench made her glad her stomach was empty.

Although the tavern itself had been set up inside an aboriginal building of stone, this back area had been constructed later, of desert burr-wood, and wasn't nearly as sturdy. She could escape it. She hoped.

To the right of the disgusting toilet was a small window, far too small to climb through. But the wall beneath the window was so thin her lenses detected a sheen of light bleeding through seams in the wood. She drew her blaster, thumbed the selector to wide beam. She fired, held the trigger down for just a moment.

The flaring red-orange beam hissed like a griddle spattered with water, and a large oval of wood ignited with a crackle, then disintegrated into fiery ash. Ginn ducked and plunged through the hole, left hand covering her mouth and nose to avoid breathing embers. She landed in a crouch on hard packed dirt. For a moment, she hesitated.

From the alley out back of Red Jac's, where the dagvyre had seemingly warned her of an ambush, a shout arose. And another. Two enemies at least. They would have heard her blaster. They'd be coming.

She could fight, Ginn thought. She wanted to fight. Then her mind centered on the vial she'd tucked inside her shirt. Her left hand reached to press against it, like a talisman between her breasts. She couldn't risk it being damaged.

She holstered her blaster, lunged up from her crouch into a run for home.

CHAPTER TWO

THE APPLE AND THE WORM

Ginn's mouth tasted foul. She tried to spit, found she had no saliva. Then she tried opening her eyes. One worked. A moment's rubbing got the other open too. Her head ached. Even the dim purplish sun coming through the skylight above was too bright, and the fact it was morning told her she'd slept a long time. She'd gone to Red Jac's almost fifteen standard hours before the Ember Star was due to rise out of Night for its own fourteen day reign.

Sitting up, she thrust blonde hair back from her face, let her bleary gaze take in her surroundings. She was at home, in her own bed. She'd managed to get off her lenses, jacket, boots, and blasters, but little else.

Terror stabbed at her then. *The vial!*

She spun around in her tangled sheets. *There.* Open on the bedside table. *The packet.*

She grabbed it up, breathed a sigh of relief at seeing the vial and syringe still intact inside. Greenish liquid moved viscously within, but not as much as when she'd opened the packet hours before.

"Four more doses," she muttered to herself. "Just four."

She started to return the packet to the table, thought better of it. She peeled off her sweat-stiffened black t-shirt and tossed it on the floor, then removed the vial from its packaging and used a strip of dura-tape to fix it to her chest over her sternum.

Rising on unsteady legs, she made her way to the bathroom,

had a morning pee and considered brushing her teeth. Even the thought made the bile rise and she spat it yellow into the sink. She rinsed her mouth, swallowed a cupped handful of water. Her stomach growled but there'd be no eating just yet.

Stepping free of the bathroom again, she pulled on a looser t-shirt, also black, and then gathered her holstered blaster from the floor and strapped it around her waist. Long habit bade her put on her light-lenses too. The BDUs were military surplus and were serviceable for a while yet. She sat on the edge of the bed to work boots onto her feet.

This apartment had once been the manager's second story office in a factory that produced hovercycles. The factory had closed; the manager had gone. Ginn had moved in. She had two rooms, three if you counted the tiny bathroom. There was a bigger main office and a smaller storeroom that she'd converted into her bedroom with scavenged materials. There was no running water, no electricity. She'd rigged a small recycler tank on the roof to provide water for the sink and toilet. She used her light-lenses if she needed to see in the dark. And no one knew where she lived.

"Are you awake at the last?" a voice called from what served as her front room.

On Kelmer, you didn't freeze if you wanted to live. The blaster filled Ginn's hand as she spun her bedside table to the floor and dropped behind it. The tabletop was thin burr-wood, but for just such an occasion as this she'd plated the underside with leftover plastisteel from the factory below. Even a blaster wouldn't cut it easily.

"There is no need for weapons," the voice from the other room called again. "I mean no harm to you. If I had, I would not have awaited your awakening."

The voice carried no accent, which she'd normally take to mean 'human.' But the tones were too soft, too lyrical, and impossible to type as either male or female. Maybe it wasn't human. But its logic was still unassailable. In her hurry to get the vial home, Ginn must have failed to take her usual precautions. She'd left her perimeter open and someone had walked through.

She didn't move.

"I have brought kaftee," the voice added. "I imagined you could use a cup."

Ginn cursed under her breath. She'd been stupid. Coming to her feet, she holstered her own blaster but plucked up the one she'd taken last Night from Red Jac's guard. She stepped cautiously through into the outer room.

A being muffled in aboriginal robes sat at one side of the office desk, which Ginn had pushed into the middle of the room and used as a dining table. A turban concealed the being's head. Its face was veiled, its two hands gloved. Ginn catalogued the fine weave of the dark purple robes, the thin threads of copper-like native metal twined through the fabric so that it draped artfully. The metal alone told her that her visitor had wealth. Metal was scarce on Kelmer. Local metal at least.

"I don't remember inviting you home so I'm gonna need to know who the hell you are," Ginn said. She waggled the blaster back and forth in her hand.

"I will be glad to tell you. First, will you not have a bit of kaftee?"

A gloved hand gestured to a tall, black plastic mug sitting in the middle of the desk, then pushed it a few inches closer to Ginn. The drink was capped but Ginn still smelled the deliciously potent aroma from it. She swallowed saliva that burst across her tongue but made no move to touch the mug.

Her visitor sighed, popped the lid off the mug and lifted it in both hands to its mouth. It took a long sip directly through its veil, leaving behind a thin wet line and a hint of foam on the soft material. Once again the mug was placed before Ginn. This time she picked it up, in her left hand, and held it a moment.

"Doesn't mean much if you've already taken the antidote," Ginn commented.

"Considering the vivum you have so recently consumed, I do not believe you need worry anyway."

Ginn's poker face was solidly in place. She betrayed nothing, but her mind filed away one more question about this being. Who was it? *What* was it? How had it found her? How did it know about the vivum? Most importantly, what did it want from her?

Sitting down on her side of the desk, Ginn took a long swallow of the kaftee. It tasted like faintly bitter molasses laced with creamed butter, chocolate, and caffeine. Kaftee was a native drink, made from the seed pods of a desert plant, but the name came from Earth. The first humans to taste it claimed it reminded them of coffee and tea together. Ginn didn't agree. She also didn't care. The stuff was incredibly good, and rich with nutrients. And, like coffee, it had a stimulating effect on the nervous system. Right now, *that* was a godsend.

Moving very slowly, the being across from Ginn slid one hand toward a faint bulge at its midsection, where natives often sewed pouches into their robes. Ginn watched the movement, her blaster pointed almost casually in the needed direction. The lower portion of the stranger's veil wrinkled, as if with a smile. The hand slowed even further, but dipped just inside the pouch and emerged with a crimson fruit, an apple. It, too, was placed in front of Ginn.

"All for you," the being said.

Ginn took another swallow of the kaftee, then set down the mug and plucked up the apple. She studied it for a moment, then bit and chewed. Her gaze never left her companion.

"Three hundred and fifteen solars to ship this from Earth," she said finally.

"Three twenty-five."

"So you've got money and you want me to know it. Why?"

"To hire you."

"I'm listening."

"I must make a journey. Through nomad lands. I am known among some of the tribes. Not all."

"I'm guessing, not among the tribes where you plan to travel."

"Not where I plan to finish. Also, the nomads I know cannot

accompany me there. It is taboo for them."

"Then it's likely to be *death* for you. As well as for me if I decided to be stupid enough to take the job."

"I have been there before and do not think so. Besides, there will be much vivum where we are going."

Ginn's heart stuttered; skin tightened all across her body. She was glad her clothing hid the goose bumps. She took another bite of apple to cover her reaction, chewed while her guest watched her from behind its veil.

"If you've been there before you surely don't need me," Ginn finally said.

"I did not go alone last time either."

"Then hire the same people."

"There are reasons I cannot."

Ginn rubbed her mouth with the back of her hand. "So that must mean...."

She paused as she heard a whisper of sound that she shouldn't hear. From outside.

"Who'd you bring with you right now?" she demanded suddenly.

"No one. I mean, they did not come into town."

Ginn surged to her feet, the apple dropped and forgotten, the kaftee spilling to the desk. She filled her free hand with her second blaster. Her visitor recoiled, hands going up toward its veiled face.

"Then you were followed," she snarled.

From below, in the abandoned factory, a door shished open. From the street outside came a sound like a sheet of paper tearing—a pulse weapon powering up.

Ginn hurled herself forward, one arm sweeping her robed companion with her to the floor.

The wall at her back exploded.

CHAPTER THREE

SMOKING BLASTERS

Shrapnel sleeted. Echoes hammered.

A burning flake of metal furrowed Ginn's left shoulder. She heard the sudden grunt of the being beneath her but couldn't tell if or how bad it had been hurt. Dust and ash roiled and the already dim Kelmerian sun did little to cut it.

Lurching into a crouch, Ginn hacked up some of the swirling grit, tried to draw shallow breathes to keep the rest out of her lungs. The light-lenses provided a quick catalog of what was left of her apartment. It wasn't pretty. Her roof sagged, smoldering. Half of it was gone. The remaining walls bulged outward. She wasn't living here anymore.

The floor beneath Ginn creaked, as if about to collapse. Her enemies weren't waiting on that. From below in the abandoned factory, running footsteps sounded. They'd expect her to try and escape that way—if she lived. But the stairs down would not belong to her anymore. Her options were narrowing.

"Follow or die," Ginn growled toward her strange visitor, who was sitting up now and coughing harshly.

She straightened and charged toward the gaping maw of what had been her bedroom. The bed was gone. The outside wall was gone. The wooden strakes of the floor shuddered beneath her boots. But for a moment they supported her, and then she leaped—outward. Kelmer's gravity was less than Earth's. She cleared the dust and ash, fell into the clean air beyond. Her light-lenses instantly adjusted.

Below in the dirt street sat an open hovercar. Two of Red Jac's bravos manned it. Both standing. Both laughing. One leaned casually against a pulse cannon mounted in the back of the car. He saw Ginn falling toward him, started a shout.

Ginn fired both blasters. The man's cry boiled in his throat as his head turned to slag. The second man lunged toward the wheel of the hovercar. The top half of him made it, screaming.

Ginn hit the ground in a roll and came to her feet. She leaped the side of the hovercar, landed on her boots in the passenger seat. The half-man lay on his side in the driver's area, one hand still clutching a steering wheel that was useless to him now. There was no blood, the awful wound having been cauterized by the blaster flame that made it. His eyes were open; his mouth worked around words she couldn't hear. She dropped into the seat beside him, slapped the door latch and shoved him out into the street.

The hovercar's engine was already running. She powered it into high, listening to the whine of energies building in the machine's central dynamo.

Most hovercars couldn't lift more than ten feet off the ground. She took this one up to its limit, spun it toward the wrecked apartment that had been her home only a few minutes before.

Her visitor in the native robes hadn't followed her leap. Standing wreathed in rapidly diminishing smoke, it seemed anchored to the last solid patch of floor in the destroyed bedroom. No walls surrounded it, only a few blackened beams.

"Come on!" Ginn shouted.

The being took a step forward, faded a half step back with its gloved hands clenched at its sides. Ginn thought she saw movement in the background, an assassin coming up the stairs maybe. She sent blaster flame scorching into the dimness but no answering fire returned. Maybe the movement had been just a board falling. In another few seconds it wouldn't be. The hunters were on their way.

Ginn tried to force eye contact with the entity who'd claimed a wish to hire her. Even from beneath its veil, the faint shine of fear-stricken eyes was clear to her lenses.

"Come on," she said, almost quietly. "Or I'll leave you."

The being gave a shudder, but then jumped, and landed hard across the back seat of the hovercar, across one man's corpse and half of another. Ginn heard it cry out, in pain or horror, but she didn't wait to find out which. She punched the throttle. The car hesitated an instant, like a beast gathering itself. Then acceleration shoved her back into the seat as the vehicle leaped forward.

Ginn had lived at Old Towne's edge, in a mostly abandoned industrial strip. The road ran a hundred yards and ended in the open desert. The hovercar wove between piles of debris and the buildings fell away as they shed the town's husk.

Seconds passed. More. Wild shouts turned Ginn's head. Blaster fire cratered the ground behind them. Too far behind them. She almost slammed the car to a stop, almost leaped into the back seat to turn her enemies' own pulse cannon against them. Then she laughed. She was alive. That's all she needed for the moment.

Wind swept past them, cold through her t-shirt. She was used to the cold on Kelmer. She called over a shoulder: "Less crowded up here. Why not join me."

A bedraggled form crawled over the back partition and slid down into the passenger seat. Its robes were bloody but it looked like most of the blood wetted the outside of the cloth.

"You all right?" Ginn asked.

The being nodded. "Bruised."

"Good," Ginn said. "Because even if your other job offer is off the table now, you still owe me for saving your ass back there."

"Red Jac's men—"

"Red Jac's men were after *you*. I knew it as soon as I saw them. A *pulse cannon*!" She shook her head. "Not for me. Jac's gonna want *me* alive. Gonna want back what I took from him. Has to be you they wanna ash."

The being shuddered, plucked helplessly at its gore-smeared

robes.

"I'll pay," it said finally. "For today. Also to hire you. If you will take the work."

Ginn smiled. "I want another apple, too," she added.

CHAPTER FOUR

UNDER THE EMBER STAR

From behind a jumble of boulders, Ginn watched the hover-car's dust recede at high speed across the flat and almost feature-less pan of the Karst Desert. If Red Jac's men pursued, and she imagined they would, they'd almost certainly follow the fleeing car by its dust plume. Too late would they discover that the car's only passengers were already dead.

She turned then and threaded her way among the boulders toward the main wall of the vast escarpment that bordered this western edge of the desert. Overhead in a sky the color of musca-dine grapes, the ember sun burned dim and dusky but seemed to provide no heat. She glanced up at it. Her light-lenses dark-ened to compensate for the glare, though not nearly as much as they would have on Earth.

Gateeri. The Ember Star.

Ginn knew the Kelmerian sun's official name. But no one ever called it that. The ember star was a dying red dwarf. Half a million years ago, long before humans had taken to space, Gateeri had provided enough light and heat to nourish a rich biosphere on Kelmer, its second planet. It had nourished a sentient species as well, a species that developed a worldwide civilization. Then, over a period of some hundred thousand years, Gateeri started to fail. The Kelmerian civilization collapsed into savagery. Life itself began to struggle. Until someone from outside intervened.

Ginn glanced away from the ember star, to the north and then the south. Not far above the horizon in each of those directions hung a brilliant whirl of luminosity that put Gateeri to shame. Humans generally called them the "Collectors." Many natives called them Gods, and believed that because they rotated in opposite directions that one represented the male energy and the other the female.

They were really machines, giant, quantum machines. Built by a race that far outstripped humanity in technology, they looked like massive, glowing hurricanes in orbit above the planet. Between them, they gathered the weak radiation of the ember star, gathered it, focused it, fed it in wide swathes onto the surface of the planet below. Without them, Kelmer would have long since become a frozen, lifeless world, as sections called the Silent Zones already had. Because of the Collectors, the Kelmerian Days were about as bright as a heavily clouded afternoon on Earth. And large areas of the planet's surface were still habitable, with normal Day-time temps ranging from twenty below to twenty above zero Celsius.

Certainly not for the first time, Ginn wondered about the race that created the Collectors. And why they'd done it. It wasn't the Kelmerians. Because of their metal poor world, Kelmer's natives had built a technology based almost exclusively on wood and stone. They'd never achieved space flight, never even mastered powered vehicles. The plentiful ruins dotting the planet proved that.

So why had some alien race decided to save life on Kelmer? Had they planned to colonize and aborted that plan? Were they just good Samaritans? Or had there been some other reason?

The mystery of the Collectors had called Ginn's physicist father to Kelmer some thirteen standard years ago. The Collectors themselves were protected by force fields no human technology could pierce, so Jake Hollis had ranged Kelmer's surface in hopes of picking up clues to their origins. That search finally killed him, leaving his fourteen-year-old daughter alone.

Ginn looked away from the sky and down to the umber dirt. She rubbed her eyes under her lenses and spat a heatless curse that combined the words of her old world and her new. Then she stalked on, coming out of the field of boulders and entering one of the many wind-scoured caves that honeycombed the Karst escarpment. Her companion, her fellow escapee, squatted quietly there, looking up when she entered. The blood of dead men had finally dried on its robes.

She tossed two nearly full canteens, a med kit and another hand blaster down beside the being. She'd appropriated a wicked looking SSK subsonic knife for herself from the hovercar, and the insulated jacket one corpse had worn. It was only lightly singed and stained around the collar.

"I set the car on autopilot after I stripped it," Ginn said. "Flat as the desert is, she might run five hundred miles before something goes wrong."

The being nodded. "A wise strategy."

"Did you contact your people?"

"I activated my signal. They will find us. They are nomads. As I'm sure you expected. Yet it may be some hours before they arrive. In the Day they will have to move quietly to avoid telltale dust."

"Good thing Red Jac's men don't have flyers."

"Are you sure they do not?"

Ginn shrugged. "Earth's navy controls Kelmer. They keep an eye on the nomads from orbit and they've got plenty of firepower. They don't allow unauthorized air travel. I suppose Jac could have bribed somebody but I doubt he'd risk a flyer on anything but the rarest emergency. He isn't stupid enough to beg attention from the military."

The other nodded again. It picked up the extra blaster, held it as if it weren't quite sure what the weapon was for.

"Look," Ginn said. "At least tell me your name. I'm tired of calling you 'hey'."

Beneath its veil, the entity's mouth twitched in what might have been a brief, faint smile. Or might have been something else entirely.

"I am Duash-tei-tei-varzan alh Corovaneen," it said. "My human...acquaintances generally call me 'Duash'."

"Acquaintances? Don't you have any friends?"

"You know as well as I that humans and '*Kelms*' are never truly friends."

"'Kelms' is not necessarily an insult," Ginn said. "I don't use it that way. And appropriating the term for yourself doesn't necessarily mean you are what you claim. Native robes have served to confuse before. Maybe you should show your new employee your face. Get everything into the open, so to speak."

There followed a long silence, but just when Ginn began to think Duash would refuse, the being reached up and withdrew some of the pins holding its veil in place. It tugged gently, and the cloth came loose at one side and slithered to the shoulder.

Ginn didn't gasp but she came close. The face was more human than any Kelmerian she'd ever seen, but it wasn't *completely* human. The gray eyes were almost unheard of, and the mouth was smaller than the Kelm norm. There was a chin, which natives lacked. She even glimpsed teeth behind the parted lips where Kelmerians carried only rough cartilage. But the nose! There was no nose, and no scars to suggest that one had been removed. Kelmerians lacked noses, though many wore prosthetics when dealing with humans.

"What are you?" Ginn blurted.

"I am that which they say cannot exist."

"And that would be?"

"A hybrid. My 'mother' was Kelmerian. My 'father,' human."

"Impossible," Ginn protested.

Duash shrugged thin shoulders. "As I said. That which cannot exist."

"Evolution doesn't work that way," Ginn argued. "For one, Kelmerians don't possess DNA. There's no genetic compatibility between our races."

Duash shrugged again. "You tell me nothing I have not known before. Yet," it gestured at its own body, "I am."

"For two," Ginn continued, as if Duash hadn't spoken, "you don't even have genders. At least not like humans. There's no such thing among Kelms as a 'mother' or a 'father.' There aren't even words in your languages for those things."

"Those who give life are seysmoern," Duash said. "They are what your race calls hermaphrodites. Male and female both. Others among us are seysbuedin."

"Neuters."

"Yes."

"So what does that make you?"

"Male. Only. As you may imagine, my existence has caused some...turmoil among the Kelms."

Ginn's thoughts roiled. "Turmoil?"

Duash's soft tones hardened. "Your people house themselves amid what was once Kelm glory. You trash it. Your scientists make occasional study of Kelm biology and Kelm ruins. Yet humans have seen too many alien races in their expansion across the galaxy to care much for the remnants of another. Certainly they do not care for what lies inside. You, yourself, have lived here for years. You treat the Kelms better than almost all your kind. But even *you* know nothing of their true spirit."

"So fucking what," Ginn snapped, her own anger igniting. "You think *anyone* knows anyone else's spirit? We're *all* alone. Every last bitch and bastard among us. Only money gives you a chance to fool yourself that there's more to life than raw survival."

Stung, Duash recoiled from Ginn's vehemence. His mouth opened as if to retort, closed again. Finally, he spoke: "You still are young. Surely you are not so cynical?"

Ginn's lips twisted into a smirk. She grabbed the two canteens and the med kit she'd dropped only moments before and slung their straps roughly over a shoulder. Then she stomped past Duash toward the front of the cave.

"We're leaving," she said. "If Red Jac's men catch the hovercar they'll backtrack it right to here. We'll follow the escarpment. Meet your people at the edge of the desert."

She didn't wait to see if Duash followed. He would. He'd admitted to having help on his last trip into nomad lands, help that must have been human in nature. Since it hadn't been her, it had probably been Red Jac. And now Jac's men were trying to kill him.

Jac only killed when it was good for business. And his business was money. That meant, no matter how wealthy Duash might be, he was worth more to Jac dead than alive. The only people who could protect Duash from Jac were the military, and Ginn Hollis. And she wasn't any too sure about the military. Duash needed her. She'd make him pay well.

Then there was the vivum, Duash had mentioned. *Vivum.* In the place where they were going. She tried not to think about that. But her body thought about it. Her belly tightened, her mouth dried, her skin flushed.

She touched her chest. Even through her jacket she felt the hard little cylinder of the vial where it nestled.

She dropped her hand to her blaster. Walked on.

CHAPTER FIVE
NOMADS

Stone above. Stone below. Stone all around.

Ginn worked her way through a nameless slot canyon at the broken edge of the Karst desert. Smooth, cool rock twisted all around her in delicate hues of salmon, mauve and pearl. Duash followed, his robes swishing lightly.

Despite feeling that Red Jac would not have flyers on the hunt for them, Ginn had taken every canyon and dry wash she could. It made her feel less exposed, less vulnerable with the sky at least partially obscured.

"Better safe than sorry," had been one of Jake Hollis's favorite sayings, even though in the end it had not saved his life.

The narrow, tortured canyon that now hid Ginn and Duash had not been made by the desert's scouring winds but by massive quantities of water pouring through a desiccated landscape. That meant it was old, because Kelmer hadn't seen a flood of such magnitude in a long time. But then, most everything on Kelmer felt old.

The swishing of robes behind Ginn ceased and she turned. Duash had stopped to swig from a canteen. He'd not re-veiled himself; she thought she knew why. She moved back a few paces toward him, took a swallow of water for herself.

"The nomads are close," Duash said.

Ginn nodded. "I know. Let's just hope it's the ones you signaled for."

"It is. Else they would not be so near human settlements."

"Not unless they were looking to burn someone."

Duash blinked, but Ginn did not wait for any reply he might make. She continued along the canyon and in another hundred paces it opened abruptly onto a boulder strewn plain dotted here and there with dry-weed and skeet-brush. She paused, her hand on the butt of her blaster. She sniffed. Not even a breeze blew today. Yet, the air was tainted with dust. There had been movement here, only moments before.

Ginn slipped her left hand into the pocket of her coat. "They're around," she whispered over her shoulder to Duash.

"Yes," hissed a voice behind her that she didn't recognize.

Ginn stiffened, but did not turn. That would have been fatal.

The voice hissed again. "The alh Corovaneen we recognize. You we do not. Dirt your weapons."

"Don't think so," Ginn said. "Figured someone might come down into the canyon behind us. I've got a bomb-bot in my pocket. Slaved to my life signs. I go unconscious and several hundred meters of this desert get vaporized. I'm gonna keep my guns."

For three heartbeats, nothing happened. Then laughter boomed. It came not from whoever had been hissing words behind her, but from the rocks all around. Five gaunt figures rose from among those rocks, as if materializing from dust itself. They wore tan burnooses over vests and trousers of Kelmerian wool. Caplets of beaded leather adorned their bare skulls. Their only veils covered their mouths as protection against blowing sand. Above those thin scraps of cloth, their eyes gleamed large and almost black.

All five were shorter than Ginn's five feet seven inches, and much thinner inside their clothing. But she did not make the mistake of thinking them weak because of that. It had been years since she'd seen nomads so close. Not since her father's death. She had not forgotten them.

These were not the Kelms of the settlements, but wild creatures who smelled of grease and fire and strange, cinnamon winds. They did not walk with heads bowed and faces covered to hide their differences from the human. They were not vying for favors or begging for solars. They did not have to accept, or even pretend to accept, that she was their superior. And they could kill her as easily as they breathed.

Their weapons were multiple bone knives strapped to their legs and the stubby dart rifles common to nomads. These were air powered and fired three-inch long spines from Kelmer's version of a cactus. The guns weren't much good at over thirty feet, but then she wasn't thirty feet away from them.

Ginn forced her body to relax. Her right hand fell away from her blaster but she didn't take her left hand out of her pocket. One of the nomads lifted an arm. This one carried the ritual scars of a chieftain just below its eyes, on a flat stretch of skin where a human nose would be.

Sand whispered with movement behind her but Ginn still didn't turn. A figure stalked past. A sixth nomad. This one was taller than the others, as tall as she. A tiny black spot of skeet-seed juice stained its mouth-veil at one side.

The newcomer had to be the one who'd ordered her to drop her guns. It stopped before the chieftain, handed over the weapon it carried. This was no dart rifle but a worn plasma pistol of older manufacture. That almost certainly meant it had been taken from some of the early human settlers on Kelmer. No doubt it had been handed down from one chieftain to another for generations.

The nomad with the skeet-stained veil turned to face Ginn. Its eyes were less black and more brown, almost yellowish, but there was hatred in them the others did not seem to share.

Ginn bristled. "I'm with him," she said into the hatred, nodding at the same time toward Duash, who stood very still and quiet with his face exposed. Ginn figured he'd wanted his face seen, to make sure he was recognized and not killed. That didn't explain how he'd come to be so accepted by the nomads. His speech, his dress, his manner. They all showed him to be a settlement Kelm and no member of the wild tribes.

"I knew they would not harm you," Duash said suddenly.

"Glad someone knew," Ginn said dryly.

The nomad chieftain laughed again, then shoved the plasma pistol into the braided twine it used for a belt.

"The alh Corovaneen is honored among us," the nomad said, speaking in its native tongue with an occasional Earth standard word thrown in. "Yet in this he is not fully correct. We might have put you to dirt. You were wise in the claim of your bomb device. Even though we knew you were bluffing. Only your military has access to such things. Yet you showed no fear. We know you now for strength. Rest and peace. We will not kill."

Ginn smiled faintly before responding fluently in the nomad's own language. "I appreciate that." She took her hand from her pocket, but added: "I think I'll leave the bot activated anyway."

The chieftain lifted both hands, fingers curled backward into a position no human-jointed digits could manage. It was the Kelmerian equivalent of a shrug. Then the being turned and strode away through the boulder field.

"We ride now," it called over its shoulder. "There is far travel ahead, and in the desert, those who do not belong."

Duash followed the chieftain, not meeting Ginn's gaze as he passed.

Ginn shook her head but trailed after the others. Mostly she was thinking about the chieftain's "those who do not belong." It had to be Jac's men, and if they found her a second time they wouldn't be so easily surprised.

Within fifty yards, the boulders gave way and they emerged onto the banks of an ancient river. A kind of purple lichen patched the dry river bed, and skeet-brush grew thicker there. She even saw some wild kaftee plants, though all were an immature blue-green and too young to bear seed.

Kelmer was veined with such dead rivers, Ginn knew. Some were only truly dead on the surface. She figured there was underground water here. Maybe even an underground stream. It would be well to remember this location.

From the river bank to the stream bed was an eight foot drop. Almost sheer. The nomad chieftain took it without hesitation.

The other nomads followed. Ginn stepped up beside Duash, who hesitated at the very edge as he'd hesitated before a similar drop back at her ruined apartment.

Surreptitiously, Ginn let her shoulder bump the Kelmerian's. His balance knocked off, Duash had to take a step forward. With a mewl of surprise, he dropped over the edge but managed somehow to land on his feet below. Ginn followed, and smiled sweetly into the glare she'd earned.

Where they stood, the river had once made a bend and the bank had been undercut. In the darkness there, well hidden unless you knew what to look for, Ginn glimpsed the outlines of seven long, lean desert hovercycles.

Yes, they would ride.

CHAPTER SIX

SAND AND CYCLES

What the horse became to Earth's eighteenth-century Native American tribes such as the Cheyenne and the Sioux, the hover-cycle became to the nomads of Kelmer. The bikes weren't just transportation. They were wealth. They were a means to obtain food and water and trade goods. They helped forge alliances. And wage war. They brought freedom.

When humans had first settled on Kelmer, some hundred and fifty years earlier, they'd sold hover vehicles indiscriminately to the locals. All Kelmerians were nomads in those days, though they lacked mounts or any pack animal bigger than a dagvyre or ceelat so their ranges were restricted to what could be covered on foot. The hovercycles, the cheapest hover vehicles to build, changed that, and the natives had paid dearly for them in local goods such as kaftee beans, artifacts from unlooted ruins, gems unknown to the jaded elites of Earth, and knowledge for the first settlers about food and water sources.

Within three generations, Kelmerian society had been trans-formed, and largely split into two distinct groups—those who settled near Terran spaceports and towns and made their living in some service capacity, and those who ran the badlands on hovercycles. The former were no longer nomads and their tribal distinctions quickly began breaking down. The latter were *truly* nomads now, ranging for thousands of miles across Kelmer's desert surface, and their tribal identities remained intact and even intensified.

At around seventy-five years into the human period, some nomads began fighting back against the increasingly voracious spread of people. Raids in force crossed into Terran settlements. Whole towns had burned. Irrigation systems had been wrecked. Many died. Most losses were on the human side at first.

Then Earth's fleet arrived in orbit from far wars and the nomads found out what destruction was really all about. Large swaths of the desert still consisted of fields of glass and slag left by the ravening energies of space-based laser cannon. The nomads pulled further back into their hinterlands. The navy returned to greater battles, leaving a skeleton force behind. The human settlers stayed closer to the main spaceports. An uneasy peace became the status quo, even though everyone knew it wouldn't last forever.

It had been declared a crime to sell hover vehicles to *any* local. But the nomads still had bikes. They didn't have the tools and raw materials to build them, but they'd become, as Ginn's father once said, "the galaxy's greatest natural mechanics." They maintained what they owned, replacing what they could—like seats—with native equivalents, and obtaining parts for engines, fans and electrical systems, and sometimes even entire cycles, on the black market. Red Jac controlled much of that market.

The seven hovercycles Ginn saw hidden now beneath the overhanging bank of the dry river were typical of nomad machines. Low slung. Predatory. They seemed molded out of rust but that was only camouflage against the umber and ochre shades of the desert rocks. Ginn noted the hand-stitched seats of local leather, the exquisite etchings in black and red that embellished every metal surface, the displays of bone beadwork that dangled from handlebars and saddlebags.

The nomads strode toward the bikes, Duash with them.

"Which one is mine?" Ginn asked.

All movement ceased. Then the chieftain turned slowly toward her, with nomad eyes as inscrutable as obsidian.

"In tow, we brought one cycle for the alh Corovaneen," the chief said. "There are no more. Yet...you may ride behind me. Or one of the others if you prefer."

Ginn shook her head. "You brought the seventh bike for me," she said. "The *alh Corovaneen* may ride at *my* back if he wishes."

"Cuakash!" one nomad snarled, and started toward her. It was the one with the skeet stained mouth-veil. Its hand lay tight upon the bone handle of a dagger strapped to its thigh.

Ginn dipped her right hand into the pocket of her coat, brought it out with the SSK subsonic knife already whining like a hornet in her fist.

The nomad drew its own knife, lunged toward her with a raptor's speed. She swayed aside. The Kelmerian's blade was of scavenged steel but sharpened to a razor's edge. The needle point tugged at the outside of Ginn's coat and sliced through. Ginn flipped the SSK from her right hand to her left, launched a back-hand slash that cut away half of one sleeve of the nomad's burnoose as he passed. Neither weapon quite touched flesh.

Ginn spun off her heel, saw the nomad already turned for another attack. She dropped into a crouch, but in that instant Duash leapt in front of her, faced the other with empty hands and shouted angrily, "Enough!"

The knife-wielding nomad snarled, but Ginn's own lips curled from a rictus into a half smile. She slowly straightened up. Duash's intensity was refreshing. She'd begun to wonder if he had any balls, felt better to see that he did. She didn't like risking her life for someone who wouldn't dirty his own hands, no matter how much she was paid.

"The human insulted the alh Corovaneen," her attacker protested. "That earns her dirt."

"I am not insulted," Duash snapped. "I am not injured. She is no enemy of either of us."

Slowly, the tension released out of the nomad, and with an abrupt grunt and thrust it sheathed its dagger. Ginn deactivated her own knife, pocketed it. She strode toward the hovercycles, pausing for an instant beside her recent attacker.

"Call me 'cuakash' again and your alh Corovaneen won't

keep me from putting *you* to dirt."

The being stiffened, but nothing more. Ginn stalked past him. Of the seven bikes, only six bore the personal cartouches of nomad warriors inscribed along the sleekly curved power packs where gas tanks had once sat on ancient motorcycles. Ginn chose the bike that lacked such a mark, swung astride and set her boots firmly on the riding pegs. She punched the button that brought the twin 2500 cc polymer-cooled Coruscant engines online. These cycles had left-handed throttles and she twisted hers, felt the vibrations strobe up her body as the surge of power beneath her lifted the bike a foot off the ground in a scatter of sand.

She cut the throttle, let the cycle settle again to earth. No rising and falling roar of sound accompanied her actions. The hovercycles' power source involved no internal gas combustion, only electrolyzed hydrogen, and the result was no more than a hum that climbed the scale as the engines cranked.

Whatever tension that remained among the nomads bled away as Duash swung astride the bike behind Ginn and grasped the passenger straps to anchor himself in his seat. The others straddled their own machines, fired their engines.

Ginn leaned back slightly, whispered over her shoulder to Duash. "I *was* insulting you, you know."

"I am well aware," Duash acknowledged. "Yet your clumsy efforts in that vein are scarcely worth noting."

Ginn found herself grinning. "Not a bad comeback. Brings me a *little* bit closer to actually liking you."

"I am getting better at *tolerating* you," Duash replied.

A short bark of laughter was Ginn's only response. She revved her machine, toed it into gear as the other bikes tore off ahead. She followed in a rapid skim along the bed of the dry river.

The hovercycle in front of her ignited suddenly as a blast of blue flame engulfed it.

CHAPTER SEVEN
DESERT FIREFIGHT

A wash of blue fire struck. From somewhere close. The nomad bike in front of Ginn was thrown sideways, burning pieces of it cartwheeling away in a shriek of superheated atmospheres.

Pulse cannon.

Even as Ginn thought it, her hand cranked the throttle open on her own cycle. Acceleration slammed her back in the seat against Duash—she hoped he was hanging on tight—and they went up in the air and over the fiery wreckage. A mist of liquid droplets hung for a moment below her; gases from ablated metal stung her nostrils. The nomad riding that bike hadn't stood a chance. Ginn smelled boiled wool and leather mixed with vaporized bone and flesh.

Her thoughts raged. *Where*? *Who*? Who had fired on them?

Then she saw. Above them along the dry river's right hand bank

Hovertrucks. Two. Armored and armed. Jac's men!

Or was it? Jac shouldn't have vehicles like these. They looked military.

Maybe decommissioned.

Ginn heard a tearing sound. She recognized it and crouched low in her saddle as she sent her bike into an evasive weave. A lightning blue lance tore the air asunder to her left. The shockwave battered her but she hung on. Duash clung like a leech to her back.

Another nomad cycle cut in front of her, the rider leaning

hard across the machine to force it into a curve back toward the enemy. She recognized the being who'd attacked her moments before. Its dart gun loosed a stuttering fire but the spines would do nothing against the armored sides of the hovertrucks. The only smart choice was to run.

Ginn cursed. She kicked her machine into a higher gear, twisted the handlebars and came around in a parabolic curve. Over her shoulder, she shouted to Duash.

"Use the blaster I gave you at the cave! Fry the bastards!"

Pulse cannons flamed. Two at once. Air sizzled. The hovertrucks were in motion now, coming around into pursuit posture. But the nomads weren't running. Darts sleeted the sides of one truck, bounced harmlessly off.

"Shoot, Duash!" Ginn screamed. She knew he carried the blaster in the pouch of his robes.

She palmed her own blaster, cut loose. The fiery bolt smoked red along the side of the same truck the dart spines had just hit, but with little more effect. A fingernail layer of metal vaporized at the impact point, but to cut *through* that armor would take concentrated fire and she couldn't stay in one place long enough to provide that and live.

The nomad chieftain swept past her to one side. A pulse cannon bolt cut close enough to fan the Kelmerian's burnoose. That would leave a flash burn, but the being reacted only by drawing its old plasma pistol and firing. A fist of flame slammed into the nose of one truck but was deflected downward by the slanted armor. Sand volatized, exploded skyward.

They had to get out of the river bed, Ginn realized. Get *above* the enemy craft. These weren't tanks. Their tops were open, vulnerable.

She thrust her blaster into its holster, yanked her cycle's handlebars hard to bring the machine slewing around into what looked like a suicide run directly into the riverbank beneath the trucks. Duash cried out in intensified fear. But Ginn knew hovercycles, had ridden them many times. At the last second she hauled back on the bars and cranked the throttle to full.

Driven into overload, no longer humming, the engines started to whine. Hover fans shrieked. For one fraction of a second the bike and its passengers were locked to stillness with the purple sky oscillating overhead. Then gravel and sand erupted away from the side of the riverbank as the fans found something to push against. The machine surged upward, climbing almost vertically for an instant.

Pulse cannon flame carved a hole in the space Ginn had just occupied. But the cycle erupted into the air over the edge of the bank, over the bow of one of the trucks. Ginn twisted the handlebars down with her left hand, drew her blaster into her right.

For a heartbeat in the lighter gravity of Kelmer, the cycle hung suspended. Below her in the hovertruck, three faces gaped upward. One man grabbed desperately at the handles of the pulse cannon, tried to swing it to bear. Ginn fired first. And fired again. Now Duash was firing, and shouting, and firing.

The hovercycle's engines stalled. The machine started to slide sideways in the air. Ginn fired. Blaster flame boiled along the hovertruck's interior. Half its pulse cannon melted. Its seats exploded like fat popping over an open fire. One man screamed, and stopped abruptly. Another threw himself burning over the side of the truck. The third? Ginn couldn't see the third.

Just as the hovercycle seemed about to roll completely over, Ginn slammed her blaster into its holster and grabbed the handlebars. She wrestled the front of the bike around. They swooped downward; they were *crashing* downward. Ginn stomped the shift lever into a lower gear, pumped the throttle. The engines caught. Rocks pinged like bullets off the undercarriage. The nose of the bike came up and they almost scraped the edge of the riverbank as they went past.

Behind them, the now unmanned hovertruck was not so lucky. Its rear end slid sideways, dragging the rest of the vehicle with it over the edge of the bank. Suddenly the machine went belly up, its own fans pile driving it into the bed of the river in a crumple of armor.

"They're running," Duash screamed in Ginn's ear.

She turned her head, saw that the other hovertruck was indeed "running." Two nomad cycles were in pursuit, but even as she watched they peeled away and circled back toward Ginn. She let her own bike settle to earth, loosened her death grip on the handlebars.

Now Ginn saw the third man from the hovertruck she'd taken down. He'd been thrown free of the vehicle. He was dead, his body twisted, the back clearly broken. The flesh had burned off his legs. She recognized him. One of Jac's men. *Tunis*. Once upon a time she'd spent a few drunk and intimate hours with him. It hadn't ended well then either.

The nomad chieftain's cycle settled beside her. A black-eyed gaze scanned hers. After a moment, the being leaned down and scraped up a fistful of friable soil. It blew across that fist, then tossed the soil over a shoulder.

Ginn understood. The nomads respected brave actions and her actions had saved nomad lives, had saved the alh Corovaneen. Dirt stood between them no longer. It was about as close as human and Kelm could ever come to being blood brothers.

They went out of that place.

CHAPTER EIGHT

QUESTIONS

"Two things," Ginn said to Duash.

They lounged around a small and nearly smokeless fire in what Ginn had decided to call a yurt for want of a better term. Three of the remaining nomads were curled up asleep a few feet away. The other two were outside, keeping watch even though the shelter was well hidden. This was a permanent way station for the nomads, or as permanent as they ever built. It nestled under a wooden framework and a webbing of knotted cord upon which sand had been heaped. It looked no different from any other of the dunes clustered around it. Ginn had never known such places existed. She imagined now that there were many more. She wondered if she were the first human to see one.

"What things do you speak of?" Duash asked.

He did not look at her but appeared to be studying a weak tendril of smoke as it drifted upward and out through the ingenious chimney system the nomads had constructed. That chimney zigzagged through the sand so that what little smoke the fire produced dissipated before being released into the purple sky. No hunters would find them *that* way.

"I wanna know why Jac's men are trying so hard to kill you? And...exactly where the hell we're going?"

Firelight painted shadows around Duash's lean face as he rubbed his stubby chin with one hand. The gesture had to be called human since no other Kelmerian had such a facial feature. His tongue licked at his lips as they parted, then fled back inside his mouth. Seconds ticked away, but just when Ginn started to fidget in want of a response, the other finally spoke.

"The questions are related. There is more than one answer to each."

"OK," Ginn said. "Maybe you better get started then. Before I get a whole lot older."

Duash's gaze flicked toward her, then down. He'd restrung his veil but left his strange gray eyes uncovered this time. Ginn had given up trying to read his moods from how he hid or revealed his face.

"Red Jac wants to kill me because of where we are going," Duash said. "Because I know the way and he can only *find* the way after I am dead."

"Wow," Ginn said. "That clears everything right up. I guess I'll have a nap now."

"I am not finished," Duash snapped. "Unless you wish to continue to delay me with your nonsense."

"Sorr...y," Ginn said.

"I needed guards. Protection. For the first trip. Red Jac could supply those guards. Without questions the government would ask. Six of his men accompanied me. Including Flavin, his lieutenant. We took two hovertrucks. It was a long journey. One truck was lost on the way, with all three crewmen. But we... found what we sought.

"If you wonder why I did not take nomad companions, it is because we first had to cross Teshkarie lands. Humans consider the Teshkarie just another nomad tribe. But *they* do not believe themselves such. They claim descent from the kings of the high Kelmerian civilization of the past. Nomads do not venture into their lands on pain of broken taboos and death."

For a moment, Duash paused. The moment stretched out.

"And beyond the Teshkarie?" Ginn prodded.

"Beyond the Teshkarie. Into the western Silent Zone. The cold zone. The deadest of places on this world."

Ginn blinked. "You can't expect to be going *there* now," she said. "We'd need a helluva lot better tech than we've got to venture into those lands. Hovercycles and jackets ain't gonna cut it."

"We will go there. Not far into the Zone, we will find a place of warmth."

"Unlikely."

"There is a city. A settlement of some kind. Neither Kelmerian. Nor yet human."

Ginn had been leaning back on one elbow. Now she sat up straight, her heart quickening. "No!"

"Yes. I believe it to be a site of those who created the Collectors."

Ginn's fists clenched on her thighs. "Dad thought.... He... suspected. Such a place. But he looked for years."

"That it is underground perhaps caused him problems," Duash said. "Yet, he was close."

Ginn leaned forward as if to pull answers from the other by force of will. "Why do you say that?"

Duash gave a long, human-like sigh. "I had wished to speak of this under other conditions. In your home. Over kaftee. That was not to be." He reached into the pouch of his robe, came out with a slender package bound in vellum. Leaning forward, he placed it gently on the hard packed soil before Ginn.

Ginn frowned at Duash, then looked down. Her hand reached out; her fingers caressed the outer layer of the package. *A book*, she realized. She picked it up, turned back the cover. A sudden weight settled over her limbs. She couldn't move, could barely breathe.

The lassitude broke and her heart started to hammer. She looked up at Duash. "There's no way you can have this. You can't have this."

"It *is* your father's journal."

"Lost! On the day he died."

"Not lost. You recall the Kelmerian assistant your father had in his last years."

"Balaen!"

"Your father's dying wish was that Balaen go to you. Aid you.

Bring you this journal. Yet, Balaen was hurt also in the crash of your father's flitter. Inside the body. The healing was long, and by that time you were not to be found. Balaen journeyed then to the settlement known as Caereden. I dwelt in that place. No word in your language captures Balaen. Mentor. Guide. These are inadequate. Avish-taa. That is the word for what Balaen became to me. When my nature began to grow clear."

"Your nature?"

"When I first showed you my face, you said I was impossible. That is true. I *am* impossible. For Kelmerian technology. Even for human technology. But for those who...."

Duash gestured toward the invisible sky and Ginn knew he meant to indicate the Collectors and those who created them.

"As a child," Duash continued, "the one I called seysmoern, life giver, many times sang a song to me. So often that I could not forget it. Only when grown did I find that the song spoke of the Silent Zone and of *two* life givers. My seysmoern died in a fire just as I was about to come of age. It was Balaen who discovered my true nature. You have said that Kelms lack DNA. Yet, they have that which functions much the same. Like your father, Balaen was a scientist. Tests showed that I carried twin biologies. That indeed I had a mother who was Kelm and a father who was human.

"Balaen told me what my song meant. Balaen also had your father's journal with its words about the Silent Zone. These things together guided us. To the alien site I spoke of. In that place I saw many machines. What *we* would call machines. Balaen thought that one such might explain how I came to be. Surely you can understand that I would wish to know such a thing."

Ginn released a long breath. Her heart had slowed. "Yeah, I suppose I can. Just as I've always wanted to know the answer to the riddle that killed my dad."

"I thought, perhaps, you would."

"I remember Balaen. Not well. But I liked what I knew. Dead now, I guess?"

"Yes."

"So that's why you came to me."

Duash's shoulders slumped. He seemed to shrink in upon himself. "Balaen made me promise that if anything happened I would try to find you. To give the journal to you as was your father's wish. More, though, I came to you because I am a coward. Without Balaen I could never have undertaken that first journey. Without you I cannot go back."

"How is that you *have* to go back? Why didn't you stay until you found what you sought?"

"Red Jac."

"What?"

"Balaen and I, when we saw the alien site, we could not risk such technology falling to a criminal like Red Jac. We used trickery. Only two of Jac's men survived to return to settled lands with us. Flavin was one. I gave him a map. A false map. Balaen and I each had a true map. As precaution, the maps were keyed to our lives. Balaen's map to mine. My map to Balaen's. Later, Jac killed Balaen. Took his map. Yet, he could not open it."

"So that's why they want so bad to slaughter you," Ginn said. "So Balaen's map will open and let them find the place again."

"Yes."

Ginn shook her head. "That whole 'keyed to your life' bit. Pretty damn stupid, if you ask me."

Duash stiffened. "A pity Balaen and I did not have your superior intellect to guide us," he said.

Ginn puffed through her lips. Balaen was obviously important to Duash and he still felt his friend's loss keenly. "I just meant you didn't think things through," she said. "No insult to Balaen."

"Not every problem can be solved by killing it with a blaster," Duash retorted.

Eyes flashing, angered herself now, Ginn spat back the first words that came to mind. "I take back what I said earlier about starting to like you."

"As I am fast losing what little tolerance for you I had," the Kelmerian replied. With a flourish of robes, he turned away and curled up on the dirt floor of the yurt.

Ginn did not move for a long time. She regretted the exchange with Duash. It was a new feeling for her. She'd learned in the time since her father's death that it was better not to regret anything.

Dad.

She looked down at her father's journal, clenched tightly in her hands. Words wanted to come, and couldn't. Tears wanted to flow, but didn't. She lay down on her side facing the fire. Sleep came by itself.

CHAPTER NINE
WE CAN GO NO FARTHER

Dust. Wind. Biting flies. Long silences. And the vibrations of the hovercycle setting every molecule of Ginn's body a-jangle. They crossed the desert—seven riders—heading west for the most part but following every bit of cover they could find to help protect them from spying eyes. That was long habit for the nomads anyway, whose movements were often tracked from orbit by Earth's military.

Along their trails, they dug for water seeps in places Ginn would never have thought of digging, and they found it. They ate the hard kernels of skeet-seed and the soft inner pads of the zahtii, the cacti of Kelmer. They fried the fat tails of volmer, the skittering beast that resembled some lizard-scorpion hybrid grown to the size of a rabbit. They ate dark-meat, a staple the nomads carried with them everywhere.

For sleeps, they found other secreted way stations, or sometimes just rolled up in their blankets and took their rest in the desert itself. Twice, Ginn chipped a little from her vial of vivum, only a drop or two each time when the black floaters started to serrate her visual field and the weakness began to lay claim. She could go on like that for a good while, but eventually she'd have to take a full dose and she couldn't do that on the move. She couldn't do it without hours to devote to oblivion.

At other stops, other times, reading in her father's journal seemed to calm her need. When she finished her first go through of those pages she went back to the beginning and started over.

Twice, also, they slept in nomad encampments, places hidden under cliff overhangs or dug out along ancient riverbanks. In those camps, Ginn watched the children play like wraiths through fields of boulders, or herd the small flocks of ceelat from which eggs and a kind of wool were taken. She studied the graceful nomad adults moving purposefully about the thousand and one things they had to do to wrest life from the wasteland. She watched them harvest the desert's meager bounty, watched them make dark-meat with a mortar and pestle and fire.

At age ten, when her father explained to her what dark-meat was, Ginn had decided like a child that she'd never eat it. Periods of hunger had long since slain that squeamishness. The one truly abundant type of life on Kelmer was bugs. The nomads ground them into a paste, mixed it with a grease that bled out of skeet roots when they were boiled. The tarry mass that resulted dried into a taffy-like toughness that was cut into strips of jerky. It wasn't fine dining but it filled a hole in the stomach.

There'd been no further sign of Red Jac's men, but Ginn took little comfort in that. The hovertrucks that had attacked them hadn't been expecting such strong resistance. Jac wouldn't make that mistake again, but he also wouldn't waste resources hunting Duash's party through lands where the nomads had every advantage. From Duash's story, Ginn knew that Jac lacked the exact coordinates of the supposed alien city but did know it lay in the western Silent Zone. She figured Jac's killers would be patrolling the border of that zone, waiting to pick up Duash and her there.

Well short of that border, with the ember sun setting slowly and only a half dozen hours of light left before Night, the other five cycles coasted to a stop ahead of Ginn. The land had been rising and growing more broken around them for a while, and Ginn had sensed a corresponding tension building among the nomads. She figured that tension had just come to a head.

She pulled her bike up next to the chieftain's, tugged down the veil she'd bought in a nomad camp to cover her face against the sand.

"What is it?" she asked.

The chieftain's gaze turned toward her; the eyes seemed webbed with a strain she didn't understand.

"Land of the Teshkarie," the nomad said. "Land of ghosts. We can go no farther. We regret this."

Ginn started to look back at Duash but felt the cycle lighten as her passenger dismounted and walked over to the chieftain. Duash's hand found the other being's shoulder.

"Ki-sahn," he said. "My friend. There can be no regret. It has been written in blood that you and yours do not enter this land. I thank you for the service already given. We would not have made it here without you."

The chieftain's head turned. One hand lifted the veil over its mouth; its lips brushed the back of Duash's gloved fingers. Ginn's eyebrows lifted. She'd seen the respect the nomads paid Duash, though she didn't understand its origins. But this? The chieftain's kiss seemed to represent much more than respect, something more like reverence.

"Beware the Teshkarie," the chieftain said softly. "They will not honor you. Nor," the being's gaze slid toward Ginn and back again to Duash, "will they understand you riding with a human into their lands."

"We will be like the dust-wraiths," Duash said. "The Teshkarie will not know that we have passed."

"I pray this so."

"I will accompany the alh Corovaneen," a third voice spoke then.

Ginn turned her head, startled. The speaker was the nomad she'd fought the first time they met. Kenzes, by name, Ginn had learned. Ginn didn't doubt Kenzes's bravery, but she didn't much like the being. The feeling seemed to be mutual.

Letting her glance slide back to Duash, Ginn saw him look... disconcerted. Beside Duash, the chieftain sat with eyes half closed in the Kelm equivalent of a frown.

"You cannot," the chieftain protested. "A nomad may not travel into the land of ghosts."

"Not even to accompany the New One?" Kenzes asked.

New One, Ginn thought, frowning herself. *What the hell is this now?* Who *was* Duash to these people?

"The laws are older than the coming of the New One," the chieftain answered.

Kenzes bowed head in acknowledgment of the chief's response, but in the being's own words there was no surrender.

"I would do you no dishonor, my chieftain. But recall, I beg, how you found me wandering in the desert. A child still. When I sought the people. Hardly knowing of them and yet yearning. I would have died on the sands. For I was born no nomad. In a hospital of the humans, I was born. In the space-port at Ahrishban. I was born to a Kelm who served the Terrans as what they name 'fire-gyrl.' A whore for their hungers. Such would have been *my* fate. Yet, even as I grew I did not flee. My heritage was forsaken. Until unclean death took the one I loved, and freed me. I am no nomad. I honor the laws but they do not speak clearly on this. Perhaps, even, I am here for this purpose. At this moment and place."

Ginn listened to Kenzes's speech, and grew appalled. Duash had told her once that she knew nothing of the Kelmerian spirit. He'd been right. She'd understood what the fire-gyrls were. She'd chosen not to think about it, or about the children they raised in their humiliation. No wonder Kenzes hated her and her kind. Her hand clenched on the butt of her blaster.

Even after Kenzes fell silent, Duash and the chieftain made no response. It seemed they did not know *how* to respond. Ginn wanted to scream at them to give in. She had not liked Kenzes, maybe still didn't. But she understood need and Kenzes had a need as strong as her own. She *forced* her mouth to stay shut.

"The New One can use me," Kenzes added quietly.

The chieftain looked toward Duash.

"There is truth here," Duash said at last. "Inside, I do not believe that Kenzes invites taboo."

The chieftain nodded, slid from hovercycle back and strode the sand to Kenzes. The gaze of the two nomads met—black against yellow-brown.

"You were not born in the desert. Nor of the people," the chieftain said. "Yet you have no more to prove to me. I chose you as child of my life. I would not lose you."

"You will not," Kenzes said.

The chieftain studied the one it had named its child a moment longer, then with a sudden movement withdrew the plasma pistol tucked into the belt of its burnoose. A lifted hand stilled Kenzes's protest and the pistol was shoved into the younger being's belt.

The chieftain moved to straddle its hovercycle, making a gesture toward another nomad who climbed from its own bike and slid aboard behind the chief. Three hoverbikes wheeled about and took off across the desert, leaving three other machines behind and three beings to ride them—Kenzes, outcast born of a fire-gyrl whore, Duash, a half-breed who should not even exist, and Ginn, with her anger and her vivum addiction. She'd never felt quite so normal before.

"All right," she said. "Let's kick in the Teshkarie's door."

CHAPTER TEN

INTO THE LAND OF GHOSTS

The Teshkarie highlands were much rougher landscapes than the lowlands where the nomads dwelt and where humans built their spaceports. In Kelmer's distant and wetter past, large swaths of the lowlands had been shallow seas while the highlands marked continents. Both had become deserts, but the lowlands still held more water under the surface, and grew more vegetation. The highlands had barren hills, barren cliffs, barren crags, with here and there an upland valley and a pocket oasis of life.

The highlands also bore most of the ancient Kelmerian ruins, and the remnants of the huge irrigation aqueducts built in the end times to try and save the cities from dry death. In some cases those desperate measures had worked. For a while.

The lowlands had ruins too, mostly on what had once been islands. Humans had chosen those places to establish spaceports. They liked combining alien structures that could be modified for human dwellings with the flat planes needed for landing fields. They liked that water tables were closer to the surface and more easily tapped.

Humans had another reason for leaving the highlands alone— the Teshkarie. As Duash had said, most Earthers considered the Teshkarie just another type of nomad. Ginn's father had known better. *She* knew better. The Teshkarie had been last to surrender civilization and return to the hunting/gathering lifestyle that was all a dying Kelmer could support. Even today, some Teshkarie maintained parts of their ancient cities. Their leaders claimed titles more akin to king and emperor than to chieftain, and while nomad religions had largely returned to more primitive animistic forms, the Teshkarie religions had continued to develop and splinter.

The nomads were tribal warriors. When they fought, they struck in lightning fast raids, looted and burned and evaporated right back into the deserts. The Teshkarie were soldiers. They fought for causes. They fought for religion and politics, and that made them far more dangerous.

The Teshkarie tribes warred constantly with each other, but in an instant would drop their internecine grudges and unify against any human expedition venturing into their land. As a result, few such expeditions existed, although a reckless adventurer occasionally attempted to loot one of the cities of enough artifacts to finance a life of ease. Most found their 'ease' in the grave.

Ginn knew the highlands as well as any human, which was to say, not very well. She'd been here half a dozen times, first with her father, who had somehow managed to explore quite a few of the ruined cities without getting killed, and later on her own, when her needs grew desperate enough to risk death for a quick grab at artifacts worth enough solars to keep vivum and life in the body.

So now, by virtue of experience, Ginn led this party of three interlopers. She didn't know where Duash's alien site lay, but she knew the way west to the Silent Zone where they'd find that site. The others seemed content to follow.

Within hours, the ember star set for its fourteen day sleep, and Ginn called a halt so everyone could don the warmer clothes packed in their saddlebags. The highlands were naturally colder than the lowlands anyway, and during Night the temperatures steadily dropped until they reached well below zero. Ginn knew she was going to be grateful for the heat generated by the hover-cycle engines.

A glance toward the horizons showed the Collectors dipping

quickly out of sight so they could cast their refocused energies onto the other face of Kelmer. Soon, they'd be no more than the dimmest of glows, and since Kelmer had no moons and only the brilliant stars to soften the Night, Ginn and her light-lenses would likely be leading the rest of the trip as well. Kelmerians had better night vision than humans, but not up to the quality provided by the lenses. The hovercycles also had headlights but it wouldn't be wise to use them when the Teshkarie could be anywhere. Progress would be slow.

About an hour into their dark ride, though, Ginn found what she was hoping for. The ancient Kelms had built good roads. Some were still passable, at least in sections, and Ginn located one that headed generally west in the direction they wanted. It had apparently been built to aid in constructing one of the great aqueducts, which ran in ruined majesty along one side of the highway. But while the aqueduct was now useless, the road still functioned as intended and Ginn and the others began making up time.

Focused on navigating, Ginn lost track of the hours until Kenzes pulled up beside her. She glanced over at the nomad, saw the head-jerk that signaled her to look back. Duash was falling behind, and from the slump of his shoulders to the way he hung on to his cycle like a drowning man, she read his exhaustion.

Just ahead, two of the stone columns that had held up the aqueduct still stood, but the span between had collapsed into a pile of debris that made a good place to hide the bikes and set up camp. They drank from their canteens and gnawed at strips of dark-meat. Duash fell asleep with food in his mouth.

Kenzes motioned Ginn to stillness when she would have risen to help Duash. She watched the nomad take the dark-meat from the smaller being's mouth and eat it so there'd be no waste. She watched the being smooth sand for Duash's bed and gently cover him with extra blankets. She wondered again at the reverence the nomads showed toward the unusual Kelmerian. Maybe it was time to ask Duash about it. When he woke up.

Kenzes returned to loom over Ginn where she sat. She

figured the looming was on purpose and she didn't like that. A few sleeps earlier, she might have done something about it, but she recalled Kenzes's story and decided to cut the being some slack. Besides, she was comfortable. She plucked up a canteen that held kaftee instead of water and poured a cold cup.

"I will claim first watch if you wish to sleep," Kenzes said.

Ginn glanced up. Was the offer a kindness? Or a challenge? She lifted her cup to call attention to the kaftee. "You sleep. I'll watch. I'll wake you in a few hours."

The nomad seemed about to protest, but then showed its hands in a shrug and rolled up in a wad of blankets a few feet from Duash. Ginn rose and walked away from the encampment. At thirty feet, looking back at her companions, all she could see were humps on the ground indistinguishable from rocks. That was with her light-lenses activated. Without them she would have seen only blackness.

Satisfied, she found one of the ancient aqueduct support columns and leaned where her outline would blur into the stone. She reached under her shirt, pulled loose the tape that fixed the vial of vivum to her skin, and drew out the drug. Fluid moved within the vial, appearing under her lenses to be faintly luminescent.

The vial had originally held five doses and she'd taken a full one immediately. She winced now to see that she'd chipped away another dose drop by drop until only three full ones remained.

Her mouth was dry; her eyes ached down in their depths. Her breathing was a little too quick, a little ragged. She *felt* shaky, even though her hands were steady when she held them out. Withdrawal hadn't truly started yet. But it soon would and she didn't want to be shaky for real if a fight came. A drop would ensure she wasn't.

Or was that just the need talking?

She thought then of the first time she'd been given vivum. Eight years old. Three weeks into a new life on Kelmer with her father. But Kelmer wasn't Earth. Besides the lighter gravity, the atmosphere was also different—less oxygen and carbon dioxide, more methane and krypton. She'd been foolish. She wasn't acclimated. She hadn't been drinking enough water, hadn't taken the pills that were supposed to help her adjust to a different world.

Out on the desert, she collapsed. They were too far from a hospital but her father had paid attention to the long-timers, the settlers who called Kelmer home. He had vivum. It was illegal for humans, but if Jake Hollis hadn't broken that law his daughter Ginn would have died.

Vivum saved lives. And sometimes it ruined them.

Ginn thumbed the cap off the vial. She drew out the syringe inside, tapped the base of it once, twice, to drive out any air. The liquid moved within the barrel of the syringe. It flowed as if alive. She started to pant.

She turned her left hand over and made a fist around the vial. The veins at the base of her wrist popped into relief, like blue rivers through the white flesh. She pricked one vein with the needle, pushed a single drop of vivum into her bloodstream. A voice inside screamed at her to push more. She trembled, but forced herself to withdraw the needle.

In a few quick movements then, she fitted the syringe back inside the vial, capped it and retaped the whole thing under her shirt. A throb of heat passed up her arm from the injection site, then spread quickly through her. Her heart steadied, her breathing slowed. She pushed away from the aqueduct column and made a circle of the camp. Kenzes and Duash slept on. She checked them before starting another circle.

An hour eroded away; the cold deepened. She passed the aqueduct columns again, paused suddenly. There was something.... Her head came up. She smelled something that hadn't been there before.

Ozone.

A low moan whispered out of the darkness behind her. Ginn spun, her right hand flashing down, coming up with a blaster ready. Beside one of the aqueduct columns grew what humans called a sponge-bush, for its resemblance to that Earthly creature. This one was much bigger than usual, boulder-sized. Through its sponge-like pores Ginn's lenses picked up a gleam of silver-blue light—there for a moment and then gone. She'd seen similar light through her lenses before.

Eye shine!

But this had been bigger than the glow from any eyes.

She circled the bush. *Nothing!* And no tracks or even a flattened place on the dry soil. That didn't matter. She felt it. Something had been hiding behind here, something that had watched her, with its voice like that of a dying man.

Land of ghosts.

That's what the nomads called this place. Ginn had never believed it, had never seen or heard such a thing in the times she'd explored here. But then, she'd never been here during Night before.

She backed away, toward the camp. A low hiss from her lips brought Kenzes up from sleep, a plasma-pistol held like a dark clot in one hand. In an instant the nomad was beside her.

"Get the cycles ready," Ginn whispered. "Something out there. I'll fetch Duash."

The nomad moved away. Ginn slipped over to where Duash slept, knelt beside him. Her hand reached for a shoulder, found only bundled robes instead.

Duash was gone.

CHAPTER ELEVEN
THAT WHICH STALKS THE NIGHT

Cold prickles of goose flesh spread across Ginn's scalp and down her back. Her gaze sought the darkness surrounding her. Her ears expanded as a thousand sounds suddenly announced their existence. Somewhere a seed dropped and rolled down a rock. Somewhere desiccated branches rattled together. She heard a scuttling in the dirt off to one side of the camp.

Coming to her feet, she snapped a single quick word: "Kenzes."

The Nomad materialized out of the shadows beside her. She pointed with her blaster at Duash's empty blankets, then gestured to the right, indicating an encircling movement.

Kenzes did not hesitate but darted away; Ginn moved left in a half crouch. A boulder loomed. She slid around it. Her light-lenses revealed a stretch of sand faintly gleaming with star-shine; a small volmer careened across it, its scorpion claws up as it hunted prey. But no volmer had stolen Duash.

Ginn hurried on. The empty desert suddenly seemed full. A sand cricket chirruped. Another answered. A gem-wing moth whipped past Ginn's face on some wild erratic flight. She flinched back, cursed herself and rushed on. A head-sized mass of blackness revealed itself as a nomad-ant nest, the bodies of the soldier ants forming a protective gall around their king-queen. She gave the thing a wide berth.

Ginn expanded her search. A finger of stone seemed to rear up out of the rocky soil. She'd seen these all along the aqueduct.

A marker of some sort. Incised with symbols she couldn't read.

The world changed. No insects now. No sound for the moment. But this place wasn't empty either. She felt cocooned. A presence brooded and watched; ozone rasped her nostrils. She twisted around.

A moan of wind—or of something else—brushed like a living thing by her ear. She froze. Light flickered in the air above her and she looked up. A meteor streaked the darkness. Only a meteor. Then it was as if a door had closed. The presence was gone, the odor gone. Insects began to call again.

Ginn sighed. For a few more minutes, she searched, knowing it was useless. Finally returning to camp, she called Kenzes to join her.

"Anything?" she asked when the nomad appeared.

A head shake answered her.

Kenzes looked beaten. The thin Kelmerian shoulders were slumped, the eyes dazed and unfocused. Ginn figured she knew what the nomad was thinking. Duash had been sleeping not ten feet away and been taken, after Kenzes had sworn to protect him.

"There might not be tracks on this dry soil," Ginn said. "But there should have been *some* sign. A kicked stone. A bush bent out of place. No town dweller like Duash walks away from a camp without leaving telltales behind."

"The ghosts," Kenzes muttered.

Ginn had expected that. She'd been thinking it herself.

"What the hell are they?" she demanded. "Or what the hell are they *supposed* to be?"

Kenzes's mouth-veil was pulled down, as if there wasn't enough air in the world to breathe. No answer came.

Ginn grabbed the nomad's shoulder, hard. Kenzes's eyes suddenly blazed. A jerk of the being's arm threw Ginn's hand away.

"Do not touch me, human," Kenzes snarled.

"Then answer me," Ginn snapped. "We both failed here. Human *and* nomad. I was on watch. You were only feet away.

But what matters is that we can get Duash back. If we don't waste time. If we know what we're dealing with. What are these ghosts supposed to be?"

Kenzes wiped its mouth with the back of a hand, replaced its veil.

"Spirits. Ancient. From when the cities fell. Those who died in the cold and the dark when civilization failed. They cannot rest. They seek...to bring the living over with them. To make the whole world as dead as they."

"I don't believe in ghosts," Ginn said.

Kenzes shrugged with his hands. "I only know what I have heard. I did not believe either. Yet—"

"Could it be the Teshkarie?"

"They would have killed or taken us all. Not one alone."

Ginn nodded. Her mind sought answers, couldn't find them. So she sought possibilities instead.

"On Earth and Kelmer both, legends often contain truths. Do you know? Is it rumored? Do the 'ghosts' associate somehow with the ancient cities?"

"I have heard that," Kenzes said. "It is one reason I did not think to fear them here in the wild lands."

"Not wild," Ginn said, nodding toward the remnants of the aqueduct. "This went somewhere. Maybe it's close."

In the nomad way, Kenzes considered possible responses for a long time. But at last: "I am a fool not to have thought of that."

"Foolishness only afflicts the living," Ginn said. "We've each had our turn at it and we ain't dead yet. I intend to keep it that way."

She moved to her bike, straddled it. "I'm figuring we go forward. Along the aqueduct. We know there's no city for a long way behind us."

Kenzes powered up another machine, then spoke: "You are not much like any human I've known."

Ginn glanced over at the nomad. "I'll take that as a compliment." She kicked her cycle into gear. They whirred off through Night.

CHAPTER TWELVE

CITY OF BROKEN SPIRES

Where the ruins lay, the wind hunted. And so did Ginn and Kenzes. From a shattered city wall where their cycles lay hidden, they darted to a broken red tower that leaned drunkenly against a building with no roof. The wind tugged at them as their gazes searched ceaselessly across buckled streets and through gaping windows and doors.

"Not far away, this place. As you suspected," Kenzes said to Ginn. "Yet I see no signs of life or movement in this accursed destruction."

Ginn heard the distaste in the being's voice, felt a little of it herself. The desert was clean; these ruins were not. She could still see signs of the fighting that had raged here in the city's last days—doorways torn open by weaponry, stones scarred with the marks of ancient fires. Many of the cities had not been merely abandoned. They had died in convulsions of rage and violence.

She spat. Her foot kicked something that moved; her light-lenses captured a faint gleam that caromed off of blackness. She bent down, picked the thing up. It was part of an obsidian sword, the blade broken, the wooden hilt almost entirely flaked away. She shook her head, lay it back where she'd found it.

"Inside the tower," Ginn whispered to Kenzes. "If the steps are OK we might get high enough to see into the city's heart."

Kenzes nodded, followed as she slipped through the tower's narrow doorway into the interior. Even with her lenses, that interior was almost completely black. From a pocket of her BDUs, Ginn drew a bright-bead, activated it but kept her hands cupped tightly around the marble-sized device so only a weak glow lit their surroundings.

They found themselves in an old guard room. A table cut from breccia lay shattered. What might once have been plates and utensils and other gear littered the dust-strewn floor. Rising in a helix around the wall were steps that would take them to the tower's top, where signal fires must once have burned.

The stairs were subtly twisted from the lean of the building, but Ginn thought them negotiable. She tucked the bright-bead into her mouth to free her hands, then started up one slow step at a time. Again, Kenzes followed. Three quarters of the way up, they came to a large window and paused.

Ginn took the bright-bead out of her mouth and deactivated it. "Far enough," she said. "The steps don't look any too safe beyond this point."

Ginn had been in a number of ruined Kelmerian cities. All were compact by Earth standards. The Kelms had never gone in for the megalopolis style of urban planning that many humans seemed to prefer. This one was small enough so they could see a long ways across it even from their current height.

"Not sure quite what to look—" Ginn started

"There!" Kenzes interrupted.

Ginn followed the nomad's pointing finger. She shivered then, and it wasn't from the cold breeze that played through the window. In the distance, a glow wove itself along a debris clogged street. Her light-lenses resolved that glow into five stalking figures. They were Kelm-shaped. Or human-shaped. She could be sure of little else.

The figures entered a building that seemed largely intact.

"Bingo," Ginn said. "That's the same glow I saw where Duash was taken."

"Bing...o?" Kenzes said. "What is this?"

Ginn blinked, then chuckled and shook her head. "You know, I have no idea. It's just something Dad used to say."

Kenzes nodded, a little confusedly. Then: "Where they entered. It is a worship place. What you would call a church. I know not what God it is dedicated to."

"Only one way to find out," Ginn said.

"That would be?" Kenzes asked.

"Let's go pray."

CHAPTER THIRTEEN

They Want

Ginn halted as Kenzes grasped her wrist.

"Do you hear it?" the nomad asked.

She listened, and she *did* hear it.

They'd worked their way through the streets to the church, found a back way in. Barren hallways guided them toward the front of the building, where the weird, glowing figures had entered. Along the way, Ginn saw where repairs had been made to the structure and that helped her feel better. She didn't think ghosts would care about having a solid roof and a floor where rubble had been cleared away.

The sound she heard now *didn't* make her feel better. It was no more than a distant cacophony at first, a babble of discordant voices wailing. Then her brain began to find rhythm and she realized she was hearing some kind of chant.

The nave of the temple stood before them, shadowy and empty except for an almost random arrangement of tall black columns. Where ever the chant came from, it didn't seem to be from the main part of temple.

"There's a second floor to this place," Ginn said. "And considering the repairs that have been made it should be traversable. Maybe we can spot these creatures' glow from up there."

Kenzes nodded. "The stairs should be just ahead."

Without waiting for Ginn, Kenzes darted forward to another column. Ginn followed. In another moment, as predicted, stairs materialized out of the gloom. The steps were narrow, in the

Kelm style, and deeply worn in the middle from ages of passing feet. The human and the nomad went up side by side, found themselves in a sort of loft, a place that in a human church might have been meant for a choir.

Dust coated everything. Ginn stepped on the desiccated shell of some insect, winced as it crunched under her boot. But the chant they'd been hearing continued, and now a dim glow suffused the air. They made their way toward it, both dropping into a crouch as they approached a balustrade at the end of the loft.

A glance over that railing revealed why they'd not seen any glow from the temple's main chamber. Recessed into the floor, perhaps some twelve feet deep by thirty feet across, stood an oval pit. Six sets of steps led down into that sanctum, and in the center rested a breccia altar. A dozen robed and cowled figures gathered around it, each glowing blue-white. Upon the altar lay Duash, his arms and legs strapped down with chains, his mouth gagged. He was awake and naked and clearly terrified.

One figure stood at Duash's left side and held a knife with an obsidian blade. That one suddenly spouted a torrent of words, contrapuntal to the chant going on around it. A second torrent followed after a short beat, as if it were some kind of prayer. It sounded Kelmerian to Ginn, but not like the language she knew.

"What's it saying?" Ginn whispered to Kenzes.

"Insane," Kenzes replied. "This one speaks the old tongue. They are Teshkarie. Yet not."

"What the hell's that supposed to mean?"

Kenzes's head turned toward Ginn. She saw the reflected glow in the nomad's eyes, read confusion and fear there.

"The one claims they *are* the ghosts of the ancients. I think it believes. I know the glow. There is a soft rock found at certain places. Eske, it is called. It makes such a light, but also causes sickness. Those exposed to it develop sores and become pale *as* ghosts. Eventually, they die."

"Radium," Ginn grunted. "Or something like it."

"These have painted their clothing and skins with it. They

are insane. They wish to die, to be ghosts in truth. I see no other explanation."

The chant from below suddenly stopped.

Then the figure with the knife stepped closer to Duash and began to speak.

Kenzes's face blanched under its desert tan.

"They did not choose the alh Corovaneen by accident," the nomad moaned. "They recognize him as the New One. They wish to take that from him. To stop the future."

Ginn would have a hundred questions when they were free of this. If they *got* free of this. Now was not the time. She didn't understand the meaning of "New One," but she knew what made Duash the New One to the nomads, and what these—whatever they were—planned to 'take' from him. They were going to cut off whatever made him a male.

Leaning closer to Kenzes, Ginn said in a fierce whisper: "Two choices! One of us has to distract them, lead some away. The other has to go down and get Duash. Which do you want?"

"Distract," Kenzes said, with no hesitation.

Ginn didn't argue. "Meet us at the bikes. We'll wait until we can't anymore."

Kenzes nodded, darted swiftly away. Ginn hefted her blaster. If the "ghost" started to cut before Kenzes made a move she'd have to fire. Then they'd all be on her. She licked dry lips, forced her rapid breathing to slow.

A moment passed. Another. The ghost droned on with its patter, loud now in the silence of the lost chant. Then it too stopped. Ginn slid her blaster forward, felt how rigid her finger curled around the trigger.

A sudden ululation of sound burst upward from the temple room with the black columns. Kenzes' distraction. The effect was electric. All movement froze for an instant among those below Ginn.

Then the creature with the knife began shrieking words. Its hands gestured wild commands. Ten of the glowing beings leaped for the stairs around them, swarmed up and away. That left two, the knife-wielder and one other, who now drew a pain-stick into its fists.

Ginn was already rising. The two remaining "ghosts" weren't in good positions for her surprise but she couldn't wait. Her right hand held the blaster, her left grasped the railing and she let it take her weight as she vaulted over and dropped from above. Something made the knife-wielder look up. Shadowed eyes widened beneath its cowl.

Ginn landed halfway between her two enemies, striving for a crouch but slipping instead to one knee. The knife-wielder was already lunging toward her, the sharp black blade of its weapon refracting the being's own light. Ginn shot it, but missed the clean kill she wanted. She'd turned the blaster to narrowest beam and the lance of orange flame drilled a hole all the way through the creature's shoulder and into the wall behind it. The knife went flying.

Ginn rolled to her right, knowing the second ghost was some-where behind her. A pain-stick crashed into the stone where she'd been. She let the roll bring her all the way to her feet, but her balance was off and she fell awkwardly against the wall.

She saw two things about to happen. The creature with the stick was leaping toward her, its weapon raised. The one she'd shot had its mouth open to yell. Ginn heard dart rifle fire from within the temple; that might cover the sound of her blaster but it wouldn't cover a cry for help. She shot the wounded being again, the beam cutting a neat hole through its throat and flash-frying the vocal chords into silence.

The pain-stick came down. Ginn managed to get her left hand up, took the blow across her forearm and almost screamed. The pain-stick was a baton-length piece of wood with thorns inserted along the last third of its length. The thorns came from the cobra-nettle. Like viper fangs, they injected poison wherever they struck. The poison could kill a human, though not swiftly. And while it worked it burned in the wound like a savage acid.

Ginn's left arm spasmed with agony, her knees weakened with sudden fear. She'd never faced venom-death before.

Desperately, she brought the blaster up in her right hand. The ghost lashed out with a foot, kicked the weapon away. The gun banged off the wall, went spinning across the floor. Ginn punched the being in the chest but had no leverage behind the blow.

The creature took a half step back on its own, then snapped the pain-stick up and around. Ginn pushed off the wall before the blow could fall, threw herself forward. The stick whipped past her ear. She head-butted the being, knocking it backward. Its hands flew up; its hood fell off, revealing the hairless skull of a Teshkarie. Ginn spun off her heel, lashed a kick into her enemy's throat. A gagging breath exploded from its mouth. It fell against the altar where Duash lay bound.

Ginn's left arm wouldn't respond to her commands but she stepped in to the attack, hammered her right fist into what would be a human's solar plexus. Kelmerians weren't built exactly like people but a punch to the gut had much the same effect. The Teshkarie doubled over and she snapped her knee up into its face. That blow would have broken the nose if there had been one. Instead, it slammed the head up and back against the rock altar.

Only half conscious, the being started the long slide toward the floor and Ginn followed it down, punching, punching, punching. An instant later and she was back on her feet. The knuckles of her right hand hurt but it was nothing compared to the agony cooking in her left arm. She glanced hurriedly about, saw her blaster and snatched it up before turning back to the altar. Her left hand and forearm began to twitch wildly, the twitches spreading upward.

Duash was looking at her. His eyes were stark and wide. She used the blaster like a fiery hacksaw, burning through his manacles with short bursts of flame. She stuffed her weapon back in its holster, then dragged Duash off the altar with her right arm. He sagged against her, remnants of his chains rattling at wrists and ankles. For a moment she supported his weight, though it was all she could do to stand up herself.

"Need clothes," he mumbled. "A robe."

"Later," she hissed.

She pushed him toward the stairs. He staggered, then righted himself. But he wasn't moving. She shoved him again and he took two steps and stopped. A shudder wracked his bony frame, and he was vomiting suddenly onto the floor.

"Damn you!" Ginn snarled. She grabbed him under the chin, jerked him upright. "We've got no time!"

His eyes cleared. "Yes," he said, thrusting the back of one hand across his mouth. Then he was moving toward the stairs.

"The cycles?" he asked.

She pushed past him, drawing her blaster. "Follow me."

"You are hurt!"

"Doesn't matter right now," she snapped.

His hand darted suddenly to her belt, pulled her second blaster free. She'd almost forgotten it.

"Together," he said, staring at her.

She managed a nod. They went up the stairs. The temple's main floor was almost black after the light of the pit. But in one direction she heard Kenzes's plasma pistol discharging. She went the opposite way, and in another instant her light-lenses picked up the dim outline of the open front door.

They burst through into the street, Ginn almost falling down the steps. Her breathing was ragged. A muscle spasm lashed her cheek. The cobra-nettle poison was surging deep into her bloodstream now. The left side of her chest burned.

"That way," she managed, pointing with her blaster.

Duash took her left arm and slid it around his shoulder. The pain arched through her nerves but she didn't protest. Together they staggered in the direction she'd indicated.

Minutes passed. Too many minutes. With every step Ginn expected to see a blue glow darting at her, a pain-stick falling. But Kenzes must have done his job well. The city's outer wall stood suddenly before them. She saw the hovercyles, gave a little cry of relief.

She pulled away from Duash. "Clothes in the saddlebags,"

she muttered.

Her breathing was harsh; the numbness was growing. It took two tries to get her blaster holstered. Then she stumbled to her bike, punched the button that brought the engines online. Kenzes's bike was next and she started it too. The hum was a comfort, a tiny one.

Duash was throwing a robe on over his nakedness, was belting it and thrusting the second blaster behind that belt. She saw him jerk an extra pair of boots from the saddlebags, then shove them back in with a frown. He wouldn't be getting them on over the chains that still clung at his ankles.

"You'll have to drive," Ginn told Duash. Her tongue was thick, the words slurred.

"Now?" Duash asked.

Ginn shook her head violently. "Not yet."

He nodded, straddled her bike. She tried to get her right leg up and over the cycle's passenger saddle, couldn't and nearly fell. Duash dismounted to help her, then climbed on in front of her. She stuffed half her right arm through his belt as an anchor, leaned forward against his back. She had to open her mouth wide now to suck breath into her lungs. And to speak.

"Wait," she muttered. "Kenzes. Coming."

"Yes," Duash said.

Then it seemed her mind itself was starting to twitch. *How much time? Where's Kenzes? Still alive? Already dead?*

"I don't know if..." she muttered.

"We will wait a little longer," Duash said.

She nodded against his back. Or thought she did.

A rush of feet sounded behind them. Ginn snapped alert, turned her head as she grabbed for her blaster. But it was Kenzes, limping on one blood-spattered leg. The nomad threw himself onto the other hovercycle. For a moment, Kenzes's gaze crossed with Ginn's. They both nodded.

"Go, go, go!" Ginn shouted to Duash.

They went.

CHAPTER FOURTEEN
BETTER LIVING THROUGH CHEMISTRY

Ginn's eyes snapped open. She lay flat on her back, on a blanket with a hard surface beneath. More blankets covered her—of ceelat wool. She thrust them off and sat up. Her jacket and blaster were gone; her light-lenses were missing.

She didn't need the lenses. A tiny fire smoked near her feet and by its glow she saw the wavering outlines of rough walls around her. She was in a cave. Her head ached but a delicious aroma wafted to her.

Kaftee. Hot.

She started to rise and a voice said softly, "Rest a while yet."

A shadow shifted on the other side of the fire. A stick-thin figure climbed to its feet.

"Duash," Ginn said.

"Yes."

"What happened?"

Duash bent for a moment by the fire, then came toward her and crouched down, offering her a wooden cup that steamed. She took it automatically, sipped and sighed. Duash lifted one hand then, showing her the light-lenses between his fingers. She let him slip them on over her eyes and the world brightened and grew detail.

"My blaster," Ginn said.

Duash nodded, reached to loosen the gun belt that looked out of place around his lean hips. He handed it to her and she took it, held it for a moment while she had a longer sip of kaftee.

"What...happened?" she asked again.

"You fell unconscious. Tumbled off the back of the hover-cycle. We found this cave. Brought you here. Kenzes went to hide our trail and to watch to see if we are followed."

"And the cobra-nettle poison?"

Duash reached into the pouch of his robe, drew out a small packet that Ginn recognized. She wanted to snatch it out of his hands but did not.

"So that's why I feel pretty damn alive," Ginn said. She drained the last of her kaftee and set the cup down.

"You would not have survived without it. The poison had gone deep. Only the vivum could overcome it."

Ginn nodded. "I reckon. How much did you give me?"

"A full dose. It took that much."

"Shit!" Ginn said. "That means...."

"You've been asleep for over twelve of your standard hours."

"Shit," Ginn said again, this time without heat.

She rose to her feet, swayed but managed to keep her balance. She held her hand out toward Duash. He placed the vivum packet in her palm. The tape was still attached to it and she lifted her t-shirt and stuck the package back to her skin. A faint hitch sounded in Duash's breathing and when she looked back at him he was watching her intently. His eyes glittered. She pulled down her shirt.

"I guess you really are a male," she said.

He jerked, his eyes going wide, and she saw it come rushing into his face, the blood that turned him almost copper. He was blushing.

"I—I—I'm sorry," he blurted. "I did not mean...."

"It's all right," Ginn said. "Not like I haven't been looked at before. Usually I don't even bother killing the guys who do."

The copper drained from Duash's face as quickly as it had come and he bounced to his feet.

Ginn laughed. "Relax. I'm kidding, I'm kidding." She couldn't resist a, "Mostly,"

"I am sorry," he said again, so discombobulated that she

didn't have the heart to tease him about having to "search" her for the vial.

Instead, she asked: "Kenzes got the chains off you?"

Duash glanced at his wrists where the remnants of manacles had hung the last time Ginn was awake. "Yes. Cutting with a blaster."

"Helpful individual. Kenzes."

Duash nodded.

Then a different thought struck Ginn and her good mood evaporated.

"Kenzes's leg. I saw blood. It's all right?"

Two Teshkarie darts. I removed them and there is no sign of infection. Kenzes says it does not hurt."

"I bet it does," Ginn said. "Not that a nomad would admit it."

She buckled her gun belt around her waist, used the thongs to tie the holster down to her leg so her hand dropped naturally to the butt of the blaster when she stood up. Then she picked up the cup she'd set down earlier and poured herself another helping of kaftee. She leaned against the cave's wall, gazed at Duash over the rim of the cup.

"Thanks, by the way. For what you did for me."

He nodded.

"Still," she said, "I think we need to have a little talk. About a lot of things. One being the difference between truth and lies."

CHAPTER FIFTEEN

REVELATIONS

Duash's narrow body stiffened beneath his robe. His face became a mask that hid his emotions as well as any veil. "I have not lied to you," he said.

Ginn deliberately arched an eyebrow. "No? You told me that my dad's journal helped you find the alien site in the Silent Zone. I've been through it. There's nothing like that in those pages. Barely a mention of the Zone, in fact."

Duash stared at her for a long time. Slowly and carefully then, he said: "Perhaps you did not read it while taking fully into account your father's personality."

Ginn bristled. "What's that supposed to mean?"

"It means only that your father was a complex thinker. Or so it is that Balaen told me."

Ginn frowned. Then her eyes widened. "A code!"

Her hovercycle stood only feet away. She rushed to it, fumbled through the saddlebags until she came out with the journal. Flipping the work open to the first page, she began scanning her father's neat handwriting. Three pages in she began to see it. After that she saw it everywhere.

"Certain combinations of letters," she muttered, half to herself and half to Duash. "Written slightly smaller. And the spacing is different. Looks natural until you know what to look for. But I don't.... Wait!"

She flipped back and forth between several pages, her eyes scanning rapidly, then looked up at Duash with a grin and a snap of her fingers. "Kelmerian," she said. "He's using Earth standard letters to write Kelmerian phrases. He's embedded them in standard words but given a visual clue with the size and spacing differences."

"Yes."

Ginn sat abruptly down by the fire. "He knew very few humans would be able to read it. Even if they figured out the pattern. I can't believe *I* missed it."

"You have not exactly had much time to think on it," Duash said. His tone softened. "I would not have noticed it myself. Balaen knew of it."

Ginn sighed. "I should have. I owe you an apology. For the 'lie' thing. Dad used to write notes like this to me. When I was a kid."

She stared into the flames. Silence settled.

Duash moved toward the campfire, sat across from her. "You miss him," he said.

Removing her light-lenses, Ginn rubbed her eyes and then put the glasses back on. "It's hard to imagine what life would have been like if he hadn't died," she said.

"It was hard for you? After?"

"Kelmer isn't easy on anyone," she replied.

"I understood from Balaen that you were in school when word came that your father's flitter had crashed and that he had died from his injuries."

"At Port Lincoln. Most of the spaceports have human schools associated with them. For diplomats' kids. Fleet officers' kids. I wanted to be with Dad."

"He was doing what he thought best for you, I am sure."

"I know he was. I needed the schooling. I was wild enough already."

"I once told you how Balaen promised your father to see to your safety. Yet, by the time my Avish-taa's injuries had healed and allowed travel to Port Lincoln, you were gone."

"I left. Right after I found out about Dad. They would have shipped me home. To Earth."

"Would that have been so terrible for you? What about your mother?" He assayed a brief smile. "I know you *human*s have such things as 'mothers.' Was she not on Earth?"

"I imagine she was dead by then. Dad took me with him because he couldn't leave me behind with her."

"She was ill?"

Ginn stood up abruptly. "She was a drunk, for one. You know, people ask me sometimes what my name is short for. It's not short for anything. It's long for my mom's favorite kind of booze."

"I am sorry."

"Don't be." Ginn shrugged. "I hate the whole sordid story but I've come to terms with it. Mom was basically a prostitute until she got her hooks in Dad. She straightened up then. For a while. But you can't keep a drunk sober, and you can't keep a good whore off her back for long."

"Your father found out?"

"I did. I caught her at it. The *fucking*, that is. She admitted it all. *Bragged* about it all. We had a huge fight. I even demanded to know if Dad was my real dad. She said she wasn't sure."

"You told your father?"

"I did. I think he knew. Kind of. He'd already planned a trip to Kelmer. To study the Collectors. He just decided to take me with him and not come back. It made it easier when he found out Mom had spent every solar on herself that he'd saved to put me through university."

"What did he say about being your real father?"

"That was the only part he seemed to get mad about. He told me he was, and to *never* question it again."

"I would have liked to have known him."

"Yes, you would."

"And after you...left the spaceport school? What then?"

Ginn shook her head, but she was smiling, even if it was a melancholy smile. "I think you've milked enough information out of me today. Time to share a little about yourself."

Duash straightened up slightly where he sat, tugged his robe into a more comfortable position. His voice sounded resigned when he asked: "What do you wish to know?"

"Who are you to the nomads? What's this "New One" stuff? And when you were a captive of the 'ghosts,' why did Kenzes say they were trying to kill you to stop the future?"

Duash nodded. "I predicted those would be your questions. Your father wrote also of this."

"What? Where? Not in another code?"

Duash held his hand out toward her. "May I see the journal?"

Ginn puffed a breath of air through her lips. She moved back to the fire, passed the journal over to Duash and sat down.

Duash paged through the book for a moment, then turned it slightly toward the firelight and read:

The most prevalent religious belief among the ancient Kelmerians was that they sprang from the union of two gods. These deities were separate male and female in their aspects. Legend is that the two wandered the universe alone until they discovered each other over Kelmer. By that time, both were old, with not long to survive. To keep their children—the Kelmerian sentients—from suffering such terrible aloneness, the gods formed them as "breeders," who were both male and female at once, and "neuters," who do not long for young themselves but are content to care for the breeders and their offspring. A thread that runs through the Kelmerian beliefs is important here, though. It is a tenet of those beliefs that in time the Kelmerians will grow into gods themselves. To do so, they will first have to be born again divided. Male and female as separate individuals.

Duash closed the book and looked up. "The New Ones," he said.

"I'd forgotten until I read the journal that Dad talked of that," Ginn said. "He thought it meant that the Kelms had once had separate sexes."

"Balaen came to believe that too."

"So...the nomads think you're some kind of god?"

"No. It is honor they do me, not worship. They believe I am

a 'harbinger,' to use an Earth term. They believe that more and more will be born like me. From among *our* children, the gods will come."

Ginn frowned. "But aren't you...like you are, in part, because you're a hybrid?"

"That may be. Yet, it is unclear. Nor does it truly matter. The nomad beliefs do not say how the new ones will come about."

"Why would the Teshkarie want to keep the new gods from coming?"

"Is there but one unified faith on your world?"

"Hmm. I see your point. Click me down for a stupid question. So these 'ghosts' are a different religion?"

"A Teshkarie splinter cult. I did not know how active they had become in their worship. They believe Kelmer was *supposed* to die, that the drying and freezing of the world was the Gods' will. To them, whoever placed the Collectors in orbit were working *against* the Gods. The eske mineral is their sacrament. They paint it upon themselves and begin to exhibit the corruption of the flesh that they believe all are destined for."

"There's something else," Ginn added. "I'm pretty sure they're in contact with Red Jac. Or have been."

Duash's body jerked. "What? How do you know this?"

"Because they came into our camp and took you. Just you. And they made no attempt to kill me. Only Jac knows we're traveling this way. He's the only one could have tipped them off. It figures though. Jac wants me alive and you not. The ghosts want only you. Dead."

Duash's shoulders slumped. "I had not considered that."

"I'm not gonna let them kill you," Ginn said.

Duash seemed about to speak when a whisper of noise from outside the cavern brought Ginn to her feet, her blaster in one hand, a finger of the other over her lips to signal Duash to silence.

Kenzes darted into the light of the fire. His words electrified the air. "The ghosts have worked out our trail! The glow betrays their coming."

"Time to fly," Ginn said, holstering her blaster.

There was little enough to repack in the saddlebags. Ginn grabbed her father's journal, the blankets that had made her bed.

"Leave the fire," she said, when Kenzes moved to douse it. "Let 'em think we're still here. It might buy us a few minutes."

Kenzes grunted agreement, and in another moment they eased the hovercycles from the cave and mounted. Ginn saw the dim blue telltales of the ghosts approaching from the east. Their speed indicated hover travel.

To the west it was almost black, though faint star shine limned outcroppings of rock and a narrow way through that might be the collapsed remnants of an old lava tube.

Ginn reached for the button to power up her cycle and a voice came splintering out of the dark.

"No movement or you die."

CHAPTER SIXTEEN
A TRAP SPRINGS SHUT

Punctuating the verbal threat out of the darkness came the physical threat of nomad dart rifles being locked and loaded. A lot of them. Ginn glanced up. The enemy hid above them in the rocks over the cave and along the top of the lava tube. Even with her lenses she could see little besides the silhouettes of limbs and here and there a slice of face. She and the others were neatly boxed.

She let go the cycle's handlebars, watched Kenzes reluctantly do the same. Behind her, Duash sat as rigid as a gun barrel.

Three figures dropped down into the tube and strode toward the front of the cave where Ginn and her companions waited. She got a good look as they closed in. These were the Teshkarie she knew, the ones she'd heard tales of and seen drawings of, the ones she'd caught glimpses of in other forays into the highlands.

They were taller than the lowland nomads, with lighter skin. They wore leather and fur over their woolen garments rather than desert burnooses. Thin circlets of bone and wood were sewn into their vests to make a kind of chain mail. These three wore headdresses of braided thorn that hung close around their narrow faces. Two of them carried modern blasters; the third appeared unarmed. It was the third that Ginn watched most closely.

"Fifty warriors cover you from above," the unarmed one said, using the common nomad tongue.

Ginn shrugged, replied in kind. "So you've got us. What

next?"

The Teshkarie speaker chuckled, a remarkably human sound although not quite with the same meaning. "Whatever I wish."

"At least until your fellow tribesmen get here," Ginn said. "Those glow-freaks seem to have their own 'wishes.'"

The speaker turned its head, spat through lips pierced with thin ribbons of bone. "The Arkossa? Fellow tribesmen of no one, those fools."

Ginn knew the word "Arkossa." It meant sick, as, in-the-head sick.

"Are they not still Teshkarie?" she asked.

"They are nothing. Soon to be less. Only I order killings in this land. They have overstepped their bounds. We will let them commune truly with the ghosts they seek to know so intimately."

"Red Jac might not like that," Ginn said. "They didn't accomplish the task he set them. Of course, I figure he spun some kind of deal with you too."

Ginn expected the Teshkarie to deny all knowledge of Jac—even though the chieftain's comment about "killings in this land" convinced Ginn she was right—but her answer came in a frank admission.

"Red Jac's 'likes' do not influence clan decisions. Besides, his information was not very reliable. He mentioned two invaders. I see three. Including a cursed Yeskatsie!"

Kenzes bristled and Ginn could imagine why. The nomad had just been called a "filthy savage." She started to say something but saw that Kenzes wasn't stupid enough to respond. The chieftain's next words were directed at Ginn anyway, and startled any other thoughts out of her.

"You are the daughter of the one named Hollis."

"You knew my father?"

"Did you?"

In the interest of staying alive, Ginn swallowed her sudden rush of anger. "Not as well as I thought, apparently."

"Hollis was fair with the Teshkarie. His information was

always reliable. Though Red Jac wished us to detain you, you may go. Also, the one the Yeskatsie call the 'New One.' It is good that we have seen him, that we have marked him. Some time we may indeed have to kill him. Yet not this time. Not for Red Jac. He may also go."

"There's only one problem," Ginn said. "You didn't mention Kenzes leaving."

"The Yeskatsie will remain to enjoy our hospitality."

"No," Ginn said. "We all three go or none of us do."

"Ginn!" Kenzes protested. "Go! The alh Corovaneen must be protected. My fate does not matter."

Ginn glanced over. "First time you've called me by name, Kenzes. But that earns you no solars now. Just shut up."

The Teshkarie chieftain wore a predatory smile when Ginn looked back at him. "You should leave before I rethink my decision," came the being's words.

Ginn smiled in kind. She had a bluff in mind. She had to run it with absolute conviction, but before she could lay out her cards, Duash took a hand.

"Perhaps a word alone," Duash said to the chieftain.

Ginn turned her head in sudden surprise. "What the hell..." she started, but Duash was already dismounting from the bike and striding toward the Teshkarie.

"Duash! Get back here!" Ginn snapped. The small Kelmerian paid no heed, and when she started to get off the bike herself two blasters discouraged her, their tips glowing faintly red as the slack was taken out of their triggers.

"This is no time to grow a backbone, Duash," Ginn muttered under her breath, but she only sank back onto her cycle and fumed as the "New One" and the chieftain bent their heads together for a long few minutes.

Duash returned to the hovercycle and climbed aboard behind Ginn. He ignored the nails she looked toward him.

The Teshkarie leader spoke: "I am no longer concerned with the Yeskatsie. All of you will go. Swiftly. West to the border of the Silent Zone. Red Jac's men patrol there but I have spoken to the New One of a way."

"What did you say to him?" Ginn whispered over her shoulder to Duash.

"Later," Duash said. "For now, we should ride."

Ginn nodded, punched the start button on the cycle. The power built beneath her. She eased the bike forward, with Kenzes following. And the Teshkarie parted for them like a pack of freshly sated carnivores.

CHAPTER SEVENTEEN

THE SILENT ZONE

The world grew colder and darker as the three riders approached the Silent Zone. They put on their gloves, layered on more clothing, and all wore veils now to keep their faces from freezing in the wind of their passage. They built fires during their stops, no longer worried about the Teshkarie seeing them, and warmed their hands often on the engines of their cycles.

Strangely though, life was more abundant around them now than before. Actual thickets of skeet and burr-wood grew here. The ground was scattered with bead-grass and bioluminescent lichen. They passed a sponge-bush as large as a hovercar. A multitude of insects leaped and flew through the air, leaving jeweled flickers of ruby and jade in Ginn's light-lenses. She saw more wild volmers than she'd ever seen together in her life.

Ginn thought she understood why this abundance existed. During Night over the Silent Zone, water vapor froze out of the air. During the weak thaws of Day the ice melted and soaked down into the Teshkarie highlands. She wouldn't have expected *this* kind of fruitfulness, but, as with every Earth-like planet, water was the key to life on Kelmer.

Ginn drove the lead cycle, but it was Duash who guided their journey now, using information apparently gotten from the Teshkarie chieftain. He changed the subject every time she tried to question him about that. It worried her.

"Here!" Duash said suddenly.

She hauled her bike to a stop. Kenzes pulled up beside her.

Duash dismounted without another word; Ginn lingered in her seat.

"An aqueduct?" she asked. She studied the row of rock supports and the old stone channel of the aqueduct itself as it ran straight west from their location toward the Silent Zone. "How does this help us?"

Duash turned. "We know Red Jac will be monitoring the border of the Zone. Yet, it is unlikely that he will be watching the aqueducts."

"For good reason," Ginn said. "The whole system broke down long ago. There are isolated pieces of the channels still standing. Like this one. But they don't lead anywhere. I bet this piece here doesn't run a hundred paces."

"You would lose that bet," Duash said. "The Teshkarie keep this one repaired. That is why there is so much life near here. They do not tell Red Jac of this."

"But they told you?"

"Yes."

"What the *hell* did you promise them? And this time you're *not* avoiding an answer."

Duash drew in a long breath, and released it. "Technology," he said.

Ginn's chest tightened. She shook her head. "I won't help you do that," she stated flatly. "It'll change the whole balance of power on Kelmer."

"What balance?" Duash demanded.

The voice shocked Ginn. The words were harsh, almost arrogant. Duash's thin native body seemed to have grown inside the robes that covered it.

"There is *no* balance," he continued. "It is humans who have *all* the power here. The wealthy humans. Those who own the ships and claim the land and water. The criminals like Jac. They take what they want at will."

"So you'd rather promote a war!" Ginn retorted. "How is that going to aid the nomads? The Teshkarie? The Terran navy will cleanse the whole planet if they feel they're being pushed to it.

And that's exactly how they'll feel if you give the Teshkarie *anything* that can be used as a weapon."

Duash took a step toward Ginn. He yanked down his veil. "Look at me!" he shouted. "Do you not see...*me*?"

"I see a face I'm about to punch in," Ginn snarled back.

Kenzes moved to get between them, froze as they each gave him a glare.

"What you *see*," Duash said, turning back to Ginn with anger carved deep into the cut of his mouth, "is a face that is neither Kelmerian nor human. Yes, I was raised by the Kelms. I have dwelt with the nomads and loved them as kin. Yet my father was no child of this world. I would not willingly destroy either race."

Duash's voice softened. "Kelmer is dying, Ginn. Slowly but surely. Despite the Collectors. If there is knowledge at the alien site that can slow that death further. Or reverse it. I will see it delivered. To the nomads. To the Teshkarie. To the human settlers who struggle to wring life from the desert. If those with power and wealth are discomfited by that, I do not care."

Ginn stared at Duash for a long time, then looked up at the dark sky. She took a deep breath. And another. Her hand slipped under her veil. Grubby nails scratched at her chin.

"Damn it!" She got off her bike, strode past Duash to study the aqueduct stretching gracefully overhead. "We'll have to leave the hovercycles. We'll take the water and food. All the clothes we can wear."

She looked around at Duash, then included Kenzes in her gaze.

"You know we'll most likely die over there, don't you?"

Kenzes nodded.

Duash shook his head. "I do not think so," he said.

"I'll cover *that* bet," Ginn said.

CHAPTER EIGHTEEN

FROZEN IN TIME

Cold.

All Ginn could think about was being cold. And about how the time riding the hovercycles through the Teshkarie highlands had seemed cold but were in reality warm as a zephyr breeze.

The Silent Zone was bone chilling and brewed a fitful but savage wind. Nothing grew there to burn. To get a drink required chipping ice free of the canteens and sucking on it until it melted and slid down the throat like an icicle. Even urine froze as it left the body, and Ginn had lost track of the last time she'd taken a crap. She wondered if she ever would again.

They'd long since left the aqueduct behind. For a while the land had continued to rise but now had leveled off. Except for the rare mountain range, the Western and Eastern Silent Zones were the highest lands on Kelmer. Each formed a dome of barren rock that had bulged up from some great pressure below.

Ginn staggered in among a grouping of boulders that cut the wind. She leaned against one while waiting for her companions to catch up. Duash fell as he joined her and she bent down with a moan of pain and pulled him to a sitting position. His breathing was jagged, his color unhealthy.

"How much farther?" she gasped.

He shook his head and she let him be. He'd told her to head straight west and that's what she had done and would keep doing. She drew her blaster, already set to widest beam, and played that beam over a boulder until its surface started to glow and radiate heat. Her body sucked greedily at the warmth.

Turning then, she studied their back trail in search of Kenzes. The air felt leaden, and even though it was still Night, the sky carried a sheen of gray that on Earth might have predicted snow. Kenzes came out of that gray. The nomad was in better shape than she or Duash but that wasn't saying much.

After bending to check on his alh Corovaneen, Kenzes leaned next to Ginn and held gloved hands out to the heated boulder. Those hands trembled.

"It's time," Ginn said, opening her robes as little as possible and reaching in under her shirt to pull free the vivum.

Kenzes nodded, which showed how far the nomad's strength had ebbed. The first time she'd suggested they use the drug, Kenzes had refused—not because of morality but because it showed weakness. There was no more refusal in him now.

Ginn held up the vial. Vivum didn't freeze and she was grateful for that. The liquid shone faintly green and flowed in its container like viscous oil. She withdrew the syringe. Kenzes pulled up his left sleeve, revealing flesh for a moment, and Ginn pricked his skin and pumped in a single drop. She did the same for Duash, with two drops instead of one.

Her turn then. She studied the syringe a moment. Even in the cold her mouth grew warm with saliva. Her chest ached; her belly knotted. She bit her lip against the urge to jam the needle into a vein and push every drop home.

They'd already used the vivum twice since entering the Silent Zone. There'd been two full doses in the vial when they'd started. About a dose remained, and no telling how much more they'd need before they reached their destination. Duash had said there'd be vivum where they were going. She didn't know if she believed him any longer, but it was too late now to turn back.

Realizing that her hand was shaking badly, Ginn quickly pushed a single drop of vivum into a vein in her wrist and then immediately put the syringe back into its vial and tucked the packet beneath her shirt. She pulled her wool coat tight but already the drug's warmth had begun to course her body. Cramped muscles loosened. She took a deep breath, gave a sigh.

Vivum had been used a long time on Kelmer for moments such as these, moments when bodies had to do more than they could normally do to stay alive. The drug would keep their cells working, keep their legs moving. Until it ran out.

Ginn thought of withdrawal then. She hoped she would freeze before the worst agony came. Powerful as it was, vivum wasn't very addicting by itself. Native Kelmerians, who had evolved with the drug over thousands of years, almost never became dependent. Humans did somewhat more frequently. But if you combined vivum with alcohol, your addiction chances went up a thousand-fold. And once addicted there was no cure.

You didn't survive vivum withdrawal. Your body shut down one cell at a time, the least critical cells first, then the more important ones. Along the way the pain grew exponentially. The first time Ginn had experienced withdrawal, she'd been just seventeen. She'd finally lain down in a trash strewn alley and waited for death.

She'd awakened in a hospital. She'd awakened with police outside her room for things she had done and been suspected of doing. But they hadn't reckoned with how swiftly a vivum addict recovered from withdrawal once a new dose was delivered. She'd stolen a supply of the drug and disappeared again into the streets. Seven years ago.

"I'm ready," Duash said, interrupting Ginn's thoughts.

The Kelmerian was back on his feet, his color much improved. Ginn nodded at his words, pushed out of the nest of boulders where they'd sheltered and plodded on to the west. The others followed. The ground turned to jagged lava, which covered large portions of the Silent Zone. The flows were ancient but erosion had done little to smooth them. Slivers of ice glittered in the crannies, and the wind moaned like a dying thing.

Hour after hour, they walked. Exhaustion turned their every thought numb, but to sleep would have been to die. They stopped again, to nibble dark-meat and heat rocks with Ginn's blaster for temporary warmth, but mostly to take more vivum. Now, barely half a dose of the drug remained. Ginn tasted the iron bitterness in the back of her mouth that always signaled withdrawal. The taste was only psychological now. Soon it wouldn't be.

They walked on. The numbness grew. And grew.

Ginn stopped. She'd heard a sound. A frown tried to crease her face but the skin and muscles beneath were too frozen to respond. She turned, almost fell. Duash stood about thirty feet behind her, off to one side of the path they'd been following. Kenzes was still coming after her but stopped when she turned. She realized the sound had been their voices calling her.

She made her way back toward Duash, who suddenly began to disappear from sight as if he were going down a flight of stairs. Kenzes was waiting when she reached that spot, and she saw that Duash had climbed down into a little hollow within the lava flow and stood on a patch of barren ground. Kenzes moved to join him and Ginn followed, though she wasn't sure why they were stopping. It was too soon for more vivum. But at least they were out of the wind.

Duash squatted down, appeared to be punching the ground. A large triangle of rock suddenly became transparent. A tunnel appeared, with a slope running down into it. A faint gleam came from inside. Ginn croaked out a "wait," but Kenzes and Duash were already staggering down the slope and she had to follow.

Three steps inside and the opening sealed behind Ginn. She felt the quick bite of terror, but her companions waited at the slope's bottom and did not seem afraid. She joined them, found herself in a triangular shaped corridor that ran farther than she could see. It was warm here, and lit by a dim glow that seeped out of the stone itself.

Duash was grinning. "This is it. The main site is down this tunnel." He gave a huge sigh and leaned against the wall before sliding down it to a sitting position. "Just need...to rest. A moment."

Snoring followed. Ginn might have laughed if she hadn't been so tired herself. She found a patch of stone flooring for herself, lay down and thought she'd never felt anything so soft in her life.

"Sleep," Kenzes said. "I'll...watch."

"Sleep yourself," Ginn muttered. "All too tired. Just have to hope...we'll be safe."

Then the sound of snoring doubled.

CHAPTER NINETEEN

WAKING TO THE STRANGE

Ginn dreamt of vivum. She dreamt a green-gold river pulsing through her veins, the color filling up the hazel of her eyes. She saw the bubbles forming in her blood, breaking again as they flowed into her cells to speed up their molecular machinery. She tasted the drug, smelled it all around her, felt the faint, oiliness of it warm on her fingers.

She dreamt of her father. They hiked in the highlands together and he busted rock with a pick to show her the glittering crystals of raw mineral that formed the basis of vivum. She dreamt that there were tears in his eyes.

The dream faded; Ginn's mind drifted toward wakefulness but her thoughts were still filled. For a while after humans discovered vivum's ability to renew and extend biological functions there had been a "gold" rush on Kelmer. Eventually, chemists synthesized a replacement more tailored to human physiology.

The synthetic, Ty-viv, didn't work on Kelmerians and lacked the original drug's psychoactive, feel-good properties. It did absolutely nothing for an addict, though it was the only legal version available for humans on Kelmer. Only the nomads and Teshkarie knew the incredibly intricate steps involved in making the real stuff. Even Red Jac had never mastered the technique, despite spending a lot of solars on the attempt.

Ginn came fully awake then, and sat up. Duash slept on a few feet away, but Kenzes's blankets were empty. Instantly, she was on her feet, but relaxed at sight of the nomad striding the tunnel toward her. Only then did she realize how badly her body ached from overexertion. Bones and muscles didn't seem to fit together any longer, and every nerve played its own tune of pain. She leaned against the wall, suppressed a moan.

Kenzes came up. "I scouted ahead. The tunnel goes a long way but the light increases. I believe we may be close to the place Duash...the alh Corovaneen seeks."

Ginn nodded slowly. She forced herself to straighten up. Stretching helped. It was hot here; she was sweating. She stripped off most of the clothing she'd needed outside and piled it against the corridor wall, leaving on her BDUs and t-shirt. Kenzes had already done much the same.

"I...would speak," Kenzes said suddenly.

She looked at him curiously.

"When we first met. I.... I regret what—"

"Forget it," Ginn interrupted. "I have. How long were we out?"

A moment passed. Then: "Not yet a third of a regular sleep."

"Three hours maybe," Ginn said. "It'll have to do. Get Duash up. I'll take the point."

Kenzes nodded, moved toward Duash. Ginn checked her blaster's charge levels. Modern weapons like hers carried almost a thousand minutes of charge to each power cell, but she'd put heavy demands on this one and it was getting low. She ejected the used cell, shoved a fresh one up the handle and clicked it home.

Better safe than sorry.

Duash moaned and groaned as Kenzes helped him to his feet. "I have never hurt so badly," he muttered.

"You'll feel better when we're walking again," Ginn told him, smiling into the glare he gave her. "Is it gonna stay this warm?"

The Kelmerian nodded. He too stripped down, retaining only his robe.

"OK," Ginn said. "We'll leave our extra gear here. Pick it up on the way out."

She didn't wait for a response but filled a small pouch with a canteen and her father's journal and slung it over a shoulder before starting down the corridor. That "corridor" cut like a triangle through the rock, running straight and smooth ahead without a speck of dust on the floor. Ginn saw what Kenzes meant about the glow increasing. Other tunnels occasionally opened off at right angles to their own, but all were dimmer and she did not turn aside. Half an hour's walk brought them to the source of the most intense glow.

The corridor ended abruptly at a large spherical area whose far walls she couldn't see. A thick pearl vapor filled most of that area, restricting vision to no more than a couple feet. Straight in front of them, however, the mist was much thinner, and about fifty yards ahead, suspended in the air like strange fruit, were dozens of geometric forms. Ginn saw triangles, rectangles, trapezoids. She saw pinwheels that reminded her of the Collectors. She saw shapes that she had no names for. All seem to float unsupported, and all were a uniform gray in color.

Duash had stopped beside Ginn, but he suddenly stepped past her, out of the tunnel into what appeared to be empty air. She shouted in alarm, grabbed reflexively for him, but he dodged away from her, and he was laughing. The vapor had solidified under his feet.

"There is no danger," he said. "This whole area. Balaen discovered. It will not let you fall."

"Asshole!" Ginn snapped.

Duash shook his head. "Perhaps you will recall a small 'joke' or two that you have played on *me*."

Ginn's lips twitched toward a smile. She fought it, then snorted. "Yeah, but my pranks were funny."

Duash shook his head again and moved off toward where the gray geometrical shapes hung. Kenzes edged after him, and Ginn finally followed, testing each step as if negotiating a tightrope. It was like moving down a steam filled hallway, with walls of silent white to either side that seemed ripe with potential threat.

To take her mind off what might be hiding in that white-out, Ginn called to Duash. "What is this place?" Her words sounded flat and atonal to her own ears—with no echo.

"A central processing unit, I believe," Duash called back. "A computer of sorts."

He approached one of the floating forms—*a dodeca-something*, Ginn thought—and touched it. A ruby red blush suffused the shape and a strange music began to play. At least it sounded vaguely like what Ginn would call music. There might even have been a voice singing along. She couldn't be sure.

"I hear words," Kenzes said.

A human-type shrug lifted Duash's shoulders. "Balaen thought it to be the language of those who built this place. Though we found no translation."

"Is there anything else you *did* find?" Ginn asked.

Duash answered by moving over to another floating shape. This one resembled a triangle with a four-spoked wheel superimposed upon it. He touched the triangle, which immediately lit up all golden. Then the Kelmerian stroked the wheel, which blinked rapidly through a rainbow of colors.

Duash muttered a word Ginn didn't catch, but before she could ask him what he'd said a small bowl materialized in the air just below the wheel and rested there, as if the mist had solidified beneath it. Perhaps it had, Ginn mused. The bowl was translucent but contained some kind of dark liquid. Duash plucked it up and offered it to Ginn.

"What the hell is it?" she asked suspiciously.

"Kaftee," Duash said. Then: "Oh, I forgot. You suspect me of wanting to poison you." He lifted the bowl to his lips and drank. Next, he handed it to Kenzes, who sipped and smacked lips in pleasure.

Ginn took the bowl from Kenzes. It felt like glass but was as light as an insect's wing. The liquid inside steamed. She sniffed, felt her mouth react to the delicious aroma of kaftee. She sipped, then turned up the bowl and finished the drink.

Duash was already stroking the machine again, and when

he turned back toward Ginn he tossed something to her. She caught it; her eyes widened.

"The apple I owe you," Duash said.

Ginn laughed in amazement. "That's incredible. It must be some kind of...matter manipulator."

"Yes. Balaen was sure that it converted molecules of the drifting mist into other substances. Yet, it is selective in who it responds to. When we were here with Red Jac's men, it worked only for myself and for Balaen. It may be that it is not attuned to the human mind. You should try it."

"How? What do I do?

"While touching the wheel, you visualize a thing you want. It helps, I believe, if you name that thing. Perhaps, also, if you close your eyes."

Ginn handed her apple to Kenzes and walked forward, paused a moment, then with a sure sense that nothing would happen stroked her hand along one spoke of the wheel. She shut her eyes, said a word. A gasp from Duash told her that something had indeed happened.

She opened her eyes. A small, green-gold marble floated in the air in front of her. Its surface swirled like the atmosphere of a miniature planet. She reached for it, hesitated, finally touched it as lightly as she could with one finger. It quivered in response and its surface spun more quickly. She drew her finger back, held it to her nose. Her heart began to pound. She touched the finger to her tongue and knew instantly from her body's reaction what she was dealing with.

"Vivum!" she said. She looked at Duash. "You didn't lie. It *is* here."

He smiled. "I am glad that it worked for you. Though I do not understand why it did not for Red Jac's men."

"Maybe because I'm a woman," Ginn said.

"Perhaps. Yet I am male. We will have you try the other machines. None," he gestured around, "worked for any of us before. A few changed in color. Jac's lieutenant, Flavin, insisted we use that machine," he pointed toward the matter changer, "to make many solars to take back to Red Jac."

"Figures," Ginn said. "Flavin never did have much imagination."

"I made many for myself as well," Duash admitted. "To finance *this* journey."

Ginn made no comment. She was busy withdrawing the almost empty drug vial from under her shirt. She pulled the syringe free and carefully inserted the needle into the floating ball of vivum. Drawing back the plunger slowly, she refilled the syringe before recapping the vial and retaping it to her chest. Her breathing came a little easier after that.

Duash stood next to a third floating shape when Ginn looked back toward him. This one resembled a diamond trapped within a helix.

"Balaen believed this to be the main control," he said. He touched it and only a brief flush of silver along the diamond's facets rewarded him.

Ginn frowned as a memory brushed her mind and faded too quickly to catch.

"If we could activate this," Duash continued, "I feel it would give the answers we search out. Now, with food and drink assured, we can stay here. Study upon it."

Once again a memory/thought brushed Ginn's mind. This time she snagged a fingernail in it.

"Wait," she said. She drew her father's journal from the bag on her shoulder and quickly began to flip through it. "Here!" She turned the journal around toward Duash. "On this page of symbols. It's the same one. The diamond and helix."

Duash took the book. "Yes," he said. "I had almost forgotten this page. See how it is drawn with a border around it. As if the symbols were incised upon a rectangular plate of some kind. Balaen told me that your father once found an artifact like this in the highlands. Near one of the aqueducts as if it had washed down from the Silent Zone. It was lost in the flitter crash."

"Then Dad made this drawing from the artifact?" Ginn asked. "Not because he was here?"

"Balaen did not believe your father ever found this place," Duash said.

Ginn took the journal back, studied the page a moment. "There's a repetition of the symbols but the sets aren't exactly the same. It's like the Collectors. The symbols seem to be—"

A sound of sudden clapping filled Ginn's ears.

CHAPTER TWENTY
RED JAC

Ginn released the journal, grabbed for her blaster. A bolt of blue flame sizzled past her head and she froze. Kenzes and Duash froze with her.

"Drop the weapons. Knives too," a voice called.

Ginn recognized it. And obeyed. Her companions followed suite. The strange surface under their feet absorbed the impacts without a sound.

Seven men walked from the corridor that Ginn and the others had taken to reach this spot. Red Jac's lieutenant, Flavin, led. Jac himself followed. All but Jac were armed with laser rifles in addition to blasters; he wore only a pair of silver handled blasters slung at his hips. The foot-soldiers spread out around the captured trio. Jac and Flavin stopped in front of Ginn. Flavin kicked their fallen weapons away.

"Hello, Ginn," Red Jac said. "How the hell are you still alive?"

"Out of hatred for you," Ginn spat.

Jac laughed. "I can imagine."

Though barely an inch taller than Ginn's five feet, seven, Jac was nearly three times as wide. In the warmth of the underground, he wore only leather pants and a sleeveless vest that revealed the bulging sinews in his arms and chest. His neck and shoulders were slabbed with muscle; his head was shaved, although she remembered when he'd had thick blond hair that he prized. The face was surprisingly average, though that changed when he smiled. Then it came alive with charm. Or menace. Depending on how well you knew him. The eyes hid behind rose colored light-lenses that had given him the first part of his name.

"How did you find us?" Ginn demanded.

Jac smiled. "Did you really think you *stole* a vial of vivum from me so easily?"

Ginn shook her head. "I ran a tracking program over it. There was no bug."

"Not in the vial. Or the syringe. In the drug itself. You stuck it in your veins with the first dose you took. Unfortunately, it is by necessity a micro-device. Doesn't have much range. I just wanted to get reacquainted. I wasn't expecting you to join up with our old pal Du-wash here. We lost you in the desert. And when we couldn't pick you up crossing the border of the Silent Zone...." He paused a moment. "How'd you manage that by the way?" Then he waved a hand dismissively. "Doesn't matter. After we figured you were in the Zone, I set a couple of flitters flying back and forth over your most likely trail until they turned up a signal. And here we are."

"How'd you get flitters past the Navy's satellites?"

"Hauled 'em all the way to the Silent Zone. The Navy doesn't scan the Zones. Nothing worth watching. Maybe you didn't know that. But the important thing is old Dooye can show us how to work this place now. Seeing that we didn't have to kill him."

"Not that you didn't try enough times and miss," Ginn said.

"You're only as good as the people you employ," Jac said. "Seems I told you that once upon a time. When we were lovers."

"You told me a *lot* of bullshit," Ginn said, shrugging. "Who remembers?"

"Ginn, Ginn. Don't you ever get tired of pretending to be a cold, hard bitch? You could have been rich by now. But you didn't have the guts for it."

"I had no stomach for you. That much is true."

Jac laughed again, reached out and stroked her chin with a

thick knuckle. She jerked her head back. From the corner of an eye, Ginn saw the stunned looks on Duash and Kenzes's faces. Duash had known of her onetime association with Jac, but not how close it had been. Kenzes was hearing it all for the first time, and disgust lay unveiled on the nomad's face. She tried not to let that bother her but couldn't quite manage it.

"I overestimated you," Jac continued. "I thought you could learn. Thought if you had enough chances you'd see that your only future lay with me." He gave her a once over, shook his head in mock sadness. "Too late now. Your body's still not bad but that *face*. What are you? Barely twenty-four? And already aging badly. The desert, I guess. I'll always remember when you were sixteen. Fresh and ripe."

"Being around you puts years on a person," Ginn agreed.

"Not to mention having to whore on the streets for vivum that I would have given you free."

"Free!" Ginn said, and smiled. "The only whoring I ever did was sleeping with you."

Jac's upper lip twitched. The humor disappeared from his voice.

"Spoken like a true addict," he said.

"Yeah," Ginn said. "Thanks for that, by the way."

"I suppose I could have mentioned the link between alcohol use and vivum addiction. But where would the fun have been in that? Besides, you would have gotten there on your own anyway. Given that mother you told me about. And your absentee old man."

Ginn punched Red Jac, the movement too swift for anyone to block. But an instant later, two of Jac's men caught Ginn by the arms and forced her to stillness between them.

Jac brushed a hand across his mouth, looked at the thin stain of blood on his fingers from a cut lip. He gave a melodramatic sigh, then spread his legs slightly for leverage and slammed a hard fist into Ginn's jaw.

She rocked backward, would have collapsed if not for the men holding her. She barely registered the second punch burying itself in her stomach, but her body jackknifed reflexively. The men released her and she fell to hands and knees as she retched.

Jac's voice came from a distance. "That wasn't very bright, Ginn. You know I could tear your pretty little jaw *off* if I really hit you."

Ginn lifted her head, spat, then pushed to her knees. Duash stood with a laser rifle resting against his cheek. Kenzes was down. She figured he'd tried to come to her aid and been beaten unconscious for it. She brought her right hand up, slid it beneath her shirt to rub at the center of agony where Jac had struck her.

Jac was speaking at Duash and ignoring Ginn. "Now," he said, rubbing his hands together as if ready to get down to the real work of the moment, "let's get you started showing me how to use these machines. That way I won't have to start cutting on your boyfriend there." He pointed at the still unconscious Kenzes. "Or your girlfriend. Or whatever you Kelm fucks like to call your humps."

Ginn's hand slid further up under her shirt; her fingers touched the tape holding the vial of vivum to her skin.

"You will not be able to use the symbols," Duash was saying, his voice defiant. "They work only for...Kelms."

"I hope you're lying," Jac said. "It's not gonna go well for your friends otherwise."

One of the guards who had held Ginn for Red Jac leaned down and dropped a big hand on her shoulder.

Ginn's fingers closed over the vial of drug, tugged it free. Her thumb popped the syringe lose. She twisted around suddenly on her knees, struck upward at the guard who was leaning toward her. The needle of the syringe stabbed into the man's carotid artery, just under his jaw. Ginn shoved the plunger all the way down, pushing five full doses of vivum instantly into the man's bloodstream.

He grabbed for his throat; Ginn powered to her feet, leaving the syringe in the wound. Her left hand dropped to the blaster holstered at the man's hip. She jerked it free, fired at point blank range into the body of the next closest guard. The man's chest exploded like overheated meat in a microwave.

Jac lunged toward her but she was already turning, running. The dense wall of white mist that clogged most of the cavern was only five feet away. Then two feet. She leaped the last foot, plunged into whiteness and threw herself down.

Blaster fire scorched the air where she'd been an instant before. But she was eeling left and right. A laser rifle on wide-beam cooked the vapor over her head, sent it eddying wildly. More fire followed but the shooters couldn't see her in the mist and the blasts kept getting further and further away as Ginn moved.

Her outstretched hand struck the wall of the cavern and she rolled against it. Now it was time to hate and wait.

CHAPTER TWENTY-ONE

COLD GINN

"Ginn! Honey!"

Red Jac's voice was smooth and oiled. No one who didn't know him would guess that he was enraged. Ginn knew him.

"I hope you didn't take those punches seriously," Jac continued. "I thought we were just revisiting old times. I remember how you liked it rough."

Ginn came to her feet, moved along the cavern wall. The mist was like a womb around her: hot, wet, uncomfortable. The whiteness diffused the light so completely that even her light-lenses couldn't help her see more than a foot or two in front of her. But the vapor also protected her. She was grateful for that.

"I needed a place to sleep; you were handy," Ginn called to Jac, and instantly darted away from her position.

No laser fire came. She smiled. She'd counted on the sound deadening qualities of the odd mist to make it impossible for Jac to locate her from just her voice. And if she kept him talking he wouldn't be torturing Duash and Kenzes.

Jac chuckled. "I was afraid you'd run away, love. It's what you're good at, after all."

"Running from you wasn't like running away from anyone I gave a damn about," Ginn called back.

"Ouch!"

Ginn remained silent but kept moving, circling gradually in toward where she thought the center of the cavern lay, where the alien machines hung in the air.

"You there, lover?" Jac called.

"Closer than you think," Ginn replied.

Jac laughed. "By the way. That dagvyre you corrupted back in Old Towne. The one who was supposed to be guarding my bar but let you pass anyway. I cut off his head."

Ginn paused for a moment, then moved on.

"Better come out, Ginn. Or I'll start hurting your friends here."

"You'll hurt 'em anyway."

"Yeah. But not as bad."

"I know how to operate the machines," Ginn called. "Let my friends go and I'll tell you."

"Tell me first."

The mist began to clear a little in front of Ginn. She glimpsed one of the alien artifacts. Then another. And a third. A body lay on the floor nearby, the guard she'd blasted. The one she'd injected with vivum might still live but five doses to the brain at once would have fried half his neurons. She needn't worry about him.

There was no sign of Red Jac or the others. She'd expected that. They'd almost certainly pulled back into the approach tunnel where Ginn couldn't get behind them. She wasn't looking to get behind them.

She hefted her stolen blaster, took careful aim at the first machine Duash had activated. The weird music chimed on from it; the words she didn't understand whispered like the hum of a dark sun. Ginn fired. Half the alien symbol went spinning away; the sound died.

"No!" Duash cried out.

"Dammit!" Jac cursed.

"I'll burn 'em all," Ginn screamed. She threw herself back into the thicker mist as blaster and laser fire erupted from the direction of the approach tunnel. A sudden sear of pain lanced her left arm and she hurled herself down, rolled away.

"Get her, get her, get her," Jac yelled.

Now Jac would send his men into the mist after her, to keep

her from destroying the alien machines he hoped to master. He'd hang back himself, holding Duash and Kenzes hostage at the point of a gun. That would leave four against one. It was exactly what Ginn had counted on.

She staggered up. Her left arm burned but her hand still worked. A glance showed a field of blisters stippled down the outside of her arm from elbow to wrist.

Near miss.

She clenched her teeth against the pain. No time for it now. She had men to kill.

CHAPTER TWENTY-TWO

GINN SHAKEN, NOT STIRRED

Blaster flame billowed the gruel-thick white mist. Ginn retreated before it, holding her own fire. Her enemies hunted her in pairs. They'd abandoned laser rifles in favor of shorter range hand blasters. They didn't know exactly where she was in the white-out but they'd set their weapons to wide beam and were fanning the flames back and forth and up and down ahead of them. She was being herded toward the cavern wall, and if she couldn't get past their field of fire they'd corner her. Then it would all be over.

Ginn didn't intend to be cornered. The cavern was too big for four men to cover every inch with fire. There had to be missed spots, places where no flame scorched. She hoped.

Ginn kept backing away, letting eddies of fog stirred by the blasters caress her body. Anyone carrying out a search and destroy mission like the one Jac's men engaged in developed a pattern to their work. Ginn began to learn that pattern from the movements of the air. She began to own it. And she retreated.

Then she stopped retreating. She darted forward, dropped to a crouch. Fire sprayed over her head. She went to her belly, rolled soundlessly on the strange floor. Flame licked the place she'd been. She came to her feet, jinked to her right. Her ears picked up the whoosh of a seeking blaster. A tingle electrified her skin, making the hair stand up. Too close for comfort but not close enough to burn.

Without hesitation, she moved. The tingle fell away. Again

she crouched, and rolled, and rose. And repeated. It was a dance with partners who could not see her but who guided her with fire. Ginn didn't know much about dancing. But she knew how to survive.

The static tingle hit her again, intense enough to hurt. She went to the floor, savaging her lip with her teeth to keep from crying out. She rolled, flattened herself on her belly. Then the firing was past her, moving still toward the cavern wall. She rose to her feet. She was behind her enemies now.

Wheeling about, she darted forward on silent feet. Two men materialized out of the mist. She was right on top of them. Their backs were turned, their focus all in front of them. One sensed something, twisted around. She didn't hesitate. Her blaster was already set to its narrowest pattern. She pulled the trigger, slashing the beam like a fiery sword from right to left across her enemies' bodies.

A line of flesh vaporized across the first man's neck. The head sagged sideways onto the shoulder. Spraying arterial blood flash-boiled away into crimson steam. The second fellow's back was still turned. He screamed as the cutting torch of the beam sliced his upper spine in two and dropped him dying to the floor.

Ginn flung herself down between the bodies, into blood. A shout came from Red Jac's other guards. They'd be here in seconds. Or faster.

The mist shuddered above her. A guard loomed. He saw the bodies, but in the instant it took him to realize that there were three instead of two, Ginn shot him right through the heart.

He sagged, started to fall. Ginn surged up from the ground, caught his shirt in her fists. Terror and rage strengthened her arms. The lighter gravity of Kelmer helped. For just a moment she held the man up and ducked behind his much wider frame, twisting her body into the smallest space she could manage.

She hadn't seen Flavin but now Flavin lunged out of the mist and saw her. He fired from no more than two feet away, perfectly willing to kill his own man to get to her. But his weapon was still on wide beam. The flare of the blast struck the corpse that

Ginn held as a shield. Clothing burst into flame; flesh boiled. The fiery backwash scorched past Ginn to either side and she screamed with the agony of it. The stench of burned meat fouled the air; some of that smell was hers.

She lurched with a shoulder against the dead body she held, shoved it toward Flavin with every ounce of strength she had left. It struck the outlaw, jarred him backward. His blaster went silent.

Ginn straightened, fired at point blank range into Flavin's chest. He jerked and shrieked. She fired again. He dropped to his knees. She dropped with him, fired again into his face. He went back and down, his eyes bubbling in their sockets.

Ginn remained on her knees, gasping hard for air that seemed unable to feed her. Pain coiled around her like a razor-scaled snake. She sobbed with it. Her light-lenses were hazed almost black from the near pass of a blaster beam. She swiped at them, knocked them off. Smoke and tears stung her eyes but she could see.

She forced herself to her feet, staggered toward the access tunnel where Red Jac would be holding a gun on beings who'd become her friends. Much of her hair was singed to a frizz. Fields of blisters spread down both arms and across her back beneath her t-shirt. The blisters rubbed as she walked, began to burst and drain and soak her clothing with pale serum. She wanted to lie down and sleep forever. But then her legs steadied. No matter how badly she hurt, she had to make it a few more minutes.

The mist thinned. She saw Red Jac and her friends ahead of her.

"Just you and me now, Jac!" she called.

CHAPTER TWENTY-THREE
REVENGE IS A DISH BEST
SERVED WITH FIRE

Jac stood calmly in the opening of the access tunnel. He held a blaster in his right hand. His left arm encircled Duash's neck and locked the Kelmerian tight against him. Duash's hands were bound behind his back. Kenzes lay at their feet, hands and feet both bound, and with a loose gag in his mouth. A third body sprawled against the wall, foam flecking its lips. The man Ginn had injected with the vivum overdose hadn't lived after all.

"Resourceful," Jac said loudly. "But it changes little. I'm still holding the ace." He jiggled Duash a bit.

Ginn gave him a lopsided grin. "No commentary on my appearance, Jac? You must be running scared." She tried to keep her voice normal but could hear how rough it sounded.

Jac sneered. "A few cosmetic surgeries and I might fuck you again."

Ginn shook her head. She too held a blaster in her right hand. Her left hand dipped into one pocket of her BDUs.

"You'll never fuck me again, Jac. Never again. Can't say the same for what I'm about to do to you, though."

She pulled a small round object free of her pocket and held it up. A scarlet telltale blinked between her fingers. "I imagine you recognize this little toy," Ginn said.

Duash's eyes widened; Jac's narrowed. "A bomb-bot," the outlaw said. "Can't be real."

"You've *always* underestimated me," Ginn said, as she

started walking forward.

"Stay back," Jac warned. He pressed the barrel of his blaster hard against Duash's head, wringing a cry of pain from the small Kelmerian.

Ginn didn't stop walking. "You kill him, Jac. I kill you. You kill *me* and this whole place goes up. Drop your weapon. Get down on your belly. I'll give you to the Terran navy. They won't execute you. You might even escape them. In time."

She shifted her gaze to Duash, let her eyes linger for an instant on his.

"I'd rather die," Jac said.

"I'd rather you would too," Ginn agreed. "But we don't always get what we want."

She was within ten feet of Jac now. With one swift movement she flicked the bomb-bot toward him. For a fraction, Jac hesitated. His gaze flashed toward the bot.

Duash, who'd read Ginn's glance correctly, twisted suddenly to one side. Ginn fired her blaster in the same instant. A narrow finger of smoldering crimson stabbed Jac in the forehead and burst out through the top of his skull. The bomb-bot dropped to the floor, rolled against Jac's boot. The crime lord crashed backward like an uprooted tree.

Ginn slumped to her knees with a moan. Duash rushed to her, knelt himself. He seemed to want to touch her but didn't know where to lay his hands without hurting her.

"I thought the bomb-bot was just a bluff," he said. "The nomads were so sure."

"They were right," Ginn said. "Only the Terran military has access to that kind of technology. That one really is a toy."

Duash barked a sudden laugh, which changed to a cry of alarm as Ginn fell unconscious into his arms.

EPILOGUE

Ginn opened her eyes. Kenzes knelt beside her wearing a tentative smile. She was lying on something soft. She felt comfortable, until the memories came back—and the pain with them. She bit down on a groan but couldn't hold it all in. Kenzes's smile faded.

"Where's Duash?" she managed after a moment, heard her own voice as little more than a croak.

"Here," the Kelmerian said. He came at a run and joined Kenzes beside her. His hand held a syringe of vivum and for a moment Ginn couldn't figure where he'd gotten it. Then she recalled the alien machine, the matter manipulator.

"You are badly burned," Duash said. "You will need a hospital. Perhaps surgeries. Yet, a dose of vivum will help a little, and make you sleep until we can get to aid."

"No," Ginn said. "Two drops. No more."

"That—"

"Two drops!" She struggled to a sitting position. She was in the access tunnel and considered using the wall as a back rest before deciding that her blisters wouldn't like it.

Duash shook his head but leaned toward her with the syringe. She caught his arm.

"I'll do it," she said.

He gazed at her. "One might think you would have learned to trust me by now."

She gazed back, and saw, in his eyes.... She released her grip. "OK."

Gently, he took her hand and turned it over to reveal a patch of unburned skin on her inner wrist. A little prick followed, and two drops of vivum purled into her veins. She sighed, sagged a little where she sat.

"More would be better," Duash said.

"No. I've gotta tell you. Show you. The machine you called the 'main control.' I know how to work it."

"What?"

"Help me up." Ginn held her hands out but neither Kelmerian moved. She sighed. "It would be nice if I didn't have to repeat everything twice. Now help me up."

Kenzes and Duash each took a hand and pulled her to her feet. She groaned all the way but managed to keep her legs steady once she was standing. Before thoughts of more vivum to kill the pain could distract her, she slogged out of the tunnel into the cavern where the alien machines drifted.

She stopped before the one that resembled a diamond inside a helix. On the floor beneath it laid her father's journal, where she'd dropped it when Red Jac surprised them. She started to bend over for it but Kenzes got to it first and handed it to her.

"I can—" she started to snap, then stopped herself. She shook her head—at herself.

"Thanks," she murmured.

Kenzes nodded, and she opened the journal, flipping through until she found the page her father had covered with symbols, including the diamond and helix machine.

"Look here," she said, showing the page to Duash. "I noticed this just before...Jac. There are two complete sets of the symbols. But they aren't quite the same."

"I see," Duash agreed. "I do not know how that means anything."

"The rotations of the symbols. They're opposites. I'm sure one represents 'male.' The other 'female.'"

Duash suddenly looked excited. "Yes. That could be."

"I think. To activate this machine we need both a male and a female. At the same time."

"You and I," Duash said.

Ginn nodded. Then she reached up and touched the symbol. Duash stepped forward, did the same.

Blue light spun along the helix pattern and each diamond facet flushed with molten silver. The cavern's misty atmosphere brightened and all the other geometrical forms lit up from within. An alien voice began speaking, and Ginn saw with wonder that the machine she'd burned in half with her blaster seemed to be "healing" itself and was working again.

Duash grinned. Kenzes grinned. Ginn grinned.

"It worked," Duash said, as if he hadn't believed it would.

Ginn's grin widened.

The alien voice changed. The words were suddenly recognizable.

"Balaen!" Duash shouted.

"Dad!" Ginn yelled at the same instant.

Incredulously, they looked at each other, then at Kenzes.

The nomad shrugged. "I hear my chieftain."

"You hear those who mean the most to you," the voice itself said. Now it seemed to come from everywhere and nowhere.

Duash recovered first. "You are the machine that runs this place?" he asked, of the air.

"Yes."

"And what exactly *is* this place?" Ginn asked.

"You have already surmised part of the answer to that. Here landed representatives of a race unknown to this world, this galaxy. These were the Sembrini. The Kelmerian sun was already far into decline. To save life here, the Sembrini placed the objects you call Collectors in orbit. Their further plans were thwarted. They were pursued. Those known as the Selkrie hunted them, and the Sembrini fled before they could be destroyed, and with them the rest of this ancient world. I remained. Their machine. Only my lower functions were left activated. Else the Selkrie would have sensed and slain me. I could not fulfill the Sembrini's hopes for Kelmer."

"What hopes?" Duash asked.

"Housed beneath us in the crust of what you call the Western Silent Zone, there is another Collector. The Eastern Zone is the same. These too should have been placed in orbit, opposite to those that now abide. As you have activated me, I will finally be able to complete that process. There will be no more Silent Zones. Heat. Light. Moisture. These will increase. Life will blossom again here. I begin as soon as you three clear the Zone so that you will not be injured."

"So that's it?" Ginn protested. "We just take off? After all the shit we went through getting here?"

For a long moment there was silence, as if the machine had not expected an argument. Finally: "I wish to fulfill my purpose. You must leave before the world can be renewed. After that, this place will cease to be."

Kenzes turned as if to go. Duash hesitated.

"No!" Ginn said. "You've waited a long time. You can wait a little longer. I've got the answers I sought, the ones my dad sought. But Duash came to find out about his mother, and *his* father. And you know the answers because it wasn't any accident that he found his way here. He was drawn here. Tell him what he wants to know and *then* we'll go."

Again there was a long silence. When words came this time, they seemed to address only Duash, and Ginn wondered if it were just her imagination that painted the words with regret.

"Duash-tei-tei-varzan alh Corovaneen," the voice said. "Little about your life has been accident. The Sembrini created using the twin energies of the universe. Those energies you call male and female are aspects of this. The Kelmerians, too, were once male and female apart."

"Jake Hollis was right," Duash said.

"Indeed," the voice continued. "Then evolution on Kelmer chose a different path. Without the separate male and female energies, I could not complete my purpose. Long before humans came here, I began to try—with the limited capabilities I was left—to effect a change that would lead to you. Or someone like you. I was unsuccessful until humans did arrive. Only hybridization could create that which was needed. Even then it took time."

"You made me," Duash said, and Ginn could not read his emotions.

"I am indeed your life giver. When you were but tiny, I called one here to take and raise you in the outside. Then I began—in the same manner—to make a sister for you. Only, the hybridization process would not work with the female. My purpose seemed as far as ever from being fulfilled. Until I became aware of Jake Hollis's daughter."

"But there's nothing of Kelmer in me," Ginn argued.

"Vivum is of Kelmer," the voice said. "It is also, intimately, of you. That is why the machines responded to you. In a way, you are a hybrid yourself."

Ginn opened her mouth to speak, closed it again with a snap. She looked at Duash.

He smiled and touched her hand. "I think perhaps I should get my 'sister' to a doctor now," he said. "I know. What I need to know."

Ginn took a deep breath, nodded.

"There is one more thing. Ginn," the machine voice said. "The vivum given to you moments ago was from an altered formula. Your body will no longer require the drug."

The words registered on Ginn's ears but scarcely sank in. She reached up and tugged at her earlobe. Then she turned and walked away. Duash and Kenzes came after. Outside the tunnel where they'd first entered the alien site they found one of Red Jac's flitters. With Ginn's instruction, Duash flew it as they headed away from the Silent Zone, and as they crossed the Zone's border into the highlands he made as if to land.

"Just keep flying," Ginn said. "Take us all the way to Old Towne."

"The military," Duash protested. "They will track us. You said yourself that unscheduled air travel was forbidden."

Ginn laughed. "I think the Terran navy is going to have more on their minds than one unauthorized flitter." She pointed behind them.

Duash and Kenzes turned, and they all saw it. Out of the rocky ground of the Silent Zone, a whirlpool of quantum light was breaking free, was spinning into the air along lines of force that sparked a brilliant aurora thirty miles across.

A third Collector.

Lifting toward orbit.

Rising over Kelmer like a new dawn.

ABOUT THE AUTHOR

CHARLES ALLEN GRAMLICH grew up on a farm in Arkansas, near the foothills of the Ozark Mountains, then moved to the New Orleans area in 1986. He's since sold several novels and numerous short stories. His tales, while mostly in the genres of horror, science fiction, and fantasy, have also included westerns, children's stories, mainstream fiction, slipstream works, and experimental pieces. He has also published poetry and nonfiction, the latter ranging from reference works to articles on writing.

After Hurricane Katrina smashed up New Orleans, Charles and his wife, Lana, moved to Abita Springs, Louisiana, where they live in the woods with many birds. Charles has an adult son named Joshua.

Charles has a long term association with REHupa (the Robert E. Howard United Press Association), and is a member of HWA (the Horror Writers Association), and the SFPA (the Science Fiction Poetry Association). He produces a regular column on writing for *The Illuminata*, an online magazine. His blog can be found at:

Http://charlesgramlich.blogspot.com

THE BATTLE FOR EDEN

A spacefaring horde of carnivorous crab-like aliens known as the Knackers is advancing toward the human core worlds, decimating outlying systems as they go. When the invaders approach Eden, one of the most beautiful and populous planets in the Human Federation, it is up to SpaceForce to make a stand.

In the skies over Eden, the battle rages—and one war-weary fighter, Major Simon Roy, falls to ground in his wounded ship. There he takes refuge with a brave family of farmers living peacefully in the idyllic countryside. When the aliens overwhelm the planet, the impromptu companions find themselves isolated and in peril. As they fight for survival, can Simon rediscover his humanity, and find a way to make his own stand against an enemy that has never been defeated?

Borgo Press Books by MARK E. BURGESS

The Battle for Eden: The Human-Knacker War, Book Three
Dog Daze and Cat Naps: A Vet Student's Odyssey

The Human-Knacker War Series

1. *Slaughterhouse World*, by Ardath Mayhar
2. *Knack' Attack*, by Robert Reginald
3. *The Battle for Eden*, by Mark E. Burgess

THE BATTLE
FOR EDEN

THE HUMAN-KNACKER WAR,
BOOK THREE

MARK E. BURGESS

THE BORGO PRESS
MMXII

THE BATTLE FOR EDEN

DEDICATION

To my wife, **Denise**,
and my daughters, **Anna & Sarah**,
without whom life in
any universe would be empty;

And my thanks to the legendary Keith
Laumer, grand marshal of combat science fiction, whose Bolo story *"The Last Command"*
captured my imagination even as a child.

CONTENTS

CHAPTER ONE

When the Knacker invasion ships materialized out of warp dimension into the Solaris II star system, humanity's space fleet was waiting for them. The decision had been made: no more running before the enemy, no more conceding system after system to the alien marauders from the galactic rim. Here the prey vowed to turn the tide against their tormentors, or to die trying.

The human ships floated silently in the inky blackness of near space, their sleek, silver predatory shapes glinting in the unfiltered sunlight. Behind and beneath them shimmered the blue and green orb of planet Eden, one of the most earth-like and heavily populated worlds of the human Federation. Whether SpaceForce's decision to stand and fight was an act of bravery or desperation was debatable, but no one disputed that the human race was running out of choices, running out of places to hide, of planets to retreat to. Humanity was also being pushed back dangerously close to their core worlds, which had to be protected at all costs.

Simon Roy reflected on this as he waited in his new Avenger class fighter, focusing his anger to help suppress the gnawing fear at the back of his mind. The glowing heads-up display floated ghost-like in front of his eyes, and he scanned it automatically while controlling his breathing. Inhale, exhale, slow and steady, while the small red blips of the enemy ships moved toward the waiting green icons marking the defenders. The alien armada was 40,000 kilometers out and closing fast. Immediately to his port and starboard floated the other members of Alpha fighter

squadron, friends and comrades all, many of whom would not see tomorrow.

The readouts before him told the harsh truth: the human fleet was badly outnumbered. Alone with his thoughts in the stillness before battle, Simon couldn't shake a feeling of inevitability. Despite SpaceForce's best efforts, Eden would likely fall today, just as with every other planet the aliens had set their sights on. If only humanity had had more time to prepare, to build ships, to develop better battle tech, then they might have been able to repel the invaders, push them back, even retake the worlds that held human populations. For truth be told, the outlying planets already overrun by the Crabs (as humans called them) had not been devastated. To the contrary, the habitat of each conquered world was left intact by the aliens, aside from the violence required to subdue the resident populations. The invaders destroyed key defensive installations, and disabled the infra-structure that modern civilization depended on. Each planet's military was overrun, its communication networks and power grids shattered. After that, the Crabs methodically "harvested" the helpless inhabitants, filling their ships' holds with living humans to process at facilities on distant worlds. Given enough time, the marauders would reduce a planet's population by 70% or more before leaving for better hunting elsewhere.

The destinations of the loaded Knacker freighters were mostly unknown, but humans had discovered a few of the factory-planets used by the aliens, and Simon knew that what they had found was a horror show of unthinkable proportions. The Crabs' processing centers were nothing less than planet-wide abattoirs that worked day and night skinning, slicing, cooking, and packaging their prey into convenient foods for the Knacker swarm.

He sighed, his exhale sounding hollow within the helmet of his environment suit, and reached his gloved hand out to touch the photo pasted to the ship's control panel. The faces of a pretty, dark-haired woman holding a young girl smiled out at him, and a

flicker of sadness touched his face. His wife and child were only memories now, part of the multitude of humanity that had been swept away in this thrice-damned war. The thought of them being served as *hors d'oeuvres* in a Knacker buffet kindled a burn deep inside him that had never extinguished. At this point he had nothing to lose, did not even particularly care if he lived or died, as long as he could take a few of the hated Crabs with him.

His expression hardened as he turned his attention back to the view outside his craft. Simon knew where the enemy should appear, from almost straight ahead of his current position, but the endless depths of space could swallow a thousand ships and reveal nothing. At least this battle would play out on the day side of the planet, so the sun's rays would highlight the combatants. Simon disliked engagements fought in deep space or in a planet's shadow, where you couldn't see friend or foe except on instrument display, unless a thruster fired or a ship exploded. And if you lost your sensors while battling in that endless black, you were blind, a sitting target. Today he would fight in the light, and he would give the Crabs reason to fear.

There!

He caught a flicker of motion in the distance, and the speck grew rapidly even as he watched. Other shapes appeared to both sides of the first ship as the shrinking distance revealed smaller vessels. The helmet speaker crackled and his commander's voice spoke crisply, "This is Colonel Hastings aboard the destroyer *Xerxes*. Heads up, everyone. Bogies at one o'clock and closing. Looks like eight or ten destroyers, three carriers, and a whole crapload of fighters. Our task is simple: engage the enemy at will when in range. Alpha and Gamma fighter squadrons, provide fire cover for our carriers and destroyers. Beta and Delta squadrons are free to range wherever you find enemy fighters. Avoid their destroyers; their antispacecraft systems will pick you off. Leave the big boys to us. Good luck, and may the gods of battle favor us this day."

Simon's hands flew over the controls in front of him,

bringing his ride to life, and he felt more than heard the deep hum resonating through the ship's hull as the fighter powered up. Scarcely had he completed the startup routine when the sky around him lit up with a brilliant blue-white flash. To his starboard side the huge bulk of the destroyer *Xerxes* had unleashed its forward energy cannons. The windows of Simon's small craft instantly cycled dark to cut the glare, and he was able to see the second salvo clearly. Twin beams of coherent energy, each more than a meter in thickness, lanced from the bow of the human destroyer and leapt across the void separating the two fleets. They appeared to impact one of the largest enemy vessels in the far distance. A brief flash obscured the target, but when the glare faded, the opposing ship was still advancing, with no damage visible to the naked eye.

The apparent futility of the human barrage was expected, and he wasted not a microsecond of his attention on it. Major Simon Roy was a veteran of five heavy naval engagements with the Crabs. He knew that these initial salvos were simply saber-rattling, as well as a preliminary testing of targeting systems and armament. There was always the chance of a lucky shot knocking out an enemy's sensor array or maneuvering thrusters, but mostly the ships were getting a feel for each other as they closed to effective striking range. Then things would get serious.

The other human destroyers, five in all, joined in the assault, and energy beams filled the void as the two forces continued on a collision course. The blunt-nosed Knacker vessels, nearly twice the size of their SpaceForce counterparts, were now returning fire, and their energy bolts came fast and accurate, each hitting a human ship dead center before winking out a second later. The Crabs possessed the superior military technology. Their energy projection weapons produced a beam more coherent than that of the humans, with less bleed-off over vast distances, therefore packing more punch over a greater range. Simon spared a glance to his right and saw chunks of debris flying into space off the *Xerxes*. The alien hit had done some damage.

No sound reached Simon's ship through the vacuum of

space. He had trained in aircraft planetside before joining SpaceForce, and he had never gotten used to the empty quiet of combat outside of the atmosphere. Once engaged in battle, the rumble of his own ship's engines and weapons would be his only companions outside of the com link. He looked forward to it; anything was better than the tension of sitting and waiting while the silence pressed in on him. No sooner had that thought brushed his mind than a cluster of Knacker fighters streaked by his craft at high speed, causing him to cringe as the nearest ship passed mere meters beyond his window. In that moment his focus shrank, and his universe became very small and very personal.

With finely-honed reflexes Simon hit the lateral thrusters and wheeled his fighter 180 degrees. As the retreating alien fighters came into his sights he kicked the main engines into high acceleration. This latest-generation Avenger possessed inertial dampeners, a technology stolen from captured enemy fighters. Even with their assistance in cushioning the blow, the pressure of fifty Earth gravities of thrust pushed him deep into his crash seat and forced the air from his lungs. He struggled to breathe as he began to run down his quarry. Icons of enemy craft were appearing all over his digital display, lighting it up like a cloud of enraged bees. Great Ares, there were so *many*!

The nimble craft maneuvered effortlessly, like an extension of his own body, as he banked hard to pursue two Crab fighters which had split off from the pack ahead of him. They appeared to be lining up for a strafing run at the nearest human destroyer, and he closed with them from astern. The ovoid shapes of the alien craft contrasted starkly with the arrowhead contours of his own ship, but their awkward appearance belied their deadly effectiveness. Nearly eighty percent of one-on-one engagements with the Knackers had ended with the human fighter destroyed. At least that was the result of battles utilizing the older Lancer class fighters; these new machines had capabilities that were an order of magnitude superior to their predecessors. The experts hoped that this would give SpaceForce a fighting chance over

Eden.

Simon felt a thrill course through him as the two alien vessels swelled in his sights. For the first time it appeared the human armada had fielded craft capable of running with the enemy even at combat speeds. Now the Knackers noticed his pursuit, and their rear energy weapons began spitting lances of fire back at him as they initiated evasive maneuvers.

The alien fighters split in opposite directions, and he tracked the one that banked left. The carapace of his ship flashed like a nova as he took a direct hit from the alien's weapons. Ghost images momentarily filled his eyes and the hull bucked beneath him. But here, too, his fighter served him well. New ablative armor deflected much of the energy of the aliens' weapons. On first detection of the attack, the navigation computer threw the ship into a jitter and zigzag pattern, jarring him within the restraining flight harness. He retained control of the general direction of flight, but the craft's trajectory took on a random element that made it difficult for adversaries to focus repeated hits on any one part of his ship. His fighter took two more glancing shots, and then the targeting computer showed "weapons lock" and fired.

The main forward guns on fighters were heavy fixed weapons; the ship had to be aligned to the target in order to score a hit. The rear weapons, such as those the alien had been peppering him with, were smaller and usually mobile, allowing targeting systems to track an opponent without turning the entire ship's hull. But the real power was to the front, and once the two ships were properly aligned, his fighter unleashed a full onslaught on the elusive alien.

The delta-wing Avengers carried port and starboard fusion-powered energy weapons, each capable of producing 50,000 megajoules of projected coherent plasma. Fired at close range and focused to a target spot no larger than the tip of a man's thumb, the beam heated the impact area to a temperature approximating the surface of the sun within 0.25 seconds. Even with the Knacker's projected defensive screens, which diffused

and absorbed some of the energy of the hit, the majority of the beam punched through. It also didn't matter that the skin of the alien ship was made of advanced, high-density alloys and refractory materials. There was only one possible reaction that a solid substance could have in the face of that amount of energy. It simply vaporized.

From Simon's viewpoint everything happened almost too fast to follow. His guns blazed, and twin gaping holes instantly opened in the alien's hull. Bits of metal and debris exploded outward from the wounds, gases jetting into space as the ship lost compression and vented its air into vacuum. The Avenger's guns fired once more, and the vessel ahead of him exploded, the heat of the plasma impact igniting the remaining oxygen within the hull. The fusion reactor containment system remained intact, or the entire ship would have instantly become a miniature sun. The Crabs did know their tech stuff. Their reactors, after which the current human versions were modeled, were marvels of efficiency and reliability, with multiple fail-safes built in to prevent loss of containment. Only a direct hit to the fusion core would usually cause it to blow.

In this case, the reactor's survival went for naught, as the explosion ripped off a large section of the Crab's starboard hull. It spun lazily away, trailing debris like confetti stretching out behind it. The main section of the crippled ship slid to Simon's port side as he shot toward it, fires still sputtering deep within the wreck. Just as he flew past, the body of a Knacker floated out of the gaping wound in the hull. The spider-like form was covered in an environment suit, and its numerous limbs were moving; the damned thing was still alive! Simon twitched his controls to the left, and his fighter swerved just enough to clip the alien with his port wing. At his velocity the blunt leading edge acted like a butcher's knife, slicing the alien neatly in two. Perhaps neat wasn't the best description, as limbs and entrails spewed outward in an organic imitation of the alien ship's disintegration. A thin smile of satisfaction touched Simon's lips.

His dogfight with the Crab had carried him close to one of

the human destroyers, and he spared a glance as he flashed by. Long blackened furrows marked the huge ship's armor where the enemy's weapons had scored it. Fires were visible in several sections of hull, but the ship was still under power, maneuvering and firing back even as he watched. That brief look was all he could spare. He tore his gaze away again to engage another enemy fighter closing in.

Simon notched four kills that day. The first dogfight was actually the hardest. The second came against a Knacker already engaged with a Delta squadron fighter; that one was easy pickings. His helmet radio relayed a quick *"Thanks, friend!"* from the other pilot, and then the speaker went silent again and he was off tracking another bogie.

The communications net was always open during battle, but comments were kept short and simple. Everything happened too fast to maintain any planned actions between fighters. Most of what came through on the com was chatter from the big ships, coordinating their efforts or issuing general direction to fighter squadrons:

"Delta group, put some distance between you and the Orion; *she needs room to maneuver, and her crew is worried about catching you in their big guns."*

"Alpha squadron, our carriers are under siege; move over to give them cover. Our destroyers will have to take care of themselves."

"Gladius and Romeo, *this is* Xerxes. *Those Knacker destroyers have us outgunned; we've already lost* Hera *and the rest of us have sustained damage. Concentrate all your firepower together on the destroyer which I've highlighted on your screens. Let's see if those bastards can take what we've got."*

Simon was too busy to pay much heed to the com. His third and fourth kills came in quick succession, one a fluke really, when a Knacker fighter jetted across his bow and his main weapons, set on automatic, locked and fired instantly. He could

hardly take credit for "his" kill, as it was over before he even knew what happened.

For awhile he continued flying cover for the two human carrier ships, one of which was home to his fighter squadron, until things got too hot and they fled back into hyperspace. He hated to see them go, but they'd return later if things went in favor of the humans. Hell, if the battle ended badly, then there would be no fighters to pick up anyway.

After they departed, he hit his thrusters and turned, powering back toward the group of destroyers, hoping to provide cover and join any remaining members of his squadron. But before he could close with them, a proximity alarm sounded and his display flashed an angry red icon closing behind him. *Damn!* He resisted the absurd impulse to turn and look over his shoulder. *How had he let that Crab get so close?* Well, nuts. There was nothing for it but to cut and run, and run he did.

His ship served him proud, responding to his touch like a fine musical instrument to a maestro. He was known among his peers as an expert pilot, and he used every trick he knew to shake his pursuer, banking hard to port and starboard, rolling and reversing mid-turn, looping up and over in a high-g climb, abruptly braking with reverse thrusters in hopes the Crab would overshoot him. No matter what he tried, the Knacker fighter stayed on his heels, never quite lined up for a kill shot, but not losing contact with him. He pushed the limits of his ship and his own endurance, exceeding the recommended maximum g-forces for the hull. Several times he neared blackout, despite the inertial dampeners cushioning his fragile body from energies that would surely have crushed him to a pulp against the cabin walls.

In a dogfight between closely matched opponents, the pursuer always has the advantage over the pursued. In the end it really was just a matter of time before the alien ship caught him in its sights. When it did, Simon's day ended as quickly as it had started. It felt like a giant hand violently slammed him into his harness. A blinding flash, a deafening explosion—the sound of

battle had reached him at last—and his controls went dead, the heads-up display flickering in and out of existence as he stared at it stunned. He was drifting powerless, an easy target.

As he shook his head to clear it, he waited for the ax to fall...but it never came. Instead he saw the Knacker fighter blur past him as it accelerated off in the direction of the human destroyers. He sat there bemused, too shaken to celebrate being alive. A human adversary would have finished off his opponent, firing an extra salvo for insurance. But the Crabs were truly alien creatures. Once his ship was no longer an active threat, they completely ignored it. This behavior had been noted in prior skirmishes as well. Knackers seemingly considered it more efficient to focus their efforts on the human ships still fighting, even if it meant leaving combatants alive. Of course, there was also the darker explanation, that the aliens were loath to destroy a potential food item that they could pick up at their leisure later.

Whatever the reason, Simon was still breathing, and he set about assessing his disabled ship's status. His main engines were junk, not a spark of life left in their controls. Likewise for his plasma guns. The hit must have knocked out the main power relays from the reactor. He could see damage to his left delta wing, but it appeared to be superficial, no major structural loss. The explosion had kicked his ship into a slow roll, and as he looked out the bubble canopy, the glowing sphere of the planet Eden rose on his left, floated over his head, and dropped out of sight to his right, leaving the endless void of star-filled space above him before reappearing a moment later to repeat the cycle.

The effect was dizzying and he dropped his eyes. As he scanned the instrument panel, a small green light caught his eye and he felt a stab of hope. Auxiliary power from the storage batteries appeared to be intact. This was insufficient to energize the weapons or main propulsion, but the batteries could fire the ship's positioning thrusters, plus operate the sensors and com unit. He stabbed the controls that shifted power from main reactor to batteries, and let out a sigh of relief as the

heads-up display reappeared. Next he hailed the *Xerxes*, then cursed when his helmet speaker returned nothing but silence. The antenna array must be fried. Ah well, there was nothing he could do about it. He'd best figure his options, if he wanted to live through this.

He had dropped low toward the planet's atmosphere during the dogfight, had even contemplated entering it at one point, as the human fighters had better handling characteristics in air than Knacker egg ships. Now his sensors told him that he was falling into Eden's gravity well, slowly losing altitude as he was pulled inexorably toward the surface. He had no way of powering free of the planet, and no means of calling for rescue. That left only one option. If he was going down, then best to not do it as a flaming meteor.

A frown of concentration knit his brows as he quickly worked calculations on the navicomputer. Yes, it was feasible—if he could avoid drawing the attention of the Crabs. The Avenger's conformation would allow a non-powered glide to the ground. But first he had to counter the spin of his ship, and level it out for approach to the planet's outer atmosphere. He hit the starboard vertical thrusters once, twice, and then lightly a third time, and brought the ship to a standstill. The planet was now steady under him, while the battle raged on above. The ship was aimed slightly nose-down toward Eden, and another judicious nudge of the thrusters pushed it forward. He nodded with satisfaction as he checked his sensors; at his increased rate of fall he would soon enter the thin outer reaches of the atmosphere. After that it was all downhill, so to speak.

Until then Simon had time on his hands, and he used it to check on the course of the battle playing out far above his canopy. His sensors painted a dreary picture. The humans had put up a good fight, in particular the newer fighters, but they were badly outnumbered. The Knackers were an ancient space-faring race, and over the course of millennia had plundered countless planets for materials to build their armada. They could attack anywhere, and often hit several star systems simul-

taneously. SpaceForce was spread too thin trying to defend the Federation.

Optimists argued that humanity appeared to be the younger, more vigorous, and more innovative species at this stage in their evolution. Whether this proved correct or not, the numbers currently favored the aliens, and true to form, the smaller human force over Eden was slowly being decimated. The defenders were down to about two squadrons of fighters, and the enemy had at least twice that many still in action. Two human destroyers were flaming ruins, one had disappeared altogether—hopefully into hyperspace—and the remaining three were fighting for their lives. It looked like two Knacker destroyers had also been damaged badly enough to render them ineffective, but that left eight ships still waging war on the human fleet. Simon cursed vehemently, beating his fists on his thighs in frustration at his impotence. The outlook was grave, and he could do absolutely nothing to help.

As he looked on, all three of the remaining human destroyers fired simultaneously on one of the Knacker ships. The combined energy impacts sheared a deep glowing gash into the starboard side of the alien vessel. Nothing vital was hit, however, and the ship returned fire, scoring direct hits with two plasma salvos on the lead human destroyer. Simon thought that it was the *Xerxes*, and he cringed as he saw flame gout from the stricken ship. It began to list sideways and its weapons went silent.

Simon hung his head, unable to watch further. A few moments later he yanked it up again as the onboard display flashed an alarm for local hyperspace activity. Something was coming out of warp very near the battle zone.

What eventually emerged into normal space was so large, and so unfamiliar, that at first Simon thought it must be an alien construct. To his surprise the ID tag on the heads-up display identified it as human: "SFS Titan, *Lamprey Class super-dreadnaught*."

Simon sat back and shook his head in wonder. *A Lamprey!* Those were still in development, had been for over five years!

This must be one of the first to see service. No wonder it had been late to the fight; there could not be enough of them to cover all the Federation planets. This ship must have responded to an urgent summons. Just how fast did that thing move in hyper-space?

He stared in awe as the interloper moved closer and its dimensions became fully evident. Simon knew the ship's basic specs, had read them in SpaceForce briefs. The Lamprey was over a half-kilometer in length, long and slender, a flattened cylinder capped at the front by a bulbous knob resembling the head of some primitive life form. Simon had heard that the class designation derived from a legendary sea creature, which the ship's conformation vaguely resembled.

Its imposing size notwithstanding, the Lamprey represented a major advance in human weapons technology. Besides heavy plasma energy guns to fore and aft, and lateral weapons nearly as powerful, the super-dreadnaught possessed a single main gun unlike anything that humans—and hopefully Knackers—had ever seen. Ironically it was based on very old technology, something which predated even humanity's journey to the stars.

At the Lamprey's core, and running nearly the entire length of the ship, was a huge modified rail gun. It was so named because the ancient models had utilized long metal rails along which a solid projectile would slide, driven along the shafts by magnetic fields and ejected at tremendous velocities. The technology had been appealing from the start. It was simple in design, required only a cylindrical metal slug as ammunition, and could deliver as much impact as missile warheads at a fraction of the cost. The striking power came from the muzzle velocities the guns achieved; with that much kinetic force delivered on target, no other explosive was needed.

The problem with the original designs, which had led to humans abandoning them as primary weapons, was that the projectiles moving at extreme speed created unacceptable heat and wear in the guns, which rapidly broke down the rail components. Small versions had been deployed on naval warships, and

these had performed adequately if used lightly, but the problems had worsened exponentially as larger models were attempted. Only now, with advances in materials science and energy manipulation, could a gun be built that enhanced the known strengths of rail guns and avoided their weaknesses.

The new weapon was based on the general design and principles of the originals, but with one important difference. Instead of metal rails, this gun utilized dense force screens which under certain conditions could be made to behave like solid matter. Magnetic fields could be propagated down their length, and the projectile slid along the energy "rails" with virtually no friction or wear. Round after round could be fired without overheating the gun.

The electromagnetic fields generated by the weapon used prodigious amounts of power, and no less than five fusion reactors were dedicated to powering the gun and the inertial dampeners arrayed along its length. Basic physics states that every action produces an equal and opposite reaction; without dampeners, the weapon's recoil would kick the entire ship backward nearly a quarter kilometer with each discharge, or more realistically, the gun would probably be blown out the back of the Lamprey's hull.

As the entire super-dreadnaught was essentially a housing for the rail weapon, the ship had to aim directly at its target in order to fire. Simon watched with intent interest as the Lamprey approached to within about ten kilometers of the alien destroyers. The surviving human ships had redoubled their attack on seeing help arrive, but the Knackers found time to begin throwing energy beams at the newcomer. Then the dreadnaught fired back.

The main gun's ammunition was a cylindrical, 100-kilogram slug of depleted uranium alloyed with titanium. This material possessed a density nearly seventy percent greater than lead. The round was further strengthened with an outer sheath of pure tungsten. The gun accelerated this projectile to a muzzle exit velocity of 223 kilometers per second, or over 800,000 kilo-

meters per hour. The round traversed the ten kilometers to its target in less than 0.05 seconds.

The kinetic force that the slug delivered to the Knacker destroyer on impact approached 2.5 million megajoules. This was equal to the energy released in the detonation of a 0.5 kiloton bomb. The alien vessel was armored with nearly three meters' thickness of high-density refractory materials in multiple sandwiched layers, designed to reflect or diffuse high levels of incoming energy. However, the Knackers had relied on energy beam weapons for much of their history, and had tailored their defensive armament to protect against same. Sophisticated as it was, the destroyer's hull was not designed to handle this type of assault. The rail gun round punched through the alien ship as if it were tissue paper.

The slug's tungsten sheath disintegrated on impact, exposing its heavy metal core. Depleted uranium has singular properties when subjected to extreme heat and kinetic forces. It instantly pulverizes and explodes outward in a cloud of fine particles. In these conditions the metal is also pyrophoric, meaning the dust cloud ignites into an intense fireball within microseconds.

In real time, the Lamprey fired, and a faint blue aura lanced 100 meters out from the bow of the ship, as the exiting projectile dragged the gun's energy fields with it into space. Simultaneously the front of one of the Knacker destroyers flared brilliant white, and then the entire ship...*expanded*...an instant before the hull split open like a cracked egg. Fire jetted from every orifice of the dying ship. The kinetic energy of the round, which continued on in the same direction as the original impact, exploded out the destroyer's stern, blowing the rear quarter of the ship off into space. The entire event took less than two seconds.

Simon sat stunned for a moment. Then he raised his arms high and shouted, "Yaa-*hoo*! That's how we cook Crabs! Get 'em, boys!" As he spoke, the Lamprey was already turning to target a second alien ship. Another blue flicker, and another destroyer became so much salvage material. A third vessel had joined its comrades in their death throes before the aliens had

time to react.

Almost as one, the remaining Knacker destroyers accelerated out of the firing path of this new threat. Then they wheeled and bore down on their attacker. The dreadnaught turned ponderously to track the enemy, but the alien ships were smaller and quicker. As a group they closed with the Lamprey and began unleashing their main energy weapons into its flanks.

The dreadnaught had considerable firepower even in its lateral plasma guns, and bright beams lanced out along its length as the humans found targets. But it was no match for five destroyers at close range, and structural debris sprayed off the ship as the enemy weapons bit glowing chunks out of its hull. In a few moments the Lamprey turned away towards deep space and began to run. The alien vessels followed on its heels like a pack of wolves hounding their prey. Simon saw the remaining human destroyers begin moving to come to the aid of their beleaguered comrade.

Abruptly his own fighter began to buffet and shake around him, and reluctantly he tore his gaze from the drama playing out in space above. A scan of his instruments confirmed that his ship had reached the outer limits of Eden's atmosphere. He had to ensure that his approach angle was proper. If he came in too steep, he ran the risk of burning up on reentry.

Once he was satisfied that he had it right, he looked up again, but the sky was hazing over with atmospheric molecules, and friction had started to glow his hull. The battle scene above faded from view until he could see nothing.

With a sigh Simon leaned back in his flight seat for the long ride down to the surface. Closing his eyes for a moment, he let the adrenaline slowly bleed from his system. He had lived to see another day. Whether he lived to regret it was a different question.

CHAPTER TWO

Sarah McKinley saw the bright streak dropping from the sky as she stood in the half-acre crop field of her rural homestead. She straightened her back, groaning as the stiff muscles protested, and pushed a lock of damp brown hair out of her eyes while she squinted up into the bright afternoon sun. Twenty years old, dressed in simple blue fabric shirt and work pants, a long handled garden shovel in her right hand, she would have looked perfectly at home on a Midwestern farm on Old Earth. Never mind that this was Eden, located in a solar system unfathomable distances from humanity's roots, and thousands of years removed from those days of yore. As much as things had changed over the course of human history, even more had remained the same.

A frown of worry creased her brow as the object descended. It was headed in this general direction, and in only moments the glowing speck had materialized into a solid object which was enlarging rapidly. It was still high up, and moving much faster than the planetary shuttles she had seen, and that was what worried her. She had a sneaking suspicion that she was looking at a spacecraft, and if so, it could mean trouble. Specifically, Knackers!

As that thought sunk in, she dropped the shovel and sprinted for the house several hundred meters away. Sarah had inherited her dad's foot speed, and her graceful stride ate up the distance quickly. As she ran she thought of calling out for her father, but then remembered he had taken her brothers to town to shop for

supplies. Her mother, her Aunt Katie, and Kate's daughter Jessie were out for the afternoon as well. Sarah was completely on her own.

She reached the house and darted into the front entrance, returning outside quickly with a farseeing scope. She dialed it to low mag, located the ship in the viewfinder, and increased the power to bring the still-distant image closer. Panting from her run, she struggled to steady the jiggling scope, scanning the interloper's conformation anxiously. After a moment she relaxed and lowered her hands. With a sigh of relief, she muttered to herself, "It's not a Knacker. Shape is all wrong."

Her papa had survived a Crab invasion on another planet, so he had taught Sarah just about all there was to know about the aliens to date. Even if he hadn't, the government on Eden made sure that everyone was educated in the basics of survival. That included recognition of friendly versus enemy craft, from space landers to fighters to ground transports. The entire planet was now on a state of alert with news of an impending invasion. So far the reports from SpaceForce were spotty, but latest word had it that at least some of the Knacker invaders would likely make it through to the planet. That was one reason her family was stocking up on supplies at this very moment.

Sarah raised the scope again and examined the object in the sky. Knacker, no, but it did appear to be a spacecraft. Now that her fear had retreated, curiosity kicked in, and her eager eyes took in every detail that the scope could provide. The unknown vessel was spewing a dark contrail that became more evident as it approached. She frowned; the ship might be in trouble. She didn't think it should be producing smoke like that.

It appeared that the craft would pass to the west of her home, and it was losing altitude quickly. But as it neared, it seemed to be slowing, its nose coming up and its descent leveling out. Sarah could now see it quite clearly without the scope, a sleek tapered shape that gleamed metallic in the sun. Not large, maybe twice the size of a private floater. A faint rushing sound came to her ears as the ship passed within a quarter kilometer

of where she stood. There was no growl of engines at all, which she thought was odd. All flying craft made noise, didn't they?

The vessel seemed to be heading straight for a low prominence just to their south. "They'd better watch it or they won't clear Roxy Knoll," Sarah whispered under her breath. She bit her lip as the ship dropped, dropped, and it seemed destined to plow into the side of the hill. But it pulled up slightly at the last second, and clipped off the tips of two Ironwood trees before disappearing over the top of the rise.

Moments later a distant rumbling came to her ears, and it continued for a handful of seconds before falling silent. Sarah stood staring numbly at the point where the ship had vanished from her sight. That noise had sounded like a crash. From what she had seen, the craft hadn't looked like it was intended to land on the ground. In that case the pilot might have tried a controlled slide, assuming a patch of flat earth could be found. And there was plenty of that around, including on the other side of Roxy. The acreage there was still on the homestead property, just barely.

Sarah hesitated, fists clenched in indecision. Then she whirled and ran toward the equipment shed. Moments later she was skimming across the fields in a floater-tractor, aiming for the notch between Roxy Knoll and the west hills. The low ground there was a kilometer-long deep ravine, cut by a small meandering creek and thick with tree cover. The locals knew it as Dark Hollow.

She found the outflow point of Byre's Creek and eased into the hollow. Her floater made no distinction of traversing land or water, allowing her to follow the stream's twisting path between the forested hills. Almost immediately the vegetation crowded in on both sides, and she was swallowed in a twilight gloom. It was markedly cooler in here than out on the grasslands. The sun peeked down between the hilltops for only an hour or two each day, and even then was filtered through the heavy canopy. Venerable Ironwood trees, for which the region was famous, reared their naked lavender trunks, streaked with black, hundreds

of meters into the sky, with feathery tufts of emerald vegetation exploding outward at their tops like giant ferns. Their massive gnarled roots were covered with small moisture-loving plants resembling bluish sea anemones. Rustles and chitters of unseen wildlife emanated from the deep shadows around her, falling silent as her vehicle approached, then resuming their secret livelihoods when she had passed. Once she heard the deep haunting cry of a Glimmer Owl echoing from far back in the forest.

Sarah had always found Dark Hollow's eerie beauty captivating, but today her attention was focused solely on the task at hand. While the floater's bulk made it ideal for towing and hauling, it was not intended for exploration, and she encountered several tight spaces where fallen trees crisscrossed the water. Add to that the fact that floaters could achieve a maximum height of only a few meters above ground level, and it made for tricky maneuvering. But Sarah was an experienced hand with all the heavy equipment on the farm, and she eventually made it through to the other side of the hollow without incident.

Once out on the flats beyond Roxy Knoll, she grabbed her farscope and scanned the countryside. After a few moments she stopped and focused. There, about a kilometer to the southwest, was a long straight line that she couldn't recall having seen in the past. By her estimation it stretched for hundreds of meters; it could easily be a landing scar. She quickly followed the strip to its termination, and there she caught the glint of something reflecting the late afternoon sun.

She put her scope away, and checked the sidearm she had donned before leaving the house. Its energy charge showed full. Sarah hoped she would have no need of it this day, but she had been taught to never take chances. Slapping it back on her waist, safety off, she gunned the floater toward the distant ship.

A ripple in the land caused her to lose sight of her goal as she got closer, and the floater ended up intersecting the landing stripe close to its midpoint. She turned right and followed it. The channel cut into the earth by the ship was at least two meters deep, and easily wide enough to accommodate two floaters.

Raw soil had been thrown up on each bank, and she could swear that she saw wisps of smoke or steam rising here and there.

Even proceeding at a cautious pace, it was only a minute or two before she saw it: a silver arrowhead buried nose-deep into the massive dirt pile that it had plowed before it. The left rear section of the craft was blackened and fused as if something had actually melted the hull. The gaping hole was pretty impressive, too.

The clear canopy on top sat open, and there was a human figure standing next to the ship, also dressed in silver. Her pulse pounding in her ears, she eased her vehicle closer, and the pilot made no threatening move. When she got to within shouting distance, she stopped the floater and slowly dismounted.

"Hello," she called out tentatively. "I saw your ship coming down. Do you need help?"

The figure was facing her, but it wore what appeared to be a heavy flight suit with helmet, and she could see nothing but reflection in the visor. After a tense few heartbeats, the pilot reached up and did something at the neck, and then pulled the helmet up and off.

The person inside was male, and he was quite handsome in a rough-hewn way. His face was long and rangy, like his build, but his strong jaw line and straight nose gave his features an appealing symmetry. He had a full head of dark brown, almost black, hair, though it was currently plastered to his skull from the combined effects of helmet and sweat. Yes, if you took away the stubble on his face and the haggard look of fatigue he currently wore, Sarah thought he would make a decent catch. Not for her, of course—he was way too old, must be at least thirty if he was a day. But her aunt, for instance....

Then he smiled, and said in a deep masculine voice, "Hi there. I'm sorry for the intrusion. As you can probably tell, I didn't have much choice."

Sarah smiled back, relaxing a bit. Over the years she had learned to trust her instincts about people, and this person didn't have a bad feel to him. His expression was open and honest,

though his eyes...his eyes seemed older than the rest of him, somehow.

She walked slowly toward him, keeping her right hand casually near her hip just in case. Not casually enough, apparently, because she saw those deep-set eyes dart briefly to her weapon before coming back to her face. A hint of amusement crossed his features, and she felt herself blushing. Never mind; if he wanted to think she was a scared civvy, then that was his right. She was not going to let herself get careless.

"Who are you?" she asked when they were only a few strides apart.

Now the pilot looked abashed, and replied, "My apologies, ma'am. I am truly forgetting protocol. I'm Major Simon Roy of SpaceForce, Alpha Squadron, 2nd Fighter Division, under the command of Colonel Hastings, currently assigned to Eden Task Force. And may I ask your name?"

"Sarah McKinley, sir," she replied formally.

Simon laughed, and it was a very pleasant sound. "No 'sirs' here, if that's all right with you," he said. "I get too much of that in the Service as it is."

Sarah grinned and nodded, then allowed herself to shift focus away from this man for a moment and take in his ship. Up close it was amazing to see. Damaged, yes, maybe critically, but a thing of beauty it was nonetheless. Sleek lines, built for speed and handling, not a wasted curve anywhere. The twin engine ports to the rear were disproportionately large, suggesting a high power-to-weight ratio. Her practiced eye recognized a highly engineered machine, even though she'd never flown so much as a commuter shuttle.

"So, this is your ship?" she said, and felt stupid the moment the words left her lips. Like, who else's ship would it be? Cripes, what was wrong with her? Just take a breath and calm down!

Thankfully the pilot didn't miss a beat. He just nodded and waved his hand at the downed vessel, smiling ruefully. "Yeah, that's my fighter, or what's left of her. Bloody shame, too. She was a sweet ride, the best SpaceForce has come up with. It'll

take a lot of human-hours and resources to replace her."

"What happened?" Sarah asked, walking around the rear of the ship to view the damage. The hole blown out of the stern was large enough to easily crawl into. A light breeze blew whiffs of smoke across her from the still-smoldering hull and she coughed as it tickled her throat. She could hear the pop and creak of hot metal beginning to cool. Whatever had done this must have been powerful. As small as the craft was, she had imagined a thin shell and more space inside, but the open wound revealed a hull thickness that astounded her. It had to be at least as deep as the length of her forearm. That didn't leave much interior room. Yet it was obvious that fuel, engines, weapons, life support, and a passenger all somehow fit into this thing. Her admiration for the minds that had engineered it went up another notch.

"What happened?" Simon echoed her question. "I'll tell you what happened, little miss. I got my butt kicked by a Knacker, that's what. Well, the whole fleet did, I fear. At least that's how it looked last I saw. Radio's dead, so I've got no way of knowing, really."

"The damage looks pretty bad," Sarah commented as she viewed the fighter from yet another angle. The hull was scored and smudged with black along the leading edges and on the visible portions of its undercarriage. But that might have been from the heat of reentry.

"It's worse than it looks," Simon said, shaking his head as he trailed her. "The energy hit took out my weapons systems and main engine. I was dead in space up there."

"And you landed this thing?!" Sarah asked in astonishment, her eyes wide. This guy must be a damn good pilot.

Simon chuckled again. God, it felt good to laugh after so long. "Well, I sort of glided it in, actually. And most of the credit goes to the navicomputer, anyway. I just handled the final approach and touchdown, such as it was."

"Wow. Just...wow." Sarah was at a loss for words, and that wasn't common for her. She stretched to peek into the open cockpit, a feat achievable if she stood on the wall of soil the

fighter had kicked up. The space occupied by the pilot was even more cramped than she had imagined. The black flight chair and harness took up most of the cockpit, and instrument panels occupied much of the rest. There was little more than elbowroom laterally. To be trapped in there for countless hours, maybe days, and in a sealed environment suit, under combat conditions...she felt claustrophobic just considering it. It would take a highly disciplined mind to do what this man did. Finally she shook out of her reverie. Turning to Simon, she inquired, "Well, what now? What do we do with your ship?"

Simon frowned and answered, "Now we leave the ship and get to shelter. She's junk at this point, and won't be easy to move. I don't know what's happening up there in space, but I've got a feeling we'll have company before long. Have you heard any news on the planetary network?"

She shook her head. "Just patchy reports, nothing solid. But if the battle just happened, then news of the outcome might not have reached the surface yet."

He nodded, one hand scratching his chin stubble. "The Crabs will track my vessel to its resting spot, most likely. If they do, then they will send a scout down at the very least. Let's not be around when they get here." So saying, he leaned into the ship's cockpit and rummaged behind the flight seat. When he straightened, he held a SpaceForce issue sidearm, a slightly more powerful version of the weapon Sarah carried, though against Knackers, it had been mediocre at best. A well-placed shot might disable one, but in a real fight against numbers it didn't pack a lot of punch. Alpha squadron had jokingly dubbed it the "suicide gun," meaning that its best use might simply be to prevent oneself from being taken alive.

Along with the weapon, and a couple of spare charge packs for the gun, he packed a small pouch of high energy pilot rations. That, along with his know-how, was all he could contribute at this point. He tossed his helmet into the cockpit, and gently pried the photo of his family from the instrument panel. Then he slammed the canopy closed, and gestured for Sarah to lead

the way.

Simon followed the girl to her shuttle, not quite able to ignore the sway of her slender hips as she walked in front of him. It had been too long since he had been around civilian women, or thought of females as more than comrades-in-arms. That part of his life had ended, and he had deliberately tucked it away, dead and buried. He intended to keep it that way.

* * * * * * *

The ride back to Sarah's home took under an hour, even at a less urgent pace than her outbound trip. While the young woman piloted the floater, Simon gazed around with interest at the landscape of this new planet. The dense forest in the hollow was primeval looking, and he imagined Old Earth might once have resembled this. When they exited the woods and flew over the savanna beyond, he took note of the wide-reaching lands, dotted with sparse trees and subdivided here and there by neat stone fences. But the fields appeared mostly undeveloped, containing neither crops nor livestock, except for a distant herd of unidentifiable animals in the far distance.

Sarah was flushed with excitement as she neared home. The two-story house stood out clearly across the flats, framed by several large trees in front. As the floater glided high over the garden crops in its final approach, she saw from their vantage that both her father's vehicle and that of Aunt Katie were parked in the carport. Her family had already returned.

Simon took in the wood and stone building with a trained military eye. Solid construction, small windows on the ground level, and heavy shutters on both stories that looked to be made of metal or plastalloy. Its large yard was surrounded by a stone wall taller than the height of a man, with a sturdy metal gate where the driveway ran through. Not a castle, but potentially defensible.

Sarah burst through the front door with Simon in tow, calling, "Momma! Papa! Come quick! We have a guest!"

A comely brunette woman in her mid-forties came bustling through a doorway to their right, and stopped short in surprise when she saw the strange man in military garb standing in her foyer. "Why, Sarah, who is this?" she blurted out, and then looked apologetically at Simon and added, "No offense, young man, but we don't get many visitors out here, and never someone from the Service. You are in the Service, yes?"

"Yes, ma'am, that is correct. Major Simon Roy, SpaceForce," Simon replied, his hands clasped behind his back in the military at-ease position.

"Ah, I knew it!" The woman looked quite pleased with herself. "My husband was in the armed forces before he retired, strictly planetside, but we met some of the Spacer folk now and then. I recognized the lightning bolt emblem on your suit, there." Then her expression abruptly turned fretful. "But why are you here? Are we being invaded? We've heard things, worrisome things. What's going on?"

Simon sighed; there was no sense in glossing over the truth. "I was just involved in a military action over Eden; it may still be in progress, for all I know. But last I saw, the Knackers had the upper hand. My fighter crashed near here; I suspect the aliens may be visiting soon to check it out. We should prepare for the worst. Travel could become difficult, and dangerous, very soon. Your best bet may be to dig in and defend this site, or hide. How many people live here?"

The woman wrung her hands, glancing over at her daughter who smiled encouragement and answered for her, "There's my dad, my three brothers, and Aunt Katie and her daughter. Besides us, of course."

Simon nodded. "Do any of you have military experience, besides your husband?" he asked Sarah's mother. "And what should I call you, ma'am?"

The woman blushed and said shyly, "Oh, you can call me Amanda, Mr. Roy."

"Simon, if you please," he replied with a grin. "Any combat experience in your family, Amanda?"

"Well, officially only my husband Tyrus; but the rest of the family has trained at home. I guess you could say we're survivalists. Especially Tyrus. He's been through this once already, and he's always sworn to not be caught unprepared again."

Great, Simon thought to himself. *A family of would-be troopers, amateurs playing at war. They'll probably wind up shooting me—or themselves—before the enemy does.* Still, it was better than finding a bunch of soft city-dwellers who pissed themselves and curled into the fetal position at the first sight of Knackers. *I wonder if we can gather more people to us.*

"How isolated are you out here?" he asked the women. "Any close neighbors? Where is the nearest town?"

Amanda answered, "Altonia is about thirty minutes away to the south by floater; Ironwood is even farther, maybe forty-five minutes off to the northwest."

Sarah added, "We've got no neighbors really close; the Towbridges live about fifteen kilometers down the road. This is pretty rural country; it's a mix of farmland and private homesteads like ours. We raise our own food to supplement what we buy in town, but we're not commercial farmers. No cash crops or livestock. Unless you include the Dire Bucks, but they're protected wildlife. We just let them live on our land." She caught herself rambling and clamped her mouth shut.

Simon nodded thoughtfully. So they were likely on their own for the duration. That wasn't all bad; one thing he had learned was that cities were hit hard and early when the Crabs came calling. Unless there were major military installations, there was no safety there. In fact, they might last longer out here, where the invaders would not think to send as many troops.

Amanda seemed to read his mind, for her next words echoed his thoughts, "Tyrus felt it would be better living in the country when the aliens came. He knew it was only a matter of time; you can't hide from them forever. We just tried to stay prepared."

"Exactly what does that mean?" Simon asked. "You're growing food out yonder, I saw that. Have you stocked supplies? What about weapons? Have you prepared hideouts or bunkers?"

The women exchanged glances, and Sarah looked like she was suppressing a grin. Her mother eventually said, "I think you should talk to Tyrus and the boys about that. They've done most of the work and planning since we moved here."

"Good idea," Simon replied. "I should introduce myself to the others, regardless. Where is everyone?"

The older woman looked thoughtful. "Well, I think my husband is out in the equipment shed. That's the big metal building with the large doors; it's out front just past the house. The boys are off checking the perimeter fences. My sister Katie's upstairs washing away the road dust."

"Well, I'll wait to say hello to her later," Simon said, somewhat stiffly.

"Yes, I think that would be best," Amanda replied with a serious face, and then she and her daughter looked at each other and started to giggle.

Simon was surprised to feel his face grow warm. He really wasn't used to socializing with civvies these days. He backed toward the front door awkwardly, saying, "I'll make for the shed, then, and say hello to Tyrus."

"Yes, go ahead," Amanda said, shooing him out with her hands. "We girls got some catching up to do."

"I'll be out shortly," Sarah called after him as he quickly exited the house.

Simon exhaled a sigh of relief as he descended the steps off the front porch. The sun was setting low toward the western hills. He stopped for a moment to take in the wide-open country, and as the warm afternoon breeze enveloped him, he breathed in deeply, savoring the sweet scent of the air. Feeling more relaxed, he reflected on the situation facing him. He missed social contact, needed it, but after years in the Service it was obvious that he was out of his element when dealing with civilians. Especially women. Great Ares, even Knackers seemed easier to understand. It would definitely some take time to get comfortable here. He wished he could shake the sinking feeling that time was running out.

CHAPTER THREE

As Simon stood outside taking in the tranquility of the homestead, he could understand why early settlers had given Eden its name. The planet's habitat so closely matched human needs that only mild terraforming had been needed, and the atmosphere and soil were compatible with a wide variety of cultivated plant and animal life. With the advent of Universal Vaccine technology, settlers could colonize a new world without major concerns about foreign microbes. In the end Eden had proven to be a perfect fit for humanity. Too bad that the serpent was about to invade paradise. The thought caused him to glance involuntarily upward at the sky, and his serene mood was broken.

Squaring his shoulders, he turned to his left and walked along the front of the house. Just off its west end stood what he took to be the equipment shed. It looked like a standard EasyFab design, similar to what SpaceForce used when setting up combat bases on new worlds. The sides and roof were of heavy construction, sturdy enough to withstand high winds and even small projectile weapons. The shed also could be set up and broken down quickly, allowing troops to move in, and then move out, of a strategic location on short notice.

This building was large enough to accommodate several pieces of earthmoving or farming equipment. The open double doors revealed what looked like a tiller and a loader parked inside, with an adjacent empty space, which he surmised belonged to the floater tractor Sarah had picked him up in.

Simon stepped through the open hanger-style doors and

strode the concrete floor between the big equipment. He could hear someone working in the space beyond the machines. The rhythmic rasping of metal on metal echoed off the walls as he moved closer to its source. When he rounded the end of the loader, he saw the man in green coveralls, standing at a workbench along the back wall.

Careless, Simon thought. *He's got his back to the door, not even aware of what is going on around him. No weapon at hand either. He's not gonna last long when things go to hell.*

Just then the man spoke up, without turning around. "And who might you be?"

Surprise tied Simon's tongue momentarily, and then he replied, "How did you know I wasn't one of your family? For that matter, I could as easily have been a Crab creeping in here to have lunch. It's unwise to leave your back uncovered."

"Oh, it was always covered," the man replied, turning around.

As he spoke, something hard that felt suspiciously like the muzzle of an energy weapon jabbed into the small of Simon's back. He froze as a surprisingly high-pitched voice spoke from directly behind him. "Should I do him now?"

The man pondered Simon for a few tension-filled seconds. After what seemed an eternity he smirked and said, "No, I think we can let him live, this time." The pressure at Simon's back eased up a bit, and he turned very slowly, being careful to keep his hands out at his sides. Whoever had ambushed him had been very stealthy, quiet, and...young! The figure holding the gun was female, and couldn't have been more than nine or ten years old. Her head barely came to his chest. A child had gotten the drop on him! Simon would have laughed at the absurdity of it, if not for the steely calm in the girl's face, and the military style two-handed grip she used to hold the weapon pointed unwavering at his chest.

"Say hello to my niece Jessie," the man said from behind him, and Simon turned again to face the speaker. The man continued with a grin, "As you say, it pays to watch your backside."

Simon couldn't help it; despite his chagrin at being ambushed

by a juvenile civilian, he grinned sheepishly in return. "I've gotta practice what I preach," he admitted. "Your niece has very good stealth skills. And you'd be Tyrus, I presume."

"Aye, that I am. Captain Tyrus McKinley, Eden Ground Defense Force, retired," the older man replied. He was solid in build, maybe in his late forties, with light brown hair shaded with gray at the temples. Exposure to sun and elements had weathered his face and arms to a leathery tan, and he flashed a lopsided grin as he asked, "And you be...?"

"Major Simon Roy, SpaceForce 2nd Fighter Division," Simon introduced himself. "My ship crashed on your acreage while you were out; your daughter was nice enough to pick me up and bring me here."

"Well then, welcome to Eden, Spacer." Tyrus wiped greasy palms on his coveralls and stepped forward to clasp Simon's hand. His solid grip testified that civilian life had not softened him. As the two men sized each other up, Tyrus narrowed his eyes thoughtfully, and asked, "It's begun, hasn't it? Otherwise you wouldn't be here."

"What's begun, uncle?" Jessie piped up, moving around Simon to stand next to her uncle. Her sidearm was now slung in a holster that she wore comfortably on her hip like a pro.

"The battle for Eden, I'm afraid, dear," her uncle told her. "You'd best round up the boys and get them back to the house. Major Roy and I have things to discuss."

The girl nodded and jogged out the door without question, and Simon grunted with approval. There was an air of discipline here not commonly encountered outside the Service. These people could prove more valuable in a fight than he had given them credit for.

Something still puzzled him, though, and he asked Tyrus, "So how did you know that I wasn't a Knacker or one of your family when I entered the shed? I don't think Jessie signaled you, and you never looked around."

The other man hooked his thumbs in his belt and replied laconically, "Well, no one in my family wears SpaceForce boots,

for one. Those sure don't sound the same on concrete as regular shoes or work boots. And as for Crabs, well hell, you can catch their stink a klick away. You start smelling like *that*, and you've got some serious personal problems. They're not big on stealth either, other than the electronic kind. Their feet click and clack something fierce on hard surfaces; I don't think a Knacker could walk quiet if you held a gun to its mama's head."

Simon nodded as the other man spoke; this guy was not dimwitted. Tyrus had been in the fire before, and he had learned from it.

"You make a lot of sense, Mr. McKinley. Well, here's the situation as I know it. At this moment the Knackers are knocking on Eden's door, and odds are they'll break through shortly. SpaceForce was losing the battle when I fell to ground. The alien forces will wait until the defenders are cleared out before bringing their big landers into Eden's space. After that the invasion will begin for real. Once the Crabs descend, they should target cities primarily, where they can find concentrated populations. But they're likely to check out where my ship landed, sooner or later. That means they'll find their way here. There's nowhere safe to run to at this late hour, and you don't want to get caught in the open. I'm thinking you're better off hiding on your property, or making a stand if you have an adequate defensive position."

Tyrus replied, "Yeah, I agree. We built this homestead with an eye to defending ourselves when the Knackers came; I knew they'd find this planet eventually. We don't plan on leaving."

"Good," Simon said. "We've got maybe a day, or a little more, before we can expect the Crabs to show up. In the meantime we should coordinate our efforts. Your family said that I should talk to you about defensive plans, weapons and the like. I'd be very interested in what you've got prepared. I don't want to intrude, but I may be able to come up with some suggestions to help out."

"Hey, any input would be appreciated," Tyrus avowed. "You've got rank on me, and I'm retired anyway. The only thing

I'll insist on is that any decisions that might put my family in harm's way will need my final approval."

"No problem there," Simon assured him. "Like I say, I'm not here to step on toes. But until I can get off-planet, I'm in the same fix as the rest of the people of Eden. Your fight is my fight. Now, about your defenses...."

The two men walked out of the shed together, deep in conversation. Tyrus occasionally pointed at various features of his house and landscape as he explained how they contributed to the homestead's defensibility. For his part Simon mostly listened and nodded, asking pointed questions here and there, and sometimes offering input when he thought it useful. On occasion he smiled as he heard something that particularly pleased him. It was a rather ferocious smile.

* * * * * * *

As evening fell, the entire family gathered in the central greatroom of the house, and Simon got his first look at its remaining members. Sarah's three brothers were tall, athletic-looking young men, ranging from seventeen to twenty-three years old. In keeping with the McKinley genes, all had dark brown hair and hazel or brown eyes. Keith was the eldest sibling, followed by Samuel, then Sarah and finally the teenager, Tyrus Junior (called "T. J." by the family).

The last person to be introduced was Jessie's mother, Sarah's Aunt Katie. Sarah had told Simon that her aunt had lost her husband two summers before. Katherine Deloria was a slender, lissome woman of understated beauty, sitting quietly in the corner loveseat with her arms wrapped around her knees. Her long thick hair was a deeper brunette than that of her older sister, but the family resemblance was unmistakable. She had the same small pointed nose, the same upward curve at the corners of her mouth, the same large expressive eyes set under delicate arched brows. Tiny laugh lines perched at the corners of those eyes, but her expression when she thought she wasn't being watched

hinted of a sadness lurking just beneath the surface. Simon wondered when she had last smiled and meant it. She mostly listened in silence as the discussion swirled around her. When she did speak, her voice was soft and soulful, like the sighing of wind in a lonely place in the mountains.

"What do you think, Major Roy?" the eldest son, Keith, asked, jolting Simon back to the discussion at hand. It wasn't like him to wander, especially when the stakes were this high.

"I'm sorry, I was thinking," he replied quickly, flustered. "What was your question?"

"Do you think we should hide out and try to go unseen, or ambush the Crabs when they show up?" the young man asked, leaning forward on the couch intently.

Simon formulated his response carefully. "If we go into hiding, then we might avoid confrontation. This has obvious advantages, but there are problems as well. Tyrus tells me you have dug cellars and tunnels for storage of food and supplies, but they lack a secondary escape route. Knacker sensors are sophisticated, and their scans may detect underground chambers. If we get caught down there, we'll have no way to run. They can simply wait us out, or gas the chambers we're in, or do a frontal assault down the tunnels. It might be wiser to defend a fortified house above ground, where our options aren't so limited."

Tyrus added, "Most of our planning has been along the lines of defending our land, not hiding passively. I tend to think like the Major here; we should not hide. We'll have to fight smart to survive, but fight we should."

As the elder of the house was speaking, Simon's attention was drawn to a small pouch that hung on a string around his neck. The family members all had them; he had assumed that they contained small communicators or something similar. But he could have sworn that the pouch had just moved, and not as a result of its wearer's motions. When it jiggled again, his curiosity was piqued. "I'm sorry, Tyrus," he said, interrupting the conversation. "I have to ask—what is in that little bag around your neck? It seems to be moving."

Tyrus grinned, and several people chuckled. "Ah, that's my little companion," he answered. "My protector. Would you like to see?"

Uncertain as to what to expect, Simon nodded. He leaned forward with interest as the other man took the pouch from his neck and loosened the string that held it closed. When he pulled it open, a small head immediately peeked out. Tyrus gestured him to come closer, and Simon got out of his chair to inspect what the man now held in his open hand. A tiny furred creature, no longer than Tyrus's palm, crouched timidly as it eyed Simon with round black eyes. It had a velvet coat that was striped lengthwise with lavender and black bands, and a long furred tail. It reminded him of tree-dwelling creatures he had seen on other planets, animals that fed on forest vegetation. But as he reached his hand toward it curiously, it bared a carnivore's tiny fangs at him, and, screeching shrilly, dived back into the pouch.

"They tend to be shy with anyone but their companion," Tyrus explained as the tiny creature continued to vocalize from its hiding place. Tyrus stroked the pouch as he spoke soothingly to the animal, and within moments it quieted. He tied the bag closed and hung it once more about his neck.

Simon asked, "What the heck is that? And why do you carry it?"

Tyrus laughed at Simon's perplexed expression, and explained, "It's called a Dawn Darter. They're arboreal, very quick, and they subsist on small insectoid life forms found in the canopy of Ironwood forests. They're most active at daybreak, hence their name. Not easy to tame unless raised from the egg, but well worth the trouble."

"Aside from the cuddly factor, why?" Simon asked him.

"Ah, now that is an interesting question," Tyrus answered. "Do you recall the first Knacker processing planet that humans assaulted? A nasty little rock not worthy of a name; they just referred to it by its catalogue number, '3G789'."

"Yes, I remember it," Simon growled. "A nasty confirmation of what the Crabs intended for us."

"Yes, and it also gave us some useful intelligence to use against them," the older man told him. "The troops there reported a number of previously unknown details about the Knackers."

"I've heard all of this," Simon said impatiently.

"Ah, but did you know that a couple of survivors from 3G789 had stumbled upon a way to evade detection from the Crabs' sensors, even at close range?"

Now he had Simon's undivided attention. "No, *that* I hadn't heard," he said.

"Yeah, a couple of SpaceForce grunts were doing recon, with the enemy crawling all over the place, and they ran into some indigenous life forms that resembled snakes. Besides being friendly with humans, they were very nasty to the Knackers. The venom from just a few of those things killed off a large Crab breeder nest, according to the reports. Scientists are still trying to synthesize the toxin from samples the boys collected in the field, to use as a weapon against the aliens."

"Yeah, I do recall something along those lines," Simon said, "but how does that relate to your little pouch pets?"

"I was getting to that," Tyrus replied. "The other item of interest in those field reports was that the soldiers carried the snake-things in their clothing for awhile, and the Crabs seemed unable to detect the humans while the critters were with them. No one was able to verify this, because the snakes were gone by the time the troops were retrieved. SpaceForce labeled the claim "unsubstantiated." Most people assumed that if it were true, then the animals must have had special physical properties that blocked sensor scans."

"But you're thinking otherwise," Simon guessed, as he began to see where this was going.

"I wasn't so sure when I read the reports, so I got on the CompuNet and asked some xenobiologists and tech people. The consensus was that Knacker sensors are usually set to detect a specific life form. When they invade worlds, they want to gather food efficiently, and the dominant species yields the highest

harvest number. Lucky us. But although they'll also reap some large stock animals, this still means that most small life forms are excluded when they run scans. If not, the sensors would be overwhelmed, detecting everything from bugs to rodents to flyers. The important thing is, close physical proximity between two complex life forms seems to confuse their equipment. The sensors treat the paired organisms as a single, unrecognized species."

"Leaving both of the pair undetected," Simon concluded with a fierce grin. "Damn! Is this confirmed?"

"Not as well as I'd like," Tyrus admitted. "There are a few reports from other planets where people claimed success when they carried a pet on their person. No official corroboration though."

"And you all carry these...Darters?" Simon asked.

The others in the room all nodded. Sarah spoke up, "What about Simon, papa? Even one unprotected person could give us away."

Tyrus looked to Katherine, eyebrows raised in silent question. She smiled slightly and said, "We've got some babies, newly independent from their mother. They're not bonded to anyone yet, and won't be tame to handle. But they will stay in a pouch just fine, so Simon could wear one."

"Fine," Tyrus said. "See to it that he gets one tomorrow. Also we need to get him a WristWatch."

Simon looked quizzical, and Sarah laughed and explained, "It's an archaic name; papa's a history buff. Basically it's like a military wrist communicator, but operates on our own private frequency. That way we can coordinate our actions in the field." She held up a small round device strapped to her left wrist.

Tyrus added, "The com links also let us know when the fence alarms are triggered, so the Crabs don't take us by surprise. We will be wearing wrist units every minute of the day from now on. No exceptions!" He looked sternly at his family, and they all nodded mutely.

Simon frowned in thought. "The aliens have good stealth

equipment, screens and the like, to keep sensors from spotting them. How certain are you that we'll know when they arrive?"

"Oh, we'll know," Tyrus answered, nodding. "We've got standard life sensors, tuned to pick up Crabs; those are the ones that they might be able to block. We've also got infrared motion detectors at key points such as the road into the property. Crabs' bodies run cooler than us, but as large as they are, a sensitive device should catch them. Thirdly, we've got line sensors along the perimeter, with invisible energy beams running between the devices; anything that steps between them and breaks the beam triggers an alarm."

"How many Knackers can we expect here?" Sarah's mother Amanda interjected from her seat next to her daughter.

Simon shrugged his shoulders. "Can't say for sure. Most likely there will be a few reconnaissance scouts at first. If those fail to report back, then the Crabs will send out a larger skirmish party. Those usually contain at least a Knacker squad of ten warriors with armored tracked vehicles or floaters."

"What should we do?" the youngest boy, T. J., asked nervously. "We'll be outnumbered and outgunned if they start sending entire squads at us."

"Yes, we will," Tyrus told his son, "so we'd better utilize our advantages. Which are?"

"*Surprise, ingenuity, and grit,*" the sons recited together, obviously having heard the question many times before.

"We'll have a couple of other advantages, as well," Simon added. "Knackers still seem to view humans as relatively dumb animals, despite our technology and improved performance against them in recent battles. They are supremely confident of their own superiority. I don't know if it's genetically ingrained, or simply the result of having defeated every race they've encountered for many millennia. But their apparent inability to visualize defeat makes them complacent and predictable, and we can use that.

"One other thing, and this is important: Knackers are reluctant to use destructive force, other than for strategic targets. It

is this, and only this, that has allowed humanity to survive this long. The aliens want us alive, for food. They're not interested in military dominance in its own right. Dead adversaries are a failure in their eyes. We must use this to our advantage, and we must kill the enemy without hesitation at every opportunity. It is the best edge we have, besides the element of surprise."

Silence greeted Simon's pronouncement for a few moments, as each person in the room dealt with the reality of the coming invasion. Finally Tyrus cleared his throat and said, "Okay, everyone. We know what we're up against, and we're ready. Let's give the Crabs a proper greeting when they come!"

* * * * * * *

They actually ended up having two days' reprieve before anything of note happened at the homestead. They used the time to rest, become familiar with each other, and prepare for battle. Simon was given a spare bedroom at the west end of the upper floor, and a wardrobe donated by the various males in the family. That first evening, Tyrus had pulled Simon aside after the others had headed for bed. He looked his guest straight in the eye and said, "There's just one thing I want us to be clear on, son. I like your feel; you don't seem like a young hotblood. But we're opening our house and home to you, and that takes trust. With that trust comes responsibility. You need to know this: I will not tolerate any impropriety under my roof. I expect you to do that uniform proud, now and always. If I hear from any of my family that they've been mistreated by you in any way, then there will be hell to pay. Is this understood?"

Simon returned the man's gaze evenly. "Completely," was all he said. Tyrus contemplated him a moment longer before nodding, apparently satisfied. He bid Simon a gruff good night, and they headed to their rooms to sleep. The matter was not spoken of again.

The next day Tyrus showed off the weapons cache he had hidden in an underground bunker, mostly military surplus that

he had accumulated while in the armed forces. Simon whistled in appreciation when his host flipped on the light switch. The walls of the small room were covered with racks of well-oiled weapons, ranging from handguns to fully automatic assault rifles. The few energy weapons were limited to small side-arms; the military kept its larger plasma guns closely restricted. He saw antipersonnel mines, small grenades, and flash-bang charges. There was even a flame-thrower, but Tyrus shook his head regretfully, saying that it was nonfunctional. Nonetheless it was an impressive collection of armament.

Simon grinned as he hefted a Milcor 22-A automatic assault rifle with infrared sighting; this gun fired heavy armor-piercing shells that should make short work of a Knacker's exoskeleton. The recoil was fierce, but a strong man could wreak some havoc with this baby. He asked Tyrus, who nodded and said that it was his to use. Add a couple of grenades slung on his belt, along with his Service weapon, and he was ready to go Crab hunting.

There was only so much preparation one could do while waiting for action. The family spent most of the remaining down time monitoring the vidscreen in the greatroom. Reports of Knacker landings were flooding in from around the planet. The AirForce valiantly fought the invaders, but the alien intrusion was massive and well coordinated. Once the aliens controlled the near space around Eden, they destroyed all the communications and military satellites. With much of the planetary info-net rendered deaf and blind, it was difficult for the human defenders to obtain field intelligence or act in concert. Owning the high ground also gave the aliens a major tactical advantage. The same destroyer-mounted energy weapons that had wiped out the human space fleet now rained down destruction on AirForce bases around the world. They knocked out many of the ground-based defenses that might otherwise have prevented landers from setting down. Then, once the way was clear, they came. By the millions, the Knackers came.

The alien lander vehicles were nothing more than massive transports. Each vessel was shaped like a giant floating pyramid,

and contained within its walls ample space to hold one hundred thousand Knackers, plus easily that number of human captives. And they descended by the hundreds. They were slow-moving, ungainly, and possessed few weapons, relying on fighter craft to fly cover for them. But the effect on a planet when they disgorged their hordes of warriors was devastating.

Simon and the family watched in horror as the news reports showed fighting on the ground and in the air overhead. The night skies over major cities lit up with the lightning bolts of energy beams and the shooting-star tracers of projectile weapons. Alien and human fighters streaked across the heavens on jets of yellow and white flame, and ruined ships exploded like fireworks high overhead, or fell spectacularly from the sky in glowing red fireballs, the flames doubling as funeral pyres for the pilots within.

On the ground, courageous reporters risked their lives providing field reports that might save others. One video crew was present almost at ground zero when a lander came down. The camera showed the noon sky darkened as the sun was blotted out, and a rushing roar drowned out the reporter's voice as if a tornado was bearing down on him. One could hear a faint, *"Oh my God"* as the man pointed frantically and the camera turned to follow his finger. The scene was from Port Helicon, a coastal city of five hundred thousand on the opposite side of the continent. The unsteady image tracked a black pyramidal shape of unbelievable mass descending from the sky, its base glowing blue as hundreds of thrusters effortlessly balanced its bulk. When it touched down in the midst of the city, the craft obliterated an entire block of buildings, crushing them flat to the ground as their walls crumbled and windows blew outward from the explosive compression. The grinding roar was accompanied by a blinding expulsion of dust and debris from beneath the craft as it settled to its final resting position. The cloud spread outward at hundreds of kilometers per hour, engulfing the camera crew within seconds. The images following were chaotic, with glimpses of men and women bent over coughing, and everything blurred through the haze. After a few minutes

the air began to clear slightly, and a woman emerged stumbling from the fog. She grimaced and turned toward the videographer, saying, "What's that smell?" A few seconds later she shrieked as she looked beyond the camera, the whites of her eyes showing clearly as she backed away. The camera view began to turn, then violently jostled as a male scream joined the woman's.

Abruptly the image shifted, and came to rest showing a close up view of the ground; it was obvious that the equipment had been dropped. The cries in the background tailed off, and for a few moments silence reigned. Then the camera's microphone began to pick up a scrabbling noise that gradually grew louder. Suddenly a jointed appendage hit the ground in front of the camera, causing everyone in the greatroom to jump. The limb was mottled green and brown, and ended in a three-pronged claw like a mutated lobster, but this was covered in coarse brown hair as well. That single detail was enough to mark it as undeniably alien; no creature in the known human worlds possessed an appendage like this.

No sooner had they taken the image in, then the camera angle shifted again, turning toward the sky. It slid quickly across something large, and they caught a brief glimpse of multifaceted red eyes aligned in a row, and large curved chelicerae resembling the fangs of a spider. Rapid popping and clicking sounds filled the microphone for a few seconds, and then the camera went dead.

The greatroom was silent as the vidscreen played static. Simon shook himself and glanced around the room. Tyrus's expression suggested he could have eaten a Knacker raw right then. His wife sat next to him on the sofa, her hand still over her mouth as she stared in shock at the silent screen. Little Jessie had her head buried in her mother's chest, and Katherine held her, making not a sound as tears streamed down her face as well. She caught Simon's glance and gazed back at him unabashed. She had a strength, that was obvious, but he knew that this conflict would reopen old wounds, and he worried about how it would affect her. He smiled sympathetically as he glanced down at

Jessie, and he caught a flash of something—was it gratitude?—in Katherine's eyes before she looked away.

The other reports they saw over the next day and a half were no better. Military defenses crumbled, cities fell, and humans were herded by the thousands into giant waiting pyramids, never to be seen again. One by one the video broadcasts winked out, as fewer and fewer networks remained on air. Simon and the McKinleys were truly on their own.

CHAPTER FOUR

It wasn't until the following afternoon that the perimeter sensors around the homestead property triggered an alarm. Simon was shaving in his room when his wrist monitor flashed red and began beeping shrilly. He threw down his razor, wiped his face hurriedly and darted out of his room. The prearranged rendezvous location was the greatroom, and within minutes all the family members had converged there. Tyrus pulled up a schematic of the property on the vidscreen, and the alarm signal winked from a point near the main road. "Just as I thought," he growled. "They came up the highway after finding your ship, instead of taking the more direct route through Dark Hollow. The Crabs were always timid when it came to tackling the deep woods. They remind me of city folk, only uglier."

"They'll likely follow the driveway up to the house, if they stay true to form," Simon offered.

"That's the idea," Tyrus answered. "Why do you think there are so many fences crisscrossing our property? It's not like we've got herds to manage. The Crabs tend to follow the easy path, and high stone fences make travel difficult. Their floaters can get over, but the tracked vehicles would have to smash through, and their foot troops climb over, each line of fencing. It's more efficient to follow the open road, and Knackers like efficiency." He grinned evilly. "They still haven't caught on to the concept of 'ambush'."

"We'd best get into position," Simon said.

"Agreed. Everyone to your stations," Tyrus told his assem-

bled family. "You all know what to do. Remember, no one fires until I do. Surprise is the key! Let's move!"

The landscaping in place around the McKinleys' home was both tasteful and tactical. A high stone wall surrounded the yard on all sides, its only gap being the gate where the main driveway came through. The large open space in front of the house included parking and rock garden areas. The latter had several widely spaced boulders, which served as focal points for the garden, and also made perfect shelters for gunners to crouch behind. The upper windows of the house had heavy shutters that could be closed down to narrow gun slits. The shutters were made of three-centimeter thick plastalloy, able to resist hand-held projectile and energy weapons alike. The house itself was constructed of wood and stone with an eye to durability. The stone was native granite, and most of the frame was cured Ironwood, one of the densest and most fire-resistant plant materials known. The home's lower windows were deliberately small, preventing direct ingress by the Knackers.

The high fence wall and the house hemmed in the north and south sides of the parking area respectively. In addition, the rock garden bordered its east end, and the equipment shed loomed to the west. This effectively turned the parking lot into a semi-enclosed courtyard, into which the defenders could pour weapons fire from three different directions. It was a great killing field, or so the humans hoped.

Knackers might be predictable, but they weren't stupid. They hadn't survived millennia of warfare by barreling recklessly into danger. Tyrus took position in his home's upper story, and eased his farscope through the slitted window to scan the driveway leading from the main road. Eventually he saw movement, and he zoomed the focus to get a good look. There they were, two Crab soldiers on foot, moving deliberately down the drive like giant spiders stalking prey. The dark forms stood out starkly against the pale gray of the gravel road. Their furred limbs moved fluidly in a complex rhythm, with several planted on the ground and several others moving forward at any instant.

It had been years since Tyrus had seen the aliens in person, and he gritted his teeth as memories came flooding back. He vowed that this time there would be payback. Looking again through his scope, he took notes on the enemy soldiers. Each was holding at least two weapons and what looked to be a sensor pack. *Ah, to have ten limbs.*

Tyrus adjusted his airwave receiver through a variety of frequencies, and eventually found the one the aliens were broadcasting on. The soft '*put-put-put*' of the alien tongue, interspersed with sharp clicks and rasps, was all too familiar, and a chill ran up his spine as the device brought the sounds close to him.

He raised his wrist to his mouth and spoke softly into the communicator. "Be alert, everyone. Two Crabs coming down the road. On foot, well armed. Should be here in a minute or two."

Simon gripped his heavy automatic tightly and took a few deep breaths. From his position in the equipment shed he had a good view of the parking area, but he could see nothing beyond the fence. He kept his eyes on the open gate, knowing that the Knackers would first show themselves there. His role in the coming skirmish was vital, but dangerous. Taking inspiration from his first encounter with Tyrus, he had offered to act as bait, sitting alone in the shed without his companion pet. This, they hoped, would make him the one human easily detected by the aliens' scanners. Seeing a lone target might make the Crabs less cautious, enticing them to move boldly to attack. Therein should lie their downfall. If not, then Simon could be in trouble really fast.

The wait seemed interminable to the human defenders lying in ambush. The three brothers crouched hidden behind the rock garden boulders, Simon behind his mostly-closed shed doors, and the rest of the family at windows on the upper floor of the house. In addition to his weapon, Tyrus held a remote control device that could trigger several different actions, when the time came.

Suddenly a clawed appendage reached carefully through the open gate from beyond the fence. It held a square device, which it slowly panned back and forth for a few moments. When it was pointed in Simon's direction, it paused, and then withdrew out of sight once again.

A clatter resembling the sounds made by hoofed animals arose from beyond the gate. Seconds later the two aliens appeared in full view. For those who had not seen them up close before, the creatures were startling to behold. As tall as a grown man, but considerably more bulky, they had ten multi-jointed limbs which sprouted out of an elongated body vaguely shaped like a human torso, but carried horizontally. The hard exoskeletons were mottled brown and black with traces of red, and covered with coarse brown fur along the top of the body, and on the lower portions of the limbs. Their large heads sported long curved fangs, jutting out just below a row of six large red eyes. Above the eyes two appendages resembling insect antennae waved randomly as the aliens eased into the open.

The Knackers' limbs appeared multifunctional. The rear six bore the creatures' weight, while the remaining limbs to the fore were currently elevated and carried weapons, plus the sensor boxes Tyrus had noted before. The two aliens crept forward side by side, still moving their scanners to left and right. Once again they paused when the scanners were pointed in Simon's direction. They turned toward each other and touched antennae for a few seconds. Then the two aliens whirled as one and rushed toward the equipment shed.

The speed with which the Knackers moved took Tyrus by surprise. Their multiple legs scuttled across the lot faster than a man could run, and they were halfway to the shed before he could react. Raising his communicator to his mouth, he shouted, "Fire!" while simultaneously tracking the lead alien with his energy pistol and squeezing off a shot. Without waiting to see its effect, he dropped his gaze to the control box in his left hand, punching two buttons on the panel. One sent out a jamming signal on the frequency that the Crabs were using, to

cut off their communications. The second button activated the driveway gate, rolling it closed behind the aliens. As it slammed shut, the defenders in the house opened fire, and all hell broke loose.

The concentrated barrage of a handful of automatic weapons was deafening in the confined area of the courtyard. A hailstorm of bullets hit the aliens and knocked them sideways midstride. They stopped in their tracks and spun with inhuman speed. All four of their energy guns came to bear on the house, and they fired even as their bodies jerked and twitched from the impact of the humans' onslaught. Brilliant plasma erupted from their weapons, lashing across the upper story windows wherein hid their attackers. The gunfire abated momentarily as the humans ducked for cover, but on cue Simon and the three brothers opened fire from the east and west ends of the courtyard, catching the Crabs in a deadly crossfire. As the beleaguered aliens turned to face this new threat, the humans in the house resumed firing down on them from above.

Despite the toughness of their exoskeleton armor, the sheer volume of high velocity slugs ripped the two soldiers apart. Within seconds both Knackers sagged sideways as multiple limbs were blown off, and their aim became erratic, the energy beams from their guns flying haphazardly in all directions. Simon had to duck back as a white-hot lance sliced across the gap in the shed doors, nearly frying him in the process. Then he resumed firing position and leveled his weapon on the Crab that seemed more mobile. It was hitching itself spastically toward the rock wall in an effort to escape. He tracked it carefully and squeezed the trigger. His heavy gun kicked as it spat a two-second burst that removed the Knacker's head from its body. It sagged to the ground, twitching weakly, and by then the other alien had joined it in its death throes.

In less than fifteen seconds it was all over. As the echoes of gunfire faded away into a deathly quiet, cheers erupted around the courtyard. The defenders had won the first round.

Simon squeezed between the shed doors and slowly walked

across the courtyard toward the smoking carcasses. He saw no sign of life in either alien warrior. Tyrus emerged from the house momentarily, and walked over to join him as he surveyed the Knacker bodies. "I must say, that's a pretty sight," the older man said, nodding with an air of great satisfaction. "We've made quite a mess, though. In a day or two these things will stink even worse than they usually do. Boys!" he hollered at his sons, who had also exited the house and stood gazing uncertainly around them, clutching their weapons tightly. "At ease," their father said calmly. "The threat is past. Give us a hand moving these Crabs out back before they spoil." The youths seemed to relax then, and they put their weapons aside and slowly came over to join in the unsavory task of battlefield cleanup.

* * * * * * *

That evening the family gathered at the long table in the dining room and shared a hearty meal. Tyrus sat at the table's head, with Amanda at his right and his eldest son to his left. Katherine was seated next to her sister, and the rest of the family were strung out along the table in no particular order that Simon could discern. He took a seat opposite Katherine and dug into the chow. It was really good, a mixture of vegetables and a meat that he couldn't identify. Being a Spacer he was used to encountering new cuisine as he moved planet to planet, but this was unusual, and he inquired as to its source.

Sarah sat directly to his right, and she grinned as she answered, "Oh, that's Dire Buck."

"I thought you said they were protected," Simon said, puzzled.

"They are," she giggled. "You can't hunt them or raise them for profit. But if you provide sanctuary on your property, you're allowed to harvest an animal now and then."

"What exactly is a Dire Buck?" Simon inquired.

Sarah frowned thoughtfully, and said, "You'd best ask Kate. She's our resident animal expert."

Simon looked across the table with an inquiring expression.

Katherine carefully put her fork down and met his eyes. Looking a bit uncomfortable at the attention, she cleared her throat and said, "Dire Bucks are the dominant herbivores on this continent. They're mammals, or what passes for mammals on Eden. They're warm-blooded and furred, but they don't nurse their young. They also hatch from eggs, like nearly every life form here. Being grazing animals, they prefer the plains where low-growing vegetation is plentiful." She smiled shyly at him as she finished, lowering her eyes once again.

As always, Simon found Katherine's voice hypnotic, the tones soft and melodic as if she were singing a soothing lullaby. And always with that faint mournful quality, hinting of depths beyond what his eyes could discern. He wanted to know more about her, to get past the public face that she presented to the world. It took discipline for him to simply ask instead, "What does a Dire Buck look like?"

She cocked her head and squinted contemplatively. "I guess you could say they resemble a cross between a cow and a New Terran kangaroo."

"*What*?" Simon sputtered, trying not to choke on his food.

Katherine laughed, and it was truly a wonderful sound, musical and throaty, and most of all, joyful. He would love to be able to inspire that in her more often. Still chuckling, she said, "Did my analogy sound bizarre? Well, I suppose they are a bit odd, at that. Dire Bucks are big, almost as large as modified cattle, and they are four-legged. But the rear legs are much larger and more powerful than the forelimbs, and they can raise their front end off the ground when reaching for fruits on trees and bushes. They also have a stout tail, which helps them balance when running or standing erect."

"Okay, I guess they would look like a cow-garoo," Simon said with a grin. "Tell me, how do you know so much about wildlife?"

Katherine looked away, and her smile faded a bit as she said softly, "I am...was...a veterinarian, in a prior life." She met his gaze again, and he saw in her eyes a silent plea to not press

further. He didn't, but as the conversation turned to other subjects, he continued to contemplate the mystery that was Katherine Deloria.

* * * * * * *

The next few days were quiet, with no incursions onto the homestead property. They waited and planned for the next Knacker move, which everyone knew was only a matter of time. Simon noticed that since the battle, the family had seemingly accepted him as one of their own, including him in their daily life and making their home his. He was surprised at how good that made him feel.

Katherine's daughter Jessie, in particular, appeared to have taken a liking to him, and she sought him out whenever he was unoccupied. In many ways she was a typical little girl, playful and silly, but she also had a hard streak that in some ways saddened Simon. No one that young should have to learn the things that she knew.

As he had found out when they first met, Jessie was a staunch little warrior in her own right, fearless when it came to combat. She had been one of the people shooting down from the upstairs windows during the firefight. She also had accompanied the adults when they inspected the remains of the Knackers, poking curiously at the bodies as if she might learn something useful to use against the enemy. The two aliens had been disposed of in a firepit out back, and their equipment confiscated. The powerful energy weapons in particular could prove useful, though awkward for humans to fire.

Simon met regularly with Tyrus to strategize and was impressed with the man's ingenuity. Guerrilla resistance seemed second nature to him; perhaps that came from having trained in the ground forces.

They were checking out the home defenses one day, and Tyrus showed Simon the large pitfall trap in the driveway just outside the yard gate. The size of the pit was impressive. It

must have measured a good five meters on a side, and it had a metal trap door that could be triggered to collapse inward via remote control. When locked and covered with dirt and gravel, it was invisible to the naked eye. Simon suspected that the door could support a heavy vehicle driving over it during peacetime. Sensors might detect the underground chamber, but an attacking force would likely be distracted and not think to look underfoot.

Tyrus and his sons opened the trap to check the mechanism and the explosive charges that were set inside. The pit was nearly seven meters deep, enough to swallow a small armored transport before blowing it to hell. The work it must have entailed to build it was considerable, but the family had had years to prepare. It was amazing what a little paranoia and a lot of time could accomplish.

After the trap door was tripped a few times without glitches, and the detonators were inspected and deemed functional, the pit was carefully closed and the door covered over with gravel and dirt. The end result looked once again like a mundane stretch of road.

Simon grinned at Tyrus as he surveyed the final product. "You know a floater will just go right over this," he commented.

"Yep, but they usually bring at least one tracked vehicle, and those don't fly," the older man countered. "Just one makes this little surprise worth the effort."

"I hear you," Simon agreed. "Now about another idea I've been considering. You know the equipment shed...." Tyrus listened as he described his concept, and the older man's expression gradually morphed from quizzical to skeptical to approving as the idea was outlined.

"You just might have something there," he told Simon when he had heard the proposal. "Let me get on the computer and check out the building specs, and if it looks workable, I'll get my boys on it right away."

Another quaint but potentially effective weapon took Simon totally by surprise. He saw the two older brothers, Keith and Samuel, bent over in the parking area in front of the house,

working with something. As he approached he saw a box of bottles filled with what looked like water, and a long piece of elastic rubber about as wide as his hand. "Ah, you're just in time," Keith told him with a grin. "We need a third person to operate this."

"Operate what?" Simon asked, looking for some other device and seeing nothing.

"Our slingshot," Samuel replied. "It fires flame bottles, although these are just water; no need to waste fuel for practice."

A light went on in Simon's brain, and he recalled an ancient device from his military history. You put a flammable liquid into a bottle that had a small open end. Cloth or a similar substance was stuffed into the hole to plug it, and to act as a fuse. The liquid inside soaked the cloth, and you lit the fuse and tossed the bottle. On impact it smashed, releasing the fuel within and creating a liquid fireball. Simple, but effective, especially given that the Crabs were surprisingly flammable.

The one drawback was the limited throwing range, and the McKinleys seemed to have solved that issue. With Simon and Samuel each holding one end of the rubber strap, Keith nestled a bottle in the homemade slingshot. The young man then pulled the rubber band back until it was a struggle just to keep his feet. Aiming carefully, he released it. He had set the trajectory upward so that the bottle would clear the stone wall, and it sailed high and far before impacting the hard ground in the distance. Simon heard a faint tinkle of shattered glass, and Samuel yelled, "Yeah!"

The boys worked for another hour, learning to gauge distance and aim the bottles with fair accuracy, before calling it a day. Simon walked off chuckling to himself at the display. Normally such a primitive weapon would stand no chance against technologically superior foes, but these were not normal times. The Knackers wanted live meals, which would limit their use of heavy weaponry. They would not be satisfied with standing back and pounding the house into submission with artillery.

The stone wall also provided the defenders protection from line-of-sight weapons such as energy guns. Behind its cover, humans could lob cocktails at the Crabs with impunity, until they got close. Other family members would occupy the aliens with shots from projectile or energy guns fired from the second floor windows. Once the aliens closed in, the slingshot crew would retreat to the house, and take up fighting positions upstairs with the others.

There was one weak spot in the plan, though, and Simon addressed this with Tyrus after he finished helping with the slingshot weapon. "I'm worried about a real assault," he confessed. "A warrior squadron will bring different weapons than those used by scouts. Knacker squads are deployed to collect food, not just survey. They'll have weapons designed to capture us alive. I'm worried about them lobbing neuro-gas over the wall."

"As you should be," Tyrus agreed. "Which is why we'll be wearing gas masks as soon as we see them coming." Simon just shook his head and shut his mouth; these folk had covered the contingencies as well as any general he had served under. He vowed never to view civilians the same way again.

After the incident with the scouts, over a week passed with no further Knacker incursions. Both Simon and Tyrus were surprised at the delay; perhaps the Crabs were preoccupied elsewhere. Tyrus ran through the channels on the vidscreen and to their astonishment, there were still a few human broadcasts on air. Their status reports were brief, but the essence of them was that humans were fighting back all around the planet. Not on a large scale, and not with any major military objective, but they were refusing to go quietly into the night.

At this stage the human-occupied worlds all knew of the Knacker threat, had known of it for years. This had caused changes in societies throughout the Federation, including beefed up military spending and a higher rate of enlistment in the armed forces. It turned out that civilians had changed their habits as well, and on Eden, many thousands had bought firearms and learned how to use them. A surprising number also

owned gas masks.

Now the Knackers were learning hard lessons first taught on Old Earth, where guerrilla troops in the past had effectively harassed much larger and better-armed invasion forces for extended periods of time. The guerrillas had utilized advantages of surprise and an intimate knowledge of their home turf to keep one step ahead of the invaders. Now humans used these same principles against an alien aggressor, and they had one further advantage—the enemy did not want to kill, whereas the defenders had no such compunction. Street by street, building by building, humans ambushed the aliens and retreated, only to set up and do it again. Their efforts were more harassing than devastating, but they resulted in a fair number of Crabs being maimed or killed, and they slowed the aliens' efforts to subdue and collect their prey. The Knackers found themselves having to devote greater resources to security and fire protection than was their wont. This took warriors away from other tasks such as investigating small-scale field incidents. Hence the delay in sending troops to the homestead when their scouts went missing.

But arrive they eventually did. One morning just after breakfast the perimeter alarms sounded on everyone's wrist coms. People dropped whatever they were doing and scrambled to gather in the greatroom. Within a minute they were all there, some still tugging on clothes as they arrived. By now everyone was getting familiar with the routine.

Tyrus identified two different breaks in the perimeter sensor system, one where the private drive left the highway, and another several hundred meters to the south. He pointed to the icons on the vidscreen, saying, "Looks like they've split up. Probably they're trying to avoid an ambush, or if one happens, they want at least one party to survive and report what occurred."

"We'll need to get to the wall and spy out what's coming," Simon offered.

"Yes, we'll send the boys out with farscopes, to watch the road and the savanna to the south of it." Turning to his sons,

he instructed them, "Use your wrist coms to tell us as soon as you know what the Crabs are bringing. I'll watch from the upper floor windows as well. Now go!" The brothers nodded and darted for the door.

A few minutes later they had their answer: two pairs of Crabs were advancing toward the house from different directions, on foot, with no vehicles in sight. Tyrus shook his head in amazement as he and Simon received the reports. "They must be strung really thin to only send two scout teams. Well, we'll not need the pitfall trap or slingshot. Let's go with the variation on the shed plan that you thought up, Simon."

A short time later Simon was again in the equipment shed, minus his furry scan-blocker. This time he wore a mask, just in case the Crabs brought neuro-gas. The air inside the face gear was stuffy and stunk of rubber, but it beat having his limbs turn to rubber from breathing the paralytic compound.

The four Knackers converged near the front gate, and cautiously peeked and probed the area inside the stone wall. They carried multiple energy guns and other devices whose purpose was unclear. Sensing only one human life form inside the wall, they advanced into the open courtyard area and turned toward the shed. This time, though, they took extra precautions. The lead Crab raised an odd-looking device that resembled a short cylindrical tube with a handle on the bottom. A hollow "poof" echoed through the courtyard as the device spewed what looked like a glass ball toward the shed. The object shattered against the shed wall, and a faint orange vapor expanded rapidly outward from the point of impact. "Neuro-gas!" hissed Tyrus into his wrist com, as he watched the action from a second floor window. "Everyone make sure your masks are fitted tight! Hold fire; wait for them to move in."

Twice more the weapon huffed as the aliens sent neuro-gas canisters toward the house and the rock garden. Finally, satisfied that they had addressed any possible ambush risk, they headed en masse toward the shed. The humans in the house remained perfectly still, watching.

Simon waited in the shed as before, and he carried his heavy automatic, but this time the plan was different. The structure was now mostly empty, the heavy equipment having been moved and parked outside. Toward the back of the shed the humans had piled miscellaneous boxes and junk. This obscured Simon from direct view (and hopefully from direct fire) where he crouched low at the rear wall. Not coincidentally, there was a small doorway in the wall, recently made by Tyrus's cutting tool, and just big enough for Simon to slither out through once the aliens were inside the shed. The key was to wait until they all were within the walls, but not long enough to actually be caught. The timing had to be perfect.

The Knackers approached the partly open shed doors, scanning the area warily with weapons at the ready. Apparently nothing alarming showed on their sensors, and the yard was utterly still. Finally two of the aliens pried the doors wide and rushed inside the shed. Within seconds the thud and clunk of boxes being overturned echoed out the shed doors. When nothing untoward happened after a few moments, the remaining two Crabs slowly crept inside to help search for the paralyzed human.

"Go!" Tyrus spat into his communicator. In that instant Simon lunged for the escape hole in the wall. A Knacker was within three meters of him by then, and only one row of boxes separated them. It heard his movement, and fired an energy bolt blindly in his direction. It glanced off the plastalloy just inches from his right shoulder, and then he was through and out of the building.

"Now!" Simon yelled at his wrist, and in the house above him, Tyrus punched yet another button on his master control panel. Then the sky came falling down.

EasyFab sheds were originally designed for the military, though a market for them had quickly sprung up in the civilian sector as well. The main design combined strength with easy assembly—and disassembly. To that goal, the sheds used by the military had been fitted with explosive bolts at the four upper

corners. Once the reinforcing connectors had been removed along the wall and roof junctions, all that was needed was to blow the four bolts, and the entire thing came tumbling down in a controlled fall. The walls were weighted, so that they fell inward, sliding inside the roof and landing flat, one on top of the other, like neatly stacked cards. The roof came last, topping off the pile. Then a lifter could slide its prongs under the stack and easily hoist the entire shed onto a waiting truck or shuttle.

The civilian version lacked the explosive bolts and had to be disassembled by hand. But Tyrus had obtained this shed, like so many of his possessions, from military surplus. Simon had noticed the bright red warning stickers on the shed's interior that first day he had met Tyrus, and he knew that the shed was the quick-drop version. That had planted the seeds of an idea, and now he was seeing it come to fruition.

The warning labels were there for good reason: it was not conducive to a person's health to be inside a shed when the bolt charges were triggered. Besides serious damage to one's hearing, there was the other problem encountered when a three-dimensional body was forced to become two-dimensional.

Military EasyFabs were sturdy in part because they were heavy. *Really* heavy, in fact. With a shed this large, the combined mass of the walls and roof approached two metric tons. As Simon leapt through the escape door in the shed's wall and desperately rolled clear of the building, Tyrus detonated the explosive bolts. The sharp crack of the small charges echoed around the courtyard, and smoke puffed out from under the roof corners. The Crabs had just enough time to look upward before the entire shed collapsed upon them.

The weight of the structure instantly drove the aliens to the ground and fractured their exoskeletons in multiple places. The impact was so fast and so heavy that only one Knacker had time to discharge a weapon, and the brief energy flash that lanced out from under the falling sections was just as quickly extinguished. Crabs had incredibly fast reflexes, however, and one had actually managed to dart for the door before being struck. It now

lay half in, half out of the shed, its body critically injured but the protruding limbs still flailing weakly. Red and yellow fluids oozed out of the cracks in its shell, and it was only a matter of time before it died. Simon rounded the shed and emptied a few dozen armor-piercing slugs into the creature's head just to be sure.

By the time the rest of the family had arrived at the flattened shed, it was all over. More Crab bodies to burn, and more weapons and equipment to add to their collection. All in all, not a bad day's work.

Once the adrenaline had worn off, Simon became aware of a gradually worsening pain in his right shoulder. A glance revealed a black scorch mark on his shirt, and he smelled a whiff of burned cloth. Gently pulling the fabric up, he found a nasty-looking wound covering nearly the entire shoulder. It appeared shallow, but the skin was an angry red, badly blistered, and was already starting to split open in several areas. He had to tend to it, or infection could set in.

Tyrus saw the damage and instructed him to have Katherine look at it. "She's the closest thing to a field medic we have; she'll get you patched up fine." Simon nodded and went to find her.

For her part, Katherine felt more than a little uneasy tending to this Spacer who had dropped out of the sky and into their lives. Oh, it wasn't that she distrusted him. For all she could tell, he was a good sort, fierce when it came to combat, but capable of kindness when the fighting was over. She had seen it in his interactions with Jessie. But his weary eyes hinted of horrors witnessed and pain endured, things that could scar a person for life. Whether such a man could ever be whole again, she didn't know. And when he looked at her with those eyes, looked *into* her...no, she definitely was not comfortable around him.

Nonetheless here he was, and he had just endured injury while protecting her family. She owed him whatever care she could provide, so she bit her lip and determined to do her best. Simon was sitting on a stool in the main bathroom, stripped to the waist, when she came in, and she almost halted involun-

tarily when she saw him. Mustering her resolve, she continued into the room with barely a pause, and approached her patient. Smiling nervously, she said, "Hi."

He grinned back and said, "Hi" in return.

This was feeling more uncomfortable by the moment, so she tried to keep up a conversation while she assessed his wound. "You've got quite a burn there," she noted as she gently palpated the area. He winced, but didn't flinch away from her touch. He had courage, that much was certain. She continued, "How did you get this?"

"I was shot as I left the shed," he replied. "I saw the beam hit the wall and thought it had just missed me; guess I was wrong."

"No, you were right," she assured him as she rinsed the wound with fortified saline. She found comfort in the reassuring familiarity of medicine, and she kept her tone deliberately clinical. "If you had been hit directly, we'd be talking about a prosthetic limb right now. The wall likely reflected the energy back at you, and even an indirect hit can do damage. You were really lucky."

"I guess so," he remarked. "It doesn't feel so lucky right now, though."

"Burns never do. The pain will get worse before it gets better. I'll give you some numbing cream for it, and some analgesic pills in case you need them. Now hold still while I clean this up and debride the dead tissue. First I'm going to spray some topical anesthetic on. This will sting a bit."

He hissed as the spray hit the raw wound, and she winced sympathetically. At this proximity she was exquisitely aware of his masculinity, the width of his shoulders tapering down to his narrow waist, the hard defined muscles of his back and chest, the faint male smell of him. It had been a long time since she had been this close to a man, other than family. Her hands seemed clumsy and inadequate as she worked, and she felt flushed, her breathing coming faster than she wanted. She was certain that he would notice her discomfiture and question her as to what was wrong, but thankfully he remained silent.

She proceeded as fast as she could without being careless,

trying to ignore his half-naked body as she focused on the wound. She heaved a sigh of relief when at last the area was cleaned and debrided. She spread some NueSkin over the lesion to speed healing, and slapped a bandage on top.

"Done," she stated as she backed away, picking up her supplies. "You'll need to change the dressing daily and put anti-biotic cream on it. Here's your medications; let me know if you need anything else." With that she practically flew out of the room, leaving her patient sitting bemused on the stool as he tugged on a new shirt.

CHAPTER FIVE

Simon anticipated an immediate response to the latest skirmish. Even with their communications jammed at the homestead, the alien scouts had doubtless reported their whereabouts and intentions prior to approaching. Their command hierarchy had to know where they had gone incommunicado. But day after day, indeed week after week, passed without incident. The family cleaned up the Crab bodies and reconstructed the shed, preparing for the next incursion. Then they waited, each of them fighting a growing feeling of dread. Something was bound to happen, and they sensed that the longer it took for the aliens to respond, the bigger the response was likely to be.

As the weeks passed, Simon gradually came to know his adopted family, and they him. Jessie followed him around like a puppy, and he found it a bit embarrassing at times. The three brothers were quite the jesters, somehow finding time for fun despite all they had been through. Simon often caught them trading friendly barbs or laughing themselves silly over an inane joke.

The youngest son, in particular, was an unrepentant prankster who delighted in tormenting his mother and aunt. One day T. J. rigged a toy Knacker about the size of a human head, complete with wiggling legs and clicking vocalizations. It dropped on a string when Amanda opened her bedroom door, hitting her right in the face. Simon heard the screeching from across the house. "*Arrgghh*! Tyrus Junior, you get back here this instant! If I ever catch you, boy, you'll be sorry! What are you trying

to do, put your mama in an early grave?" Such was life in the McKinley home.

Sarah continued to question Simon about his travels, SpaceForce, and life in the Service. She had never been off-planet since the family had moved to Eden ten years earlier, and her imagination was captured by images of interstellar flight and far off worlds. She had a good head for tech stuff, too, and he wondered if she might find her way into an engineering curriculum. If she couldn't afford a private institution, there was always military-sponsored education, with the possibility of a non-combat assignment after graduation. They sure needed engineers right now.

As he became more entwined in the daily lives of these people, he gradually began to feel a sense of belonging. It was something that he had long since forgotten, but had desperately missed nonetheless. His personal life had been so barren these past years, so lacking in meaningful human contact outside of his squadron, that what he was experiencing now felt like awakening from a deep coma. He had spent long years fighting, and only at this late hour had he found something worth fighting for.

His new friends seemed to accept him without reservation, and he spent time with each as he became comfortable socializing. But most of all, he tried to learn more about Katherine. Something about her drew his attention, he had recognized that from the start. Maybe he was overthinking it; after all, she was the only single female close to his age in the family. And she was damned attractive; he found himself watching her just for the sheer pleasure of it. The graceful way her body moved, the snug fit of her clothes on her slender frame, the supple lengths of her arms and legs, they had him mesmerized whenever she was near. And her face possessed an ethereal beauty that he could die for.

But no, it was more than that. Maybe it was the story her eyes told, the depth of experience they hinted at, some of it tragic, yes, but not so different from his own. That sense of melancholy he got from her, which his instincts told him was not her natural

state, made him want to hold her, to wipe the sorrow away, to see her laugh with joy. And maybe if he could make her whole, he would somehow heal himself as well.

Damn it, he had vowed to not get involved with a woman again, not while this accursed war was still being fought. There was too much potential for loss, he knew that all too well. It was better to have nothing than to hold everything in his hands and lose it. He could not go through that again, nor could he ask someone else to chance going through it with him. He could see how personal tragedy had already injured Katherine; it would be cruel to risk involvement of any kind now. The only problem was, he couldn't stop thinking about her.

* * * * * * *

One hot midsummer day Sarah took Simon with her in one of the family floaters to inspect the defenses. Unlike the open tractor she had retrieved him in, this vehicle was fully enclosed, so they rode in air-conditioned comfort. There was a lot of area to cover, and they moved at a fast clip through the open terrain. The homestead lands were bordered by the main highway to the east, and by a large, meandering stream to the north. A line of hills formed a natural barrier at the property's western extent, and a small extension off the hill range cut east across the family's lands just a couple of kilometers south of their dwelling. That finger-like extension of high ground included Roxy Knoll, and it divided the property into two sections, with about a third of their acreage lying to the south of the ridgeline.

Sarah and Simon surveyed the perimeter of all the homestead lands north of Roxy Knoll, carefully avoiding the area south of the hills where Simon's ship lay. The border fencing and sensors appeared to be intact, and they turned at the north limit of the family property, following the stream due west.

As they headed toward the rolling green humps of the western hills, Simon spied something on the plains in the distance. He recalled having seen what looked like an animal herd when

Sarah had first brought him to the house, but it had been too far away to clearly identify. This looked similar. He squinted against the heat waves rising up from the sun-baked land. "What are those dark objects near the foothills?" he asked Sarah.

"Those are what I was hoping to find, when we got done with the security checks," she replied, grinning over at him. "You're gonna like this."

They flew toward the cluster of dark dots far ahead, and as the distance shrank, the objects grew larger and more clearly defined. And the better he saw them, the more bizarre they appeared.

What Sarah had chosen to show him was a herd of wild Dire Bucks. She slowed the vehicle as they came within one hundred meters of the herd, and they eased forward carefully. "They're skittish and can easily be induced to stampede," she cautioned. "Even though they've grown accustomed to seeing us, their instincts are to run first and ask why later."

The animals were unlike anything Simon had ever seen. Modified cattle were used for food and milk on many human colony planets, so those were quite familiar to him. And he had seen vids of many of the famous animals from the core planets, including kangaroos. Although Katherine's description of Dire Bucks as a cross between those two species was vaguely appropriate, it did not begin to capture the reality.

They stopped the vehicle and the animals gradually drifted toward them. One came up alongside the floater, and Simon's eyes drank in the exotic sight. Viewed this close, the animal was impressively large, and it had rich brown fur marked with vertical white pinstripes over the abdomen. Most of the animal's bulk seemed devoted to the massive rear legs and hips, which looked as if they could propel its body into orbit. A fat, kangaroo-like tail protruded from the rounded rump, the tip just touching the ground as it grazed. The narrow head tapered to a protruding nose framed by two small horns. Golden eyes with horizontally slitted pupils watched them warily, and mobile ears flicked constantly this way and that, listening for any sign of

danger.

Simon saw a long tongue darting in and out of the pointed snout as it sucked in vegetation close to the ground. The fore-limbs were comparatively small, and seemed to be used partly to sift through vegetation, pulling choice shoots toward the eager mouth. Perhaps the oddest aspect of the creature was the rear foot, which had three large clawed toes and looked more bird-like than mammalian.

"See those feet?" Sarah said, pointing. "Those are their most dangerous feature. The rear legs are very powerful, and when threatened they can trample you, or leap up in the air and kick out forward, disemboweling an attacker with one stroke. You do not want to stand up to a Dire Buck; lie down if they attack you and take your stomping; at least that way you might live."

"I'll try to avoid having to make that decision," Simon assured her. "They don't look like animals to be messed with." Which begged another question.

"What makes them so shy?" he asked his tour guide. "I can't imagine anything posing a threat to the herd, if they're protected from human hunting."

She gave him a fierce grin. "Trust me, there are predators here that can take down a Dire Bock."

"Oh? Like what?" Simon asked, intrigued.

"Well, the dominant carnivores in this region are called Groons."

"That doesn't tell me much," he chuckled. "I don't know anything about Eden's flora or fauna."

"All you need to know about a Groon is that it's very big and very nasty," Sarah said. "It's a solitary hunter, and nocturnal. They stick to the forests by day, but will venture out onto the plains at night."

"What do they look like?" he asked.

"Solid black, long muscular frame with a forked tail, clawed feet the size of dinner plates, and a head that's all teeth and eyes. Nearly invisible at night."

"I'm sorry I asked," Simon said dryly as he contemplated the

unpleasant image.

Sarah nodded. "They're the main reason we don't venture far out at night, unless we're in a covered floater. Groons usually avoid humans, but have been known to attack people when hungry. And they're always hungry."

"I'm surprised they let them run wild, if they're that dangerous," Simon commented, shaking his head.

Sarah shrugged. "This area is designated national sanctuary land, other than the private homesteads out here. The animals are protected, even the large predators."

They watched the herd awhile longer, and then Sarah slowly backed the vehicle until they achieved some separation. Suddenly she tooted the floater's horn, and the animals broke into a headlong run away from them. Simon stared in surprise, and turned to Sarah, asking, "Why the heck did you do that?"

She giggled, saying, "We weren't just here for fun. The herd has grazed this area for days, and the vegetation needs a break so it can recover. I've got to move them to a different section." So saying, she gunned the floater and followed the galloping animals, herding them with the vehicle. She used the horn sparingly when needed to adjust their direction of travel. In full flight their locomotion was unexpected; they raised up and ran primarily on the large rear legs, but did not hop like a kangaroo. Rather, their limbs moved similarly to those of a sprinting human. The forelimbs were carried mostly aloft, although they touched them to the ground occasionally, especially when changing direction abruptly. Honks and snorts echoed between the animals as they loped effortlessly across the grassy savanna, gracefully leaping small bushes and darting around trees. Simon was amazed at how fast they could move; he'd hate to get caught in front of a stampeding herd of those things.

In a very short time their destination came into view. Up ahead there was a small gap in the rock fence that hemmed in this section of land. It was probably less than ten meters across, but the herd seemed to know where they were supposed to go, and they obediently funneled through and into the grassland

on the other side. Sarah stopped the vehicle at the wall, and they watched as the animals continued some distance into their new grazing grounds, eventually slowing and coming to a halt. There they stood, blowing hard, until one or two reached down to nibble the fresh forage underfoot. In a few minutes the entire herd had joined in, and it was as if the humans had never interrupted their meal.

"Looks like they're settling in just fine," Sarah told him. "We'd best be getting back."

"Thank you for bringing me along," Simon said with a smile. "This was fascinating, and it's nice to get out of the house once in awhile."

"No problem," Sarah replied, her eyes glancing his way before returning to the view ahead. "It's great to have someone new to share the sights with. I'm the only one in my family who seems to enjoy coming out here just for the fun of it. My parents are always busy with work and such, and the boys do guy stuff, playing games on the vidscreen, chatting with girls from town, looking for summer jobs, anything but this. I guess maybe they associate the outdoors with chores, I don't know."

"Your parents work?" Simon asked, puzzled. "I thought your dad was retired."

"Retired from the military, yes," Sarah said. "He still works from home, mostly on the CompuNet. Mom helps him run the business."

"Which is?" Simon asked.

"Security consulting for businesses, and for individuals also. Much of it in recent years has been advising people on how to prepare and protect themselves in the event of a Knacker invasion."

"Ah, ha...," Simon said as things began to come into focus. No wonder Tyrus was so prepared for the Crabs. Not only did he have a military background, but also he had made a living thinking of ways to fend them off. Simon probably couldn't have found a better household to hole up with on all of Eden. His getting shot down and crash-landing was looking more and

more like a stroke of luck.

They had covered about half the distance to the house when they both heard a noise over the hum of the floater engine. It sounded like the faint rumble of an aircraft, and it was getting louder. Frantically they looked out the windows and up. In the sky to the southwest a small shape was rapidly approaching. It was the ovoid form of a Knacker vessel. Sarah instantly slewed their vehicle to the left, slamming Simon against the right side door. "Sorry," she said as she gunned the floater toward one of the scrub trees dotted sparsely across the landscape. Within seconds they had reached its cover, and she braked the vehicle to a stop beneath the spreading limbs.

Breathlessly they waited, and the aircraft approached their position, passing almost directly overhead. It was flying at relatively low altitude, its shape and markings clearly visible from the ground. Either it had not spotted them or it had other business, for the ship never slowed, and in moments it had dwindled to a speck headed toward the northeast.

They exhaled as the danger passed, and looked at each other in silence. Sarah finally said, "Do you think they saw us?"

Simon pursed his lips and shrugged. "No way to tell. In any event, the Crabs already know we're here, so probably no harm done." He gestured toward home, and Sarah nodded as she eased the vehicle on its way once more.

* * * * * * *

Despite the sighting of the alien craft, things remained quiet on the homestead. Part of each day was usually spent training for various combat contingencies, or in planning new ambushes for the Crabs. When not thusly occupied, the members of the household caught up on day-to-day chores, or pursued whatever interests they had.

Tyrus was tinkering with some of the devices they had confiscated from the dead Crabs, hoping to make sense of them. He also was working to modify the captured energy guns for

easier use by humans. The heavy firing triggers of the weapons, designed to be squeezed by the Knackers' tripartite claws, were recessed into the guns' frames and difficult to manipulate. Tyrus attached a metal extension to each trigger, which protruded out of the body of the gun enough to grab and pull it, similar to the standard trigger mechanism on most human guns.

One of the more important pastimes for the humans was feeding and caring for the little animals that they carried in pouches around their necks. Katherine's veterinary background had made her the logical choice for overseeing the Darters' care. The family had obtained their original animals when a female carrying young had fallen from an Ironwood tree. Sarah had found the dying animal and had seen movement in its belly pouch. The four babies inside had been very tiny, and only Katherine's attentive nursing had allowed them to survive. Once the babies had grown, putting a receptive female in a live trap had quickly netted two eager male suitors from the woods, and they had been able to breed additional offspring. Now every family member had a Darter.

Simon had, to his surprise, developed an attachment for the volatile little creatures. It had begun after the last Knacker attack, when he had peeled off his gas mask and a thought had struck him. When he had mentioned it to Sarah, she had checked her Darter, and sure enough, the little animal was totally para-lyzed within its pouch.

Every Darter outside of the house that day, and some of those indoors, had been affected by the paralytic agent. For most of the next twenty-six hours (the length of Eden's day) the animals were unable to fend for themselves, and had to receive food and water via tube feedings. Simon had volunteered to help Sarah and Katherine with this task. Every eight hours or so, they had lined up all the stricken Darters, and Simon held each animal while Katherine carefully slid a rubber tube down its throat. Then she syringed an appropriate amount of gruel into the stomach. The food mix was essentially pureed invertebrate creatures and warm water, a slop that looked as nauseating as

it sounded. Come to think of it, the stuff didn't smell too good either. Sarah mixed up the potion in measured syringes, and handed them to Katherine one by one as she moved down the line of motionless animals.

The supportive care had kept their diminutive patients alive, and a day later they were regaining voluntary movement, and soon after, their coordination. They seemingly had no lingering effects from their misfortune.

The juvenile that Simon carried was still only partially tame, and he met with Katherine in the breeder room regularly so that she could assess its health. This week he sought her out in the kitchen where she was preparing lunch for herself and Jessie. She looked up inquiringly as he stood watching, and he grinned and jiggled his pouch. With a smile and a nod she said, "I'll see you in the animal room once I get Jess fed. Give me ten minutes or so." Jessie grinned and waved from the dining table as he sauntered back out of the room.

Soon after, Katherine came into the animal ward where Simon lounged waiting. Clearing her throat, she took a seat at a small desk cluttered with papers and several instruments, including a digital scale. Much of the small room was taken up with storage cabinets, plus a refrigerated cold bin filled with perishable medications. One corner was dominated by a large floor-to-ceiling aviary-style cage, wherein lived a mated pair of Darters and their offspring. Within the habitat several nest boxes hung suspended by rope from the ceiling. Pans of food and water lay on the floor below. Gnarled branches led from the floor to the nests, allowing the nimble animals to run up and down in their environment for exercise, while having a safe retreat high above ground. When someone first entered the room, the small creatures would live up to their name, shooting skyward in a blur to vanish into the nests. After a few minutes, if things remained quiet, they would peek out cautiously, their small faces corkscrewing around to check their surroundings before they ventured slowly back out. Eventually they would be chirping and squawking as they cavorted around their enclo-

sure, leaping and climbing with sure-footed grace.

Along the wall opposite the habitat ran a long countertop. It was covered with terrariums for raising Darter food items, mostly worm-like creatures called Gusanos. These insectoid natives of Eden were fed a fortified diet to enhance their nutritional content. Thus modified, they provided a balanced diet for the Darters, without the need for offering the diversity of prey consumed in the wild.

Katherine looked up from the growth chart in her hands, and motioned Simon over. With an inward sigh he approached. She had acted so detached with him lately, so clinical, that he wondered if he had done something to anger her. He was afraid to ask, for fear that he was imagining it and she'd think him a complete fool. When he stopped obediently in front of the desk, she asked, "How's your little guy been doing? Is he eating decently?"

"I'd say so," Simon replied with a grin. "He almost takes my finger off every time I hand him a grub."

"Let's get a weight on him and see where he's at," she said.

Reaching to his neck, Simon untied the string holding the cloth bag, and handed it to her. She took the pouch, animal inside, and plopped it on the scale at her desk. The empty bag had been weighed previously; all that was needed was the combined weight of pouch and occupant, and simple subtraction gave them the animal's current size. All without the stress of removing the shy creature from its hiding place. It would also have been nearly impossible, without anesthesia, to keep an unconfined Darter on a scale long enough for its weight to register.

"Sixty-five grams," Katherine reported with a smile. "He's getting big."

"Positively monstrous," Simon replied sarcastically. "I've got to admit, they're pretty cute little guys, especially once they get past the screeching phase."

"Well, he's getting used to you," she told him. "At first he probably thought you were going to eat him."

"At first I was tempted to, just to shut him up," Simon retorted. He laughed at her offended expression, and she eventually gave up trying to look angry and chuckled as well.

"They can get on your nerves occasionally," she admitted. "During breeding season I could hardly stand to be in here. With new babies in the nest, they wouldn't stop screaming at me until I left, no matter how long I sat here."

Simon said, "I read that they normally dwell in small holes in trees. Is that why cloth pouches work so well for them?"

"Partly," she answered, nodding. "Maybe also because they spend their early lives in momma's belly pouch. Soft bags probably remind them of security and safety. Okay, let's see your boy."

So saying, she eased the bag open to peek at the furry bundle inside. It began to screech, then quickly quieted when it saw Simon. He held out a squirming Gusano, and the Darter eagerly snatched it with tiny sharp teeth. Using its forepaws like miniature hands, it held the succulent treat and nibbled it like a human eating an ear of corn. Within seconds the tidbit was devoured, and the Darter came partially out of the bag, looking for more. Simon put out his hand, palm up, and the little animal jumped onto it without hesitation.

"Wow, you've really made progress with him," Katherine marveled. "He's a lot tamer than last time."

"He's my little buddy," Simon murmured, using one finger to stroke the creature's velvety spine. Its eyes partly closed as it held perfectly still, obviously enjoying the attention. Katherine eyed the two of them speculatively, a trace of a smile playing on her lips. She hadn't expected the pilot to be this empathetic with his assigned pet. He continued to be full of surprises.

Simon eventually looked over at her and asked, "I'm curious, how did you decide to be a vet?"

Caught off guard, Katherine smiled shyly and shrugged. "I just liked animals, you know, I loved going to the zoo as a child, loved going camping with my parents, watching vids about wildlife, all that stuff. When I got older I just followed my heart

and eventually became an animal doctor."

"I'll bet you were good at it," Simon said.

"Yes...I guess I was," she answered. A cloud passed over her face then, and he saw that the conversation had taken her somewhere she didn't enjoy going.

"Kate," he began hesitantly, "I...if you ever want to talk about anything, I'm willing to listen. With no judgment, comments, or anything, just listening. People tell me I'm good at that, for a military guy, anyway," he finished lamely.

The guarded look she wore vanished for a split second, replaced by something—affection, longing, he wasn't sure. Then the shield slammed down again, and she turned away, saying, "I'm all right, Simon. Really. We should probably go see if the others need us. It's almost time for our daily meeting."

It was clear the conversation was over, at least for now. He nodded silently, and rose to follow her out of the room.

* * * * * * *

"Eureka!" Tyrus shouted a few minutes later as he walked into the greatroom. In his raised hand he clutched a small rectangular device. The remainder of the clan was already assembled for their scheduled strategy session. Everyone looked up as one, and Jessie piped up first, "What is it, Uncle?"

Tyrus looked down at her and smiled. "It's an alien translator, my girl. It's a wonderful gift, that's what it is. We can understand the Crabs' language with this little beauty!" He was so excited that he was practically dancing, and the others looked at each other with widening grins. Everyone had heard the pop-and-click vocalizations of the aliens, but to be able to actually understand what they were saying! No one had even contemplated such an eventuality. It seemed almost too good to be true.

Simon cocked his head appraisingly at the gadget, and asked, "Is it likely to be of use in combat? I can't imagine getting close enough to overhear Crab conversations during a battle. Unless you plan on using it to interrogate a captured prisoner; that

could be interesting."

"I plan to spy on their communications," Tyrus answered him without hesitation. "Now observe and learn, oh young apprentice." With that he turned on the airwave monitor, basically a more sophisticated and versatile version of the radios employed by humans throughout their history. Deftly tuning it to the frequency they had most often found Knackers using, he listened for transmissions, adjusting the sensitivity and range settings on the tuner. Before long the "put-put" sound of soft pops, interspersed with high pitched clicks, came through the speakers. Everyone by now knew they were listening to the enemy's speech.

Tyrus then flicked a switch on the alien device, and a blue light lit on the box. "Power's on," he commented, and then he set the device near the airwave receiver. As the Knackers' vocalizations continued to emanate from the radio, the box suddenly began to spit words, *recognizable* words, out its own speaker.

"Attack...Soft-Shell...weak city defenses...need shuttles and weapons at city Teotetoplon...move four quadrills Soft-Shells... coordinates 509 155...send to harvest ship...rendezvous in 232 segmons...."

The communications rambled on, bits of recognizable words combined with gibberish. The family looked at Tyrus with questioning expressions, and he shuffled his feet and said, "Ah, yes, the translator doesn't always have human equivalents available for species-specific points of reference. For instance, I believe that quadrills are a gross number value used by the aliens, somewhat like our 'ton' or 'bushel,' and they haven't provided the translator with an equivalent in our numerical system. Their global coordinates likewise might not easily translate. Segmons are a time unit, from what I can determine. City names such as Teo-whatever-they-said are again species dependent, and the machine doesn't know the human equivalent name. It could be any human city they were discussing."

"A 'harvest ship'...they must mean a lander," Amanda mused, looking unhappy.

"Yes, that would follow," Simon agreed somberly.

"What is a soft-shell?" Jessie asked, looking around at the adults for an answer.

"I'm afraid that's us, I mean humans," her eldest cousin Keith replied, looking to Tyrus for confirmation.

"Yes, you are unfortunately correct," his father agreed. "That apparently is the Knacker name for humans, or at least how it translates into our language. Sort of makes sense, I suppose."

"It's creepy hearing those things discussing their plans for us," TJ said. "There's not much point in listening to their broadcasts; we'll get more from watching whatever human updates we can find."

"Perhaps," Tyrus answered. "But it would be very useful to know if the aliens are coming for us, now wouldn't it? Or what they might be planning when they do arrive?" His son nodded reluctantly, and Tyrus continued, "To that end, I plan on monitoring their broadcasts as often as I can, especially those originating within forty kilometers or so. We may get lucky and learn a thing or two. Any advantage we can gain may be critical. Well, that's it for today's meeting," he concluded. "I'm going to work with this for a few more hours." With that, the group separated, most of the family filing out of the room in silence as people digested this new development.

* * * * * * *

A few days later, Simon was back in the greatroom, this time reclined in a plush easy chair. It was evening, just after dinner, and he was busy with the tasks of relaxing and digesting. The room was spacious but cozy, replete with everything from a traditional fireplace at one end, to the large vidscreen that was used for entertainment in happier times, to an old-style billiards table. Lighting was recessed, and controlled with a dimmer that could set whatever mood the user wished. Currently he had it adjusted comfortably low.

The beautiful walls of dark polished wood were adorned with

numerous family portraits. Some pics showed a younger Tyrus standing with buddies in military garb; others captured him with Amanda and the kids at various ages. And a few photos featured a smiling Katherine and a smaller Jessie with a dark haired man in dress uniform.

Simon was lost in the history displayed there when he abruptly became aware of a presence at his right elbow. He turned and startled involuntarily as he saw Jessie's smiling face beaming at him from inches away. *Ares,* how did she sneak around so quietly? Her grin broadened when she saw that she had surprised him, and she said, "Whatcha doin', Uncle Simon?"

Despite his irritation at having been caught off guard again, he couldn't help but grin back. She was just too damn likable, and today her mouse brown hair was done up in pigtails, maximizing the cuteness beyond belief. And calling him uncle, well that pretty much sealed the deal. No doubt she knew that, too, the little vixen. "Not much, little Jess," he answered. "Just relaxing and thinking about that great meal your Aunt Amanda fixed up. I haven't eaten this well in years."

"Don't ya have a wife or someone?" Jessie asked him, crawling onto the armrest of his chair.

"Nope, no one," he replied. "And I'm no good cook, and the SpaceForce food is even worse!"

"Yeah, I remember my papa telling mama how good her food was compared to Service rations," Jessie nodded. She pointed at a picture on the wall. "That's my papa there, see? He was killed fighting Knackers."

Simon nodded somberly. "You must miss him."

She nodded, then frowned. "I do miss him, but I'm starting to have trouble remembering what he was like, in real life, you know, not just in pics or vids. I think mama misses him more; they were married a long time and she remembers everything. I wish I could remember more."

Simon's heart ached at the little girl's matter-of-fact statement. The words were right, but they were said with such scant emotion that he wondered if Jessie had ever had the opportunity

to properly grieve. He suspected that her mother was grieving enough for the both of them.

"Mama likes you," Jessie interrupted his thoughts. She was grinning mischievously. "I can tell from the way she watches you, and sometimes she smiles when she sees you."

"Oh, she does, does she?" Simon replied, taken by surprise and not entirely certain what to say.

Jessie looked from Simon to the wall photos, and said, "You're kinda like my papa. He was brave and fought in the Service, just like you. When I get older I want to join up and fight Knackers, too."

Simon stroked her hair and said gently, "No, Jess, you'll do something better. Fighting is ugly, it's dangerous, it's...necessary sometimes, but it's never something that a person should look forward to."

"What could I do that's better?" the child asked him, and he could tell she was totally serious. Damn, this war had caused so much damage beyond the physical casualties.

"Well, you could have a family, for one. Create life, instead of death. Be a good friend to others, help people live happily. Maybe be a doctor or a vet like your mom, and save lives. There is a galaxy full of opportunities, Jessie, if you open your mind to them."

She looked thoughtful for a few moments, then said, "Maybe I could be a vet...."

"Maybe. Just remember, your papa fought not because he liked it, but because he was protecting things that are more important. Things like family, loved ones, and freedom. Those things matter. The fighting is meaningless without the reasons behind it."

"Okay, I understand. But I can still shoot Crabs when they come to the house, can't I?" she asked hopefully.

Simon laughed and said, "If it's okay with your mom, then I guess so."

"And mama says it's bedtime right now," Katherine's voice intruded from the doorway, startling them both. "You're up late,

little girl. Get upstairs now and get ready to be tucked in."

"Yes, mama," the girl said contritely, and she slid off the chair, but not before giving Simon a quick kiss on the cheek.

As she ran out the door, her mother looked at Simon with a half smile, and said, "We'll talk further," before following her daughter upstairs.

Awhile later Simon was beginning to doze off when Katherine returned and sat down in the chair next to his, sighing deeply as the cushioned softness worked its magic. She leaned back and closed her eyes for a moment, then looked sideways at Simon and offered, "She likes you a lot, you know."

He nodded, and said wryly, "Yes, I got that impression."

Katherine smiled tiredly. "Jessie has always been pretty forward. You never have to wonder what she's thinking."

"True," he agreed. "But her mother is a different story, isn't she?" Katherine's eyes widened and he looked at her steadily. "I would really like to know your thoughts right now, if you're willing to share."

She dropped her eyes, fidgeting self consciously with a thread on her sweater, then she swallowed and said quietly, "I overheard part of that conversation you had with Jess. I want to thank you for the way you handled it. She misses her father more than she can say, and I think she's subverted her grief into something darker." Her fingers picked harder at the fabric as she continued, "I don't like how vengeful she's become, almost bloodthirsty. Having someone in the military tell her that there's more to life than killing, well, she really needed to hear that, and I'm thankful." She lifted her gaze again to meet his, and he could see the conflicted emotions on her face.

"You're welcome," he replied carefully. "But that's not all, is it?"

"No." She hesitated before continuing. "I—I'm not sure whether it's healthy for Jessie to spend a lot of time around you," she admitted, sounding unhappy at saying it. "It's not you," she added hastily, giving him a weak smile. "Or rather, it's not who you are, it's what you are that worries me. Okay, I can see now

that you're not all macho warrior and blood lust. There's a depth to you that is, well, surprising and rather nice. In another life...." She shook herself and continued, "She needs a father figure, I know that. But you're too much like her papa was, and that could make her vulnerable. I don't want her getting too attached to you and then feeling abandoned once again when you return to SpaceForce. That could break her. And if you got killed in action...." Her voice tailed off and she looked again at her lap.

"It's not just Jessie's needs we're talking about here, is it?" he asked gently. When he got no reply, he said, "Katherine, this war has damaged all of us, in one way or another. I won't lie to you, I don't know if I'll survive this conflict. Hell, I don't know if any of us will, poor Jessie included. But I do know one thing. If we allow fear to win, if we stop living because we're afraid of dying, then the Knackers have already won. What is the point of fighting, if there is nothing of value worth fighting for?"

Katherine looked at him, and her eyes were moist with unshed tears. He continued softly, "A few weeks ago I didn't care if I lived. I existed only to take revenge on the Crabs. They had destroyed everything I valued, and I had nothing left. Now, being here in this house, watching your family, I remember what it was like to have someone, to care about something other than vengeance." He looked at her fiercely. "*Live* this life, Kate, and live it to the fullest, and tomorrow be damned. Because it's the only life we have, and tomorrow might not come."

She sat silently, tears now coursing down her cheeks, and he thought about saying more, then bit his tongue. She would have to come to grips with her own demons; no one could do that for her. He would try to help but only if she asked him. Finally she wiped her arm across her wet face, and said haltingly, "Thank you, Simon, for being here. Jessie and I both appreciate you, and I want you to know that. But anything more is not mine to give at this time. I'm sorry." Then she stood and walked from the room, her head down as she choked back a sob. Simon stared after her, wondering if he had just done more harm than good.

CHAPTER SIX

In the days following, Simon's energy was focused on implementing some new defensive preparations that he and Tyrus had been cooking up. In one of their recent strategy meetings Tyrus had presented a list of their assets that had potential military applications. One item that had seemed particularly useful was the large volume of liquid fuel stored in barrels in an underground cellar. Its primary purpose was for powering the house generators if the regional power grid went down. But Tyrus had accumulated a surplus of the flammable liquid, and given the aliens' combustibility, it seemed too good a resource to ignore. They had already put it to use on a small scale, filling dozens of Molotov cocktail bottles. But Simon and Tyrus wanted to find another way to employ the fuel, something that could make a sizable impact on an attacking force.

After discussing the logistics, they set some of the younger family members to digging a shallow ditch along the inside of the rock wall in front of the house. A similar ditch was also dug along the rear wall bordering the back yard. Then they lined the trenches with Duraplas sheeting to prevent liquids from sinking into the soil. All that remained was to pour flammable fuel into the ditches when the time came, and light it from a distance with a kiss from a plasma gun. Anything coming over the walls would be treated to a royal barbecue.

Tyrus sought Simon out the morning after they had completed the firewall preparations. He found the spacer in the front yard helping the three brothers with yet another defensive project.

He approached the group with an anxious energy, and Simon stopped what he was doing when he saw the look on the older man's face. "What's up?" he asked when they were within easy conversational distance.

"Not sure. Maybe nothing," Tyrus replied, looking worried. "Maybe everything. I'm picking up a lot more local chatter from the Crabs today. It sounds like their numbers have increased in this area. I also caught translated words that sounded like, 'Rural softshells.' I'm concerned that an attack may be imminent."

Without waiting for further elaboration, Simon turned and told the brothers, "Get this project done quickly. Once the charges are set on those trees, gather the equipment and get back inside fast. We may not have much time." They nodded and scampered to complete their work. Simon turned back to Tyrus and said, "So what is your best estimate of things to come?"

"Truthfully? I don't know, but my gut tells me to expect action within the next two days," Tyrus said.

"Then we'll work on that premise," Simon declared. He had learned to trust Tyrus's instincts; the man had an uncanny feel for ground warfare.

"You know, Major, it might be time to implement that idea you had mentioned awhile back, after your jaunt into the country with Sarah."

"Do you think it's worthwhile?" Simon asked him. "I wasn't sure if it was even feasible."

"Your plan has merit," Tyrus replied. "In the best case scenario, it could be very effective."

Simon scratched his cheek reflectively. "Well, we'll need to prepare ahead of time, obviously."

Tyrus nodded. "Yes, I'll send Sarah out right away. She likes riding around in the fresh air anyway."

"Sounds good," Simon replied, then he added with a chuckle, "Whether it works or not, one thing is for certain. The Crabs are going to be in for a helluva surprise!"

The next twenty-six hours passed uneventfully. The

following evening the family shared a delicious dinner, laughing and conversing around the long dining table. Jessie sat next to Simon, and between mouthfuls she kept up a running conversation about catching bugs and killing Knackers and anything else that came to her mind. As he listened with one ear, he felt Katherine's eyes on him several times, but she quickly looked away whenever his gaze met hers. Once he could have sworn she actually blushed.

The three brothers were also going at it, trading barbs and good-natured insults back and forth as they consumed prodigious amounts of food. Their mother gently scolded them for their antics, and they laughed and began teasing her instead. Tyrus was chuckling out loud, until a stern look from his wife made him paste a not-too-convincing scowl of disapproval on his features. His sons weren't buying it, and before long Tyrus's features were twitching as he tried in vain to suppress a grin. Amanda just shook her head resignedly, which incited further laughs at her expense.

At times like this Simon could almost imagine that this was an average family in normal times. But he knew they sat in the deceptively calm eye of a storm, and the tempest would be coming to them soon. After the meal, the family settled in for the evening, and as the hour grew late, one by one they headed off to bed.

Around midnight, Simon's wrist alarm jarred him from a sound sleep. As he fumbled momentarily, caught between the dream world and reality, he heard voices coming from outside the bedroom door. He forced himself to awaken, sitting up and shaking his head before swinging his feet to the cool floor and grabbing his clothes. He was still pulling his shirt over his head as he exited his room.

In the upstairs hallway people were milling around with wrist alarms sounding, and more were appearing from behind bedroom doors as he watched. Some still were clad in pajamas, whereas others were fully dressed. Tyrus and little Jessie actually wore sidearms as well, and looked alert and ready for battle.

Simon shook his head in admiration; he was supposed to be the professional here.

"Okay, everyone, downstairs quickly," Tyrus said in a loud voice, waving his arms toward the staircase. "Trouble has arrived; we have very little time." With that he headed down toward the great room, and everyone followed on his heels.

Powering up the vidscreen, Tyrus scanned the defense grid with the others crowding in behind him. In a moment he growled, "They're here all right, and this time they're coming in force. We've got four different perimeter breaches, all from the general direction of the highway. Predictable bastards."

Turning away from the screen, he barked out instructions to his family. "Everyone grab their gas masks. Jessie, get upstairs with an infrared farscope and start watching for them. Keith and Samuel, get outside and pour fuel into the trenches. The tree charges are set?"

His sons nodded, and Tyrus said, "Good. We've no time to double-check the setup; let's hope there are no glitches. Now go!"

As they scooted out the door, he turned to Sarah. "Are your troops ready, girl?"

"Yessir!" she replied.

"Then get out there and be ready. I'll signal you on wrist com when it's time."

"On my way," she called as she ran to take her position.

"The rest of you, get upstairs and grab your weapons," Tyrus commanded. "T. J., you'll get one of the alien energy guns, along with your mother and aunt. Each of you take one window, and be careful! I'll be up in a minute; Simon and I have to discuss our plan of action."

As his family headed to the upper floor, Tyrus turned to Simon and said, "I hope we get this right; we'll not have a second chance."

"I know. What should we do first, do you think?"

"That depends on them, in part. If they have floaters, they could fly them right over the wall. We'll open fire if they do. A

tracked vehicle will probably move up the road to the gate; we'll take care of that when the time comes. I'll be upstairs coordinating things and manning the remote controls for our various surprises. I expect they will attack mostly on foot as usual. This time they'll have numbers, at least a whole squad, so we've got to expect they'll get over the wall. When they do, we'll need to light the ditches. That should slow them down. We'll also have to time Sarah's contribution exactly right, and then maybe follow it with the trees."

"What would you like me to do?" Simon asked.

"Go get the boys once they've filled the ditches. Put them upstairs with the slingshot and cocktails; being out in the yard will be too dangerous with the numbers the Crabs are bringing against us. T. J. can help them fire the sling. You get in a window and use your weapon of choice; you can have T. J.'s energy rifle if you want, since he'll be spending the early part of the battle helping his brothers."

Simon shook his head. "I'm kind of partial to old faithful," he said, referring to the heavy automatic rifle that he had used in the prior skirmishes.

"Good enough. Just be sure you have your Service pistol," Tyrus said. "I want you to be the one to set off the ditch fires when the time comes. Wait until they're almost over the wall."

"What about the rear of the house?" Simon asked.

"I've got sensors out back; if they come that way, we'll have time to get to a rear window and ignite the firewall along the back fence. I doubt they'll send many troops out there; we've got antipersonnel mines all over the place in back of the house. Their sensors will detect them, so it should deter a major assault on that front. We also have no lower-floor windows on that side, so it's not as inviting to attack us from there."

"Got it. I'll grab the boys. Happy hunting!" Simon added as he jogged out of the greatroom.

Simon found the two older sons outside, one in front and one in back of the house, straining to empty large barrels of fuel into the prepared ditches. He added his strength to theirs, and

the task was quickly finished. Then he ran with them upstairs, seeing them to a bedroom where they set up the slingshot and bottles. They called T. J. to join them at the window as Simon continued on to his room, where his trusty guns awaited. He strapped the Service energy pistol to his waist, grabbed the automatic rifle, and settled in at the window to watch for the enemy. He could see nothing in the inky blackness beyond the wall.

They didn't have long to wait. Within minutes little Jessie spoke over the com links, sounding very grown up. "Crabs approaching, on the road and also east of it. Looks like three separate groups, each with a vehicle. The aliens don't show up real well on I.R., but their machines do. I think it's two floaters and a ground transport. The floaters are coming overland, not on the road."

"How many soldiers?" Tyrus replied over his wrist link.

"Not sure. Ten or twelve, maybe more."

"Simon, are you getting this?"

"Yeah, Tyrus. It sounds like a Knacker squad, with a couple of extras, officers maybe."

"Well, they mean business this time. Be ready to hit them hard. Masks tight, everyone!"

A night attack gave the aliens an advantage; they had good infrared technology, and humans emitted more heat than Crabs. It was believed that Knackers also had inherently better night vision than humans did. But once again Tyrus had anticipated just such a contingency. He spoke softy into the com link, "Jess, tell me when they get about one hundred meters from the wall."

"On it, uncle," she replied. "They're approaching steadily. Maybe two hundred meters out now. I can hear the transport on the road." Indeed, the faint murmur of an engine now came to Tyrus's ears across the still night air. "One hundred fifty meters; they're getting close. The floaters are a little farther away, but they're moving to catch up with the land vehicle. Looks like one is approaching east of the driveway, and the other is swinging to come in on the west side, with the ground car in the middle."

Tyrus said, "Ready on the slingshot, boys. Light some cocktails. I'll brighten things up in a moment. When you can see 'em, fire away."

Jessie's voice cut in, "One hundred meters out, and closing."

"Here we go," said Tyrus, and he hit a button on his control panel. Banks of lights mounted around the outside of the fence wall flared into brilliance, bathing the landscape beyond in stark relief. What met the humans' eyes was almost surreal.

Several powered vehicles loomed in the near distance, surrounded by what seemed to be scores of scuttling creatures. Simon was reminded of a scene that he had witnessed years earlier, in a rundown barracks on a little backwater world. The place had been infested with vermin, and when he had flicked on the light switch, the floor had been covered with multi-legged critters scattering this way and that, trying to find cover. It had given him the creeps, and here it was all over again, only this time the creatures were larger than he was. And they carried weapons.

In reality there were maybe fifteen Knackers, heavily armed, and three transport vehicles. When the lights hit them, the forward aliens raised weapons and multiple *thunks* sounded. A second later a flurry of glass spheres cascaded over the wall and into the front yard of the house. The delicate tinkling sound as they shattered on the ground belied their danger. "Neuro-gas!" Tyrus shouted into his wrist com. "Fire the slingshot! Fire all weapons!"

On his command, multiple energy weapons lanced across the wall and played across the oncoming ranks of the aliens, along with the *pop, pop* of a conventional gun, likely Jessie's sidearm. At the same time a flaming object shot out of an upper story window. It arced gracefully toward the advancing troops and fell on the ground in front of them, bursting into a small fireball. "Aim higher!" Tyrus commanded, and within seconds another bottle flew outward from the house. This one hit a floater head on, instantly covering the vehicle's front half in liquid flames. Some of the fuel spilled over onto a soldier crawling alongside

the machine. The unfortunate Crab lit up like so much flammable paper, flailing and spinning spastically as the flames engulfed it. Its comrades quickly backed away as it careened off into the night, eventually collapsing in a glowing mass in the distance. The two soldiers aboard the burning vehicle abandoned their ride, jumping off and leaving it floating in place.

The plasma beams from the humans' weapons, the same ones stolen from the Crab scouts, were also wreaking havoc. Several hit their targets, and the aliens began losing pieces of themselves as limbs were amputated and cauterized by the hot blades of the beams. One Knacker took a shot directly to its head, just under the eyes. It dropped instantly, twitching, and didn't move again.

The deadly effectiveness of the initial human attack apparently caused a change of plan on the part of the aliens. Abandoning their non-violent assault strategy, the soldiers and vehicles opened up with their own barrage of energy gun fire, and they rushed toward the wall, seeking the relative safety of its cover. Glowing plasma bolts slammed into the house, some hitting the windows wherein human defenders crouched. Chunks of wood and stone flew from the structure, and the humans had to duck as hot stabs of energy probed the slits between the protective shutters.

As the attackers charged forward, the soldiers on foot outran the vehicles, leaving their protection behind in a scramble for the wall. Another Molotov cocktail exploded in their midst, touching two Knackers with flame. They frantically waved burning limbs but managed to keep moving forward. Suddenly a staccato roar reverberated through the night as Simon let loose with his heavy rifle. His aim was true, and a lead Crab exploded in a mass of disconnected body parts, its right half mutilated. It hit the ground still trying to run, but its left legs spun its body in a tight circle as the limbless right side dragged the ground.

Already he was tracking another target, and a second Knacker went down under his fire before the remaining attackers on foot reached the wall and ducked out of sight. The two vehicles still

under power continued their approach, firing both hand-held and mounted plasma cannons at the defenders. The house was taking a beating, with glowing holes and gouges ripped out of its solid walls. An upper story window frame was blown open, leaving a ragged crater where the shutter had been.

Following a planned script, the family concentrated their firepower on the floater, leaving the ground transport free to approach the gate. The combined energy beams, along with Simon's weapon, smashed into the oncoming craft. Despite the aliens' desperate attempts to return fire, the defenders were able to sweep the floating vehicle free of its crew before it reached the wall. The two Crab soldiers dropped off the transport, one in multiple pieces, as the onslaught chopped them apart. The unpiloted craft eventually drifted to a halt, just meters outside the yard.

The remaining vehicle continued to approach the gate, firing its plasma cannon, and the heavy metal barrier proved no match for the Knackers' firepower. The gate blew off its hinges, and the ground transport lunged forward toward the inviting gap in the defenses. Tyrus tracked the vehicle closely from his vantage point. Just as it approached the wall, he stabbed a button and the ground gave way beneath the aliens. The transport lurched and paused for a split second, its tracks churning in place, and then it dropped out of sight, seemingly swallowed by the earth. Two seconds later Tyrus hit a second switch. A deafening explosion threw dirt and debris skyward from the pit, as the final stage of the trap was sprung. The blast shattered a few windows in the house, and knocked nearby Crabs backward, leaving them stunned and in momentary view of the humans on the second floor. The defenders opened fire, but the aliens recovered quickly and scrambled back under cover of the wall.

From there, the Knackers began peeking up at intervals along the barrier, firing their weapons and ducking down again as the humans tried to pick them off with return fire. Neither side was able to aim effectively with such brief engagements, so no real damage was being done. It amounted to a stalemate.

That only lasted a few minutes before the Crabs decided to take the battle to the defenders. From behind the wall came multiple soft detonations resembling the *thunks* of gas canister guns, but this time there was no gentle puff of released toxin on impact. Instead a series of detonations rocked the yard; the aliens were lobbing grenades! A few of the weapons impacted against the house, and Tyrus felt the foundations shake beneath him. If it weren't for the over-engineered construction of his home, the explosions might have brought the entire front of the structure crumbling down. As it was, the assault breached the wall of the building in two places, leaving openings large enough for a human to scramble through, but too small to allow entry by a Crab.

Tyrus was worried that more such hits could accomplish serious damage, but the attackers were apparently using the grenades to soften up the defenders, not as a siege weapon. After a few more detonations, the remaining Crabs swarmed up and over the wall in a coordinated push. Each warrior appeared at the top of the barrier carrying multiple energy guns, which they used to lay down suppressing fire at the defenders. Bright beams crossed paths through the air as the two forces stepped up their barrage. The crackle of plasma discharges and the stink of ozone filled the yard. Soon the loud reports of traditional firearms joined in as the brothers, having finished with lobbing cocktails, grabbed their guns and began shooting.

Simon kept close watch on the wall while firing brief bursts from his automatic rifle. When the aliens came over the top, he was ready with his Service pistol. As the first Knackers began descending the inside of the wall, he aimed and fired a single energy bolt from the handgun. The hot touch of the plasma instantly ignited the fuel in the ditch at the wall's base. A gout of yellow and red flame erupted skyward, and it leapt down the length of the wall, spanning fifty meters in a matter of seconds. The yard was lit in flickering amber as a sheet of fire material-ized in front of the surprised attackers. Two of the aliens were engulfed immediately, and the remaining Crabs backpedaled

furiously to avoid certain death.

As the unlucky pair of Knackers added their fuel to the inferno, the survivors disappeared once again behind the stone barrier. For a moment all was still, as the humans, lacking targets, ceased fire. The only sounds were the roaring of the flames and the crackle of roasting Crab meat. Then the remaining five aliens rushed through the open gate, firing everything they had. Their multiple limbs allowed the warriors to wield several plasma guns and launch grenades simultaneously. Explosions rocked the house once more, and a piece of wall broke loose from the upper story, falling with a crash to the ground below. A few neuro-gas spheres also discharged their yellow vapors into the smoky air.

The human defenders were forced to seek cover as lances of hot plasma sought their locations. Their defensive fire waned briefly, giving the aliens time to spread out into the yard. The Crabs' speed and mobility made them difficult targets. This was especially true when the humans were forced to fire quickly from cover, with no time to track the enemy.

Tyrus cursed as an energy blast came through his window and struck the opposite wall, igniting a fire in the wood there. His was the room that had lost part of the window frame and shutter, so he had less protection from enemy rounds. At that moment he heard another muffled explosion from outside, and it sounded like it had come from behind the house! He realized that one of the land mines has been triggered, and expletives flew from his mouth as he barked through his mask into the com, "Simon! We're being hit from the rear! Get to a window now, and light the firewall!"

"*On it,*" came the brief reply.

Simon rushed out of his room carrying his rifle in his right hand and the plasma pistol in his left. He swooped through the doorway and crossed the hall, darting into a rear bedroom and across the floor as fast as he could run. He left the room lights off to avoid painting himself as an obvious target. Once at the window, he fumbled with the latch and slid the clear pane aside.

Carefully he eased the shutters open. His breath was loud in the gas mask as he peeked out into the night.

At first he could make out nothing in the pitch black. As his eyes strained to adjust, he began to see the dim pale stripe of the rock wall where it ran from left to right across the yard. A faint scrabbling sound came to his ears. There, off to the left, he thought he caught a flicker of dark motion against the lighter gray of the rock. Carefully he raised his pistol, setting his rifle aside and using both hands to steady the gun. Holding his breath, he aimed at what he hoped was the base of the wall, and squeezed off a plasma round.

His shot was on target, and the brief flash of the energy beam flared into a gout of flame that lit up the darkness. Mimicking the front fire trench, the burning pillar expanded rapidly left and right to engulf the entire length of the wall. As the scene was lit, Simon saw with grim satisfaction the two Knackers caught in the inferno, twisting and flopping as they beat in vain at the hungry flames consuming them. Within moments their movements weakened and they collapsed, their limbs curling under them like dried insects.

He tore his gaze from the twin pyres and glanced around the yard. Just beyond the wall hovered an unoccupied floater. Damn it, they should have suspected this. There had been four perimeter breaches on the monitor. This group must have separated early from the others, and moved around back without being detected. What if there were more than just these two soldiers? He risked sticking his head out between the shutters, and as he looked left and right, he caught the limbs of a Knacker disappearing around the east side of the building.

"Crabs in back!" he hissed into his wrist com as he pulled back inside. "At least two dead, and another one or more coming around the east side. Watch yourselves up front!"

He left the window and ran back the way he had come. Upon arriving at his front station, he found that indeed, two additional soldiers had joined the front five, and all seven were firing multiple weapons at the house. He saw that the aliens were

occupied with fire from the other defenders, leaving his window momentarily ignored. He used that to his advantage, squeezing off a few dozen rapid-fire rounds from his rifle. The alien he targeted was driven to the ground by the impact of the heavy armor-piercing bullets, and when it went down, it stayed there. A second later Simon had to duck behind cover as multiple lances of plasma slammed into his window shutters. A blast of superheated air washed over him as he huddled on the floor to one side. That had been close!

"Tyrus," he called through the com.

"I'm here," came the answer.

"Time for Sarah's contribution," Simon said.

"Definitely. Sarah, are you ready?"

"Any time, papa," she chimed in.

"Then do it," Tyrus commanded. "Everyone, cease fire!"

The hail of bullets and energy lances stopped raining down from the house, and the aliens, after a moment's continued barrage, also tapered off their attack, possibly in confusion over whether the defenders had been defeated. In the midst of that brief lull came the sharp crack of a distant firearm, once, twice, three times, in rapid succession. Then a rumbling sound like low thunder grew out of the west, punctuated at intervals by what sounded like the beep of a floater horn. The Knackers turned toward the stone wall, their weapons silent as the humans in the house were momentarily forgotten. One or two of the aliens raised sensor devices, scanning back and forth as they tried to divine the origin of the sounds.

In a few moments they had their answer, as a score of Dire Bucks burst through the front gate, heads forward and eyes wide. The blare of a horn behind them spurred them on at a breakneck pace, and once past the confines of the gate they dispersed at a full run. In the process they ran headlong into the waiting Knackers.

The Crabs themselves were fairly large creatures, but much of their diameter was comprised of legs. The Dire Bucks out-massed them, and there were over twenty of the stampeding

herbivores in the herd. The impact as the two groups collided was audible, and Knackers and Dire Bucks alike went down in a melee of flying bodies and limbs.

Energy bolts flew out of the crowded yard as the aliens fired off shots at the oncoming beasts. Some found their mark, and Dire Bucks went down in flaming heaps. But the sheer number of them made it impossible to stop their charge, and the Crabs were literally overrun. Simon saw aliens trampled until their exoskeletons were smashed and split open. A few Crabs reverted to their instincts, grappling and biting the herbivores with their large fangs. Knacker venom was highly toxic, and no known antidote yet existed. The bitten animals bleated in pain and fell within mere seconds.

One Dire Buck saw its way blocked, and stopped just short of a Knacker. As the alien tried to level its weapon for a kill shot, the herbivore reared up, jumping in the air, and kicked forward with both rear feet, landing a direct strike to the face of the Crab. The alien's head imploded, its eyes driven back into its skull, and it dropped like someone had shot it with a plasma rifle.

Tyrus quickly counted three aliens down, but that left three alive and scuttling toward the gate in retreat. He triggered the last buttons on his control panel, and small explosions *whuffed* as charges detonated at the bases of two trees. The family had planted Indigo Oaks around the front yard when they had first built the house. These were native to Eden, and resembled Old Earth oak trees in their general shape and branching. As their name suggested, the leaves shone a pleasing and unusual shade of dark blue, and the saplings grew extremely fast. The trees in the McKinleys' front yard now approached fifteen meters in height, with considerable weight in their thick trunks and branches.

The two trees with charges set on them grew near the rock wall, just to the east side of the gate. Tyrus had learned about explosives while in the military, and he had used shaped charges that would cut the trunks in a specific direction. The detona-

tion blew out a deep wedge from the wood, similar to the cuts created by old time lumberjacks using primitive axes or saws. One could direct the fall of a tree via precise placement of the wedge cut.

In this case, the trees were intended to drop across the front yard toward the west, blocking egress through the gate and crushing anything that chanced to lie beneath them. The charges worked perfectly, and bits of wood and dust flew outward from the bases of the oaks an instant before they began to topple. The trees leaned slowly at first, almost elegantly, as if they were bowing in reverence. Their rate of fall increased as they deviated further from vertical, and by the time they hit ground, the speed of impact was many meters per second. Two of the fleeing Knackers darted sideways from under the fall zone, but one was too slow. The brittle sound the creature made as the oak smashed down upon it resembled that of a nutshell cracking under a boot heel.

Unfortunately a few Dire Bucks were also caught in the tree falls, but most of the surviving herd was scampering to the west beyond the tool shed. "Open fire!" Tyrus shouted into his com link, and as one the humans unleashed multiple energy rifles and automatic weapons on the lone remaining pair of Knackers. With the numbers that lopsided, it was over in a matter of seconds.

The night was suddenly hushed as the guns ceased to fire. As the dust and smoke cleared, Simon commed, "Looks like they're all down. Is anyone hurt?"

Keith's voice came over the com, sounding strained. "I took a near miss to the head, and my hair caught on fire. I put it out fast, but I've got burns."

One by one the other family members checked in, and everyone was alive, and for the most part, undamaged. "Masks remain on," Tyrus told everyone. "They released a lot of neuro-gas; it will take some time to dissipate."

Simon took his weapons and roamed the upper floor, doing a routine check of each room. He paused when he came to the

bedroom from which he had lit the rear firewall. The window and shutters still hung open; he had left in such a hurry that he hadn't had time to secure them properly. Leaning his rifle against the wall by the door, he crossed over to the window, reaching out to close the shutters.

As he did so, a clawed appendage whipped into view, grabbing his wrist in a vice grip. Pain lanced through his arm, and he was helpless, unable to pull back as a large spider-like head slowly rose into view, filling the window. A tiny part of his brain screamed that this, too, they should have anticipated. Knackers had been known to scale nearly sheer cliffs; the rough rock wall of the house would have scarcely provided a challenge. Now he was face to face with a creature that he loathed with every gram of his being.

Long curving fangs worked slowly open and closed in front of his face, a half dozen red eyes glaring at him malevolently. The surface of the creature looked shiny hard, but was softened by tufts of short hairs around the eyes and antennae. Those sensory organs now reached out and stroked him lightly on the head and chest. Simon cringed at the contact; the soft caress felt somehow revolting, like the touch of an unwanted lover.

The creature examined its catch from close range, pulling Simon even closer as it regarded him with an inscrutable gaze. At such intimate proximity, the inhuman strangeness of the Knacker was overwhelming, and Simon fought down the bile rising in his throat. For a few long moments they remained unmoving, almost touching as they stared at each other. Suddenly the alien's jaws opened wide, then wider, and it leaned back slightly. He could see pearl-like drops of venom beading on the sharp tips of the fangs. In that instant Simon sensed the creature's intent, and he knew that he would not live to see the end of this skirmish.

As if to verify his intuition, the Knacker began to pop and click in its undecipherable tongue, and the translator box strapped to its carapace sputtered before emitting three distinct words: "You...now...die."

"You first," a high pitched voice said from behind Simon, and the alien looked up in surprise just as a plasma round punched a smoking hole exactly between its antennae. It spasmed and fell backwards, its fangs snapping shut an instant too late to impale Simon. They grazed his cheeks and snagged his gas mask, however, tearing it forcefully from his face as the creature's momentum carried it out and down. Simon heard a distinct crunching splat as the heavy body impacted the ground below.

Staggering, he reeled back from the window, and turned to see his benefactor. He had just enough time to take in Jessie's small masked figure holding an impossibly large energy weapon, before his legs turned to jelly and he crumpled limply to the floor.

What followed was a jumbled admixture of images, as his brain continued to function but his body was unable to respond. After he went down, he saw close up views of the floor and adjacent wall, as he lay with his left cheek plastered to the hardwood. Then he felt hands on his body, and someone rolled him onto his back. Concerned faces clustered over him, peering down. He heard voices, hollow and far away, as if he were at the bottom of a well. *Was he bitten? Does anyone see bite marks? He needs medical attention. Get Kate now!"*

The last thing he remembered before he lost consciousness was Katherine's sweet face looking into his, her eyes streaming tears as she cried, *"Stay with me, Simon! Don't you leave me, don't you dare leave!"* But he was indeed leaving, going somewhere quiet and warm, and he wanted to take her with him, longed to tell her that he didn't want to go alone, and then the peaceful blackness claimed him.

CHAPTER SEVEN

Simon remained immobilized for nearly a day. He had fallen victim to neuro-gas, not the Knacker's deadly venom. The treatment was simple: keep him warm, administer intravenous fluids, and wait for the effects to wear off. Until then he was an invalid, and he could not recall ever feeling this helpless.

Various family members took turns watching over him. Within six hours he could mumble slurred words, and soon after that he was able to swallow gruel when held in a sitting position. Although nearly everyone sat by his side at one time or another, Katherine spent by far the most time with him.

She would drag a comfortable chair close to his bed, and read a digital novel while he lay there smiling at her. Sometimes she would get chores done to pass the time. He was pleasantly surprised to watch her break down and service his Milcor rifle like an expert, sighting down the barrel, running a cleaning rod through it, checking the firing mechanism and oiling it, then reassembling it deftly. Layers upon layers, this woman had.

The night after the battle, Simon lay resting in bed. He was exhausted after having taken his first tentative steps that afternoon. By the following day, they expected him to be back to his old self. He fell asleep with Katherine nearby, feeling her warmth there with him as he floated away to unconsciousness.

Late that evening, Sarah wandered outside onto the back porch to catch some air. The veranda was on the second floor for safety reasons, although height had proven to not be a big deterrent to the Crabs. As she stepped through the door, a gentle

cool breeze soothed the perspiration from her brow. It had been a blisteringly hot day, typical of late summer at this latitude, and the house's air conditioning had been turned off to conserve energy. The local power grid had finally gone dead, and they were existing on stored fuel and generators for the duration.

She sighed as the evening air caressed her skin through the thin nightdress. Both moons were visible in the velvet sky, having just come out of their dark phase. Romuli was a thin yellow crescent almost directly overhead, while its smaller brother, Remi, hovered near the western horizon like a slitted red eye. The analogy caused her to shiver, and not from the cold.

She heard a small sound to her right and whirled with a start, relaxing when she saw a slender female form outlined against the porch railing. "Kate?" she asked, approaching.

"Yes," came the quiet reply.

"Nice night, isn't it?" Sarah said as she carefully stepped up to the veranda's edge.

"Beautiful. It reminds me of Antigua," her aunt replied wistfully.

Sarah glanced at her with surprise; Katherine never spoke about her former life on that planet, the life she had shared with her husband Jeremy. Although they stood close to each other, the contours of the other woman's face were obscured in the dark. She appeared to be looking up at the sky, perhaps at Romuli where it floated overhead.

Sarah opened her mouth and closed it again; in truth she had no idea what to say. Katherine spoke again, softly, "I still can't believe that he's gone."

"You mean...Jeremy?"

Her aunt nodded, the motion barely visible in the starlight. "It was a night like this, you know, when I got the news. A beautiful new moon, like a slice of pure silver in the sky. Antigua only had one moon, but it was so lovely."

Katherine turned toward her then, and Sarah could see her aunt's shoulders shaking, hear her ragged breaths as she sobbed quietly. Without thinking she reached out her arms and pulled

her close, Katherine returning the embrace with a desperate strength.

They remained that way for a minute or two, simply sharing each other's warmth. Sarah had an intuition about what was troubling her aunt, but she hesitated to broach the subject. Finally she ventured, "He'd have wanted you to be happy, you know."

Katherine nodded against Sarah's shoulder, exhaling deeply as her breathing calmed. "You're right, of course. If it were just me, things would be simpler. But I have Jess to think about."

"Do you think that ignoring your feelings will keep either you or Jessie from getting hurt?" Sarah asked.

"That's what I told myself. Then, when I saw Simon lying there, and I thought that he'd been bitten...I realized right then that whether or not you admit your feelings, they are with you nonetheless. That night I imagined how I would have felt if he were truly gone. Chances lost can never be regained. I promised myself that if he lived, I would not let that opportunity slip through my fingers again."

Sarah nodded, understanding. "It must be difficult, wanting to create something when it could be taken away at any moment."

Katherine stepped back and held her niece at arm's length, speaking softly but intensely. "Love is worth having, Sarah, even with the risk of losing it. The loss is hard, very hard. But I would never trade that loss for the alternative, of never having known Jeremy, never having borne Jessie. Remember this always, and keep it close to heart. Love is worth it, even in these times. Not letting yourself experience it would be the worst loss of all."

Her aunt hugged her again, before pulling away with a soft "good night" and drifting silently back into the house. Sarah stayed on the veranda awhile longer, pondering Katherine's words, seeing their wisdom. But she couldn't shake the nagging feeling that Kate had spoken them more for herself than for her niece.

* * * * * * *

Simon awoke the next morning and sat up, stretching the kinks out of his back. Then he stopped and grinned; he had moved effortlessly, without even thinking about it. Cautiously he turned and slid his legs off the bed, touching his feet to the floor. He felt good, so he leaned forward, putting his weight on his legs as he slowly elevated to a standing position. One step, two, and he felt his confidence growing as the world remained stable beneath him. On then to the bathroom, where he blissfully took care of business unassisted for the first time in two days. He looked at his image in the mirror, and grimaced at the unshaven stubble and matted hair. Time for a shower and shave, and a new change of clothes. He set about his morning routine, eager to see the others and catch up on what he'd missed while he'd been out of commission.

Simon came downstairs awhile later, and was greeted with a chorus of welcomes from the family members seated at the dining table. Amanda and Katherine were there, along with Sarah, Jessie, and Samuel. The two other brothers were out helping Tyrus clear the fallen trees. Most of the dead Knackers, Simon learned, had already been disposed of in a large burn pit. The Dire Bucks that had died had been cleaned, carved into steaks, and frozen for future use. In time of war, nothing was wasted.

"We're all happy to see you up and around again, Simon," Amanda said with a broad smile. "We've missed you, some of us more than others, I think." Her mischievous grin made Simon wonder what exactly he had missed while immobilized.

Jessie clarified that issue a second later, blurting out in the joyous innocence of childhood, "She means mom and me!" Her mother elbowed her in the side, which elicited a loud, "*Ouch, mom, why'd you do that?*" Katherine gave up at that point, covering her eyes while her face turned a pretty shade of pink. Simon tried his best to avoid choking on his breakfast sausage, while appearing to not be overly interested in the exchange.

After a solid breakfast he headed outside to find Tyrus and offer whatever help he could provide. He found the elder

McKinley with Keith and T. J., cutting the downed oaks into workable sections. Most of one tree was already dismantled and piled into neat stacks of firewood, and the other was being attacked with gusto. Simon approached and said, "Hi, all. How's it coming out here?"

The three men paused in their work and greeted him with broad smiles. "Simon! Good to see you looking like your old self!" Tyrus exclaimed, stepping forward and clapping Simon on the shoulder.

"He had it easy," Keith retorted as he threw a stack of lumber on the woodpile. When he straightened and turned, Simon saw that much of the hair on the left side of his head was gone, and the skin at his temple was fiery red and covered with blisters. Even his left eyebrow seemed to have been singed off. He continued with a grin, "All Simon had to do was lie on his lazy back for two days, while Aunt Kate spoon fed him and gave him sponge baths. Now that he's had his vacation, he's as pretty as ever. Not like us real warriors," he added, pointing to his own battle scars.

"Well, you've certainly earned your lightning bolts," Simon declared, chuckling. "SpaceForce could use a few more like you. I'll put in a good word if you ever want to sign up."

"And do this sort of thing for a living?" Keith said with a frown. "I don't think so. I want to have *some* hair left when I'm forty!"

They shared a good laugh at that, and Simon said, "I came out to give you a hand, if you can use it."

"Are you up to it?" Tyrus asked. When Simon nodded, he shrugged and said, "Well, then, we can always use some extra muscle. T. J. has been cutting up the trunks and branches with a zip blade. He's handy enough with it that we're having trouble piling wood as fast as he's producing cuts. You're welcome to help us haul and stack."

"Fine by me," Simon answered. "I'm happy being able to do any physical activity right now."

"Better make use of him before the joy wears off," T. J.

quipped. His right hand gripped the curved handle of a black rectangular device, about the length and width of a work boot. Its upper surface featured several control knobs, plus a plethora of red arrows and cautionary labels warning users to point the device away from oneself when operating. The working end had little to distinguish it, other than what appeared to be a short glass rod protruding from the surface.

Simon watched with interest as T. J. pressed a red button and the clear rod instantly flared with brilliant light. The young man then fiddled with the controls, and the glowing tip appeared to slowly elongate. When he was through, there was a solid band of pulsing energy about a half meter long extending from the device. Satisfied, he then twirled another control, and the beam focused down to the width of a thread along its entire length. Properly adjusted, the zip blade was able to make cuts only a few atoms thick, and could slice through most materials with almost no resistance.

"Here we go," T. J. said, hefting the saw. "Let's cut this beast down to size." He walked over to the downed oak, stopping where a main branch joined the trunk. Lifting the glowing blade, he placed it across the width of the branch and dropped his arm. The thin band of energy slid through the tough wood as if it weren't there, with only a faint sizzle and puff of smoke to hint at the forces being employed. The branch sagged free of the trunk as he pulled the blade out from below. Stepping to the right, he made another cut on the now-horizontal limb, and a smooth section the length of a man's forearm dropped to the ground, ready for stacking. Additional cuts followed in quick succession as he moved down the length of the branch, pausing at times to shear off smaller offshoots and twigs from the main limb.

Simon and the others pitched in to gather and pile the logs, and with all four of them working, the tree was conquered by noon. Only a brush pile of cast-off twigs and small branches remained, and this was incinerated in the fire pit that had previously consumed the Knackers.

By the time they were done the sun was beating down from the cloudless sky, and the temperature outside was steadily rising. Tyrus wiped sweat from his brow and said, "I don't know about the rest of you, but I could go for a cold brew." His idea was met with enthusiastic approval from all present, and soon after, the men sat on the upstairs veranda enjoying the shade with bottles of cold alcoholic beverages in their hands.

As humans had moved out among the stars, they had carried with them their love of fermentation. New planets had offered up an endless diversity of plant life, which in turn yielded novel varieties of spirits to imbibe. Despite the competition from various newcomers, the traditional Earth drinks had maintained a revered place in the taste buds of humanity. Colonists had quickly discovered, however, that grapes were finicky about growing conditions, and the flavor of wines produced offworld was often compared to that of industrial cleaning products. The hops and grains that made up the backbone of beer production were more forgiving, and consequently, as humanity's territory had grown, so had that simple beverage's status in the hierarchy of recreational drinks. The Human Federation worlds resided in a globular star cluster at the edge of the Milky Way Galaxy, so far removed from Old Earth in both time and space that the mother planet was almost a legend. Nonetheless, the draughts that Simon and company now hefted were not all that different from old Irish ales of ages gone by.

As he nursed his drink, Simon plied the others for information about the latest Knacker attack and its aftermath. "It was a full two squadrons they sent against us," Tyrus stated, confirming Simon's suspicions. "We found one dead Crab out back of the fence, blown to bits by a land mine. That made twenty total soldiers, with four transport vehicles. All well armed with multiple weapon types."

"That's a pretty heavy assault team," Simon commented. "They must have taken us as a serious threat."

"Well, not a major military target perhaps, but for a rural resistance group, we've certainly garnered some attention,"

Tyrus agreed.

"How do you think they'll respond to this latest defeat?" asked Keith, taking a swig of his brew.

"That's what worries me," Simon said. "Knackers don't tend to repeat unsuccessful tactics. Their usual response to failure is to escalate the action. This has worked for them countless times in the past, due to their numerical superiority in most engagements."

"So you expect that it will get worse," Tyrus nodded somberly. "I figured as much. The next question is, when?"

"That may be the only saving grace here," Simon answered. "It took them weeks to bring two squads against us. We have the rest of humanity on Eden to thank for that; they've been making things more difficult than the Crabs are used to. But sooner or later, as the planet is tamed, they will allocate the resources to deal with us. And that doesn't bode well for our survival when they come again."

"What do you suggest?" T. J. asked him, frowning.

"I suggest we have a backup plan," Simon responded. "That is your motto, isn't it?"

"True," said Tyrus. "But what sort of plan would you propose if they come with a large force?"

"That's pretty simple. We run." Simon tipped his brew back to get the last dregs of the bottle. The empty clanked hollowly on the table as he set it down and wiped his mouth.

"I thought we had decided to hole up here and defend the homestead," Tyrus said, looking displeased. "You yourself said that travel was dangerous when the Crabs occupy a planet."

"And it is," Simon nodded. "Staying here has been the best choice, up until now. We've got food and ammunition, a defensible building, and time to lay traps for the aliens. Out on the road we'd have far fewer advantages."

"Yet you would contemplate leaving. Tell me why now you suggest giving up my family's home to those creatures," Tyrus growled. "When did being here suddenly become worse than taking our chances in the open?"

"It hasn't, yet," Simon replied. "But what happens if they bring an entire division at us? Or if they wise up and decide to lob mortars at the house until it crumbles? The main disadvantage to being here, at this stage, is that the Knackers know where 'here' is. We're an easy target, stationary and well marked on their maps. They can take their time gathering the forces to wipe us out, and they know we'll still be here when they get around to it. It might be wise to plan on being somewhere else, if they bring an overwhelming force."

"And where would we flee to?" Tyrus asked him. "We've not got a secondary hideout. Running without a destination would be close to suicide."

"That will take some planning. Whether we find another homestead or remote dwelling, or simply take to the hills, we'll need supplies packed ahead of time. There's a good chance we'll have to leave in a hurry, if it comes to that."

"It's going to be hard to convince the family to go," Tyrus said, sounding uncertain. "We've built our lives here."

"Your family is what matters, not a building or piece of land," Simon answered. "I don't think anyone here loves the homestead enough to want to turn it into a mass grave."

No one had a response to that, and the men sat in silence, their enjoyment of the beverages tempered by the contemplation of things to come.

The family members met in the greatroom the next day, and Simon outlined the possible scenarios that could be looming in the near future. "It's pretty simple," he began. "We may have won a brief reprieve, but they will hit us again eventually. If they hold true to their past history, the next assault will be much more brutal than anything we've experienced so far."

"Bring 'em on!" T. J. retorted, raising a clenched fist. "We've shown those bugs a thing or two already; we'll kick their tails back into space every time they come!"

Simon had to admire the kid's bravado, but he needed to make the family see reason. Their lives all depended on it. He chose his next words carefully. "Do you know who the Tonn

are?"

The younger man looked around at his family, confused. He returned his gaze to Simon and shrugged. "I dunno," he said. "I've never heard of them."

"That's not surprising," the spacer said. "They were a highly advanced race, with a civilization that spanned at least a dozen star systems. They're also extinct, courtesy of the Knackers during their last visit to our region of the Cluster. An entire civilization, countless millions of creatures with powerful military and defensive technologies, all wiped out. They put up a good fight, too, which is what forced the Crabs to exterminate them. But in the end, the Tonn ceased to exist. We only know of them, and of their end, through archeological digs on mostly-dead planets."

He paused for a moment to let that sink in, then continued, "Now humanity is up against the Knackers. SpaceForce is learning fast, and we're picking up tricks from the enemy every day. We've also come up with some new innovations that have given us an edge, here and there. But our species is in jeopardy. The Crabs outnumber us badly, and they wage war as a way of life. Eden is one of a handful of planets under siege as we speak. There are fewer systems between the aliens and our core planets every month. Their massive war machine just keeps chewing up worlds, and nothing has stopped them in countless millennia."

Now Simon had everyone's undivided attention. As much as the family had followed the war, they knew that he was the one among them who had best seen its true face. He alone had gone head to head with the Knackers, and he knew the enemy as well as anyone could. Not a word was spoken as every pair of eyes was locked on his face.

Now it was time to drive his point home. "That is what we're up against, here in our little house in the country. Do you think we've had some good victories? Sure we have. It's a testament to the courage and skill of every person in this room that we're still alive to talk about it. Many trained soldiers haven't done as well.

"But we've been playing chess with a grandmaster who's been distracted by other opponents. Because of that, we've been able to avoid checkmate so far. Make no mistake: when the virtuosos of the war game turn their full attention on us, it would be folly to think that we'd stand any chance. If we wish to live, we'd better have a fallback plan and be willing to use it."

The room was silent after Simon stopped talking. Several family members looked expectantly at Tyrus, and eventually he cleared his throat and offered his thoughts. "When Simon first broached the possibility of leaving," he said, "my instinctive reaction was, 'Hell, no!' How could we abandon our homestead? Where would we go? How would we survive on the run? But on reflection, I have to admit that his words ring true."

Tyrus gazed fondly at Amanda, and at his sons and daughter. "You all are my treasures, my reason for fighting and wanting to keep living. All of this," he gestured around them at the greatroom and the surrounding building, "means nothing without you being here to fill it with life. We can't move our home to hide it from the Knackers. We can only move ourselves. I say it is always wise to hope for the best, but be prepared for the worst."

Multiple heads around the room nodded, and no dissenting opinions were offered. Simon breathed an inward sigh of relief. He had grown more and more fond of his "family," and only now did he realize just how anxious he had been at the thought of them choosing to stand and fight. Even though they had been total strangers two months earlier, he felt a sense of responsibility toward these people, a need to protect them as best he could. Especially Kate and Jessie.

Even as he thought it, he found his gaze drawn to Katherine, as seemed to be happening ever more often lately. She sat across the room from him, clad in yellow shorts and a sleeveless shirt, her sleek legs curled under her as she reclined comfortably in the cushioned chair. Her long dark hair was unbound tonight, and it cascaded over her bare shoulders in luxurious waves. He slid his gaze to her lovely face, and to his surprise he found

her eyes already on him. Her head was cocked slightly to one side, her full lips curled in a slight smile as if she were contemplating something pleasing. Then, when she saw her attention was being returned, she blushed but held his gaze steadily, not shying away from the contact. Her smile widened, warm and genuine, and that wordless communication made him happier than he would have thought possible. Could it be that she was having second thoughts about him? He guessed that only time would tell.

Later that evening Simon was in his room, getting ready to sleep, when he heard a light knock at his door. He hesitated, then decided not to bother donning a shirt. Clothed only in lightweight shorts, he padded barefoot to the door and opened it.

What met his eyes was entirely unexpected but very welcome. Katherine stood before him, clad in the same thin shirt and shorts she had worn in the greatroom. He could have sworn, however, that the top three buttons of the shirt had not been undone previously. It also appeared that certain aspects of her anatomy were more discernable through the material than before. Katherine usually dressed casually but modestly, downplaying her physical assets, and now with only the thin cloth of the shirt over her skin, Simon was getting a new appreciation for her curves. And she had more curves than he had imagined.

It had been a long time since he had been this close to a woman thusly garbed, and it took all of his military-ingrained discipline to keep his gaze focused on her face. She smiled at him, her eyes soft and inviting. In a voice that sounded slightly breathless she said, "Hi, Simon."

"Hi, Katherine," he said, his pulse suddenly pounding like a hammer.

Her cheeks flushed just a little as she said, "May I come in?"

"Yes, please, by all means," he said, clumsily backing up and opening the door wide for her to enter.

She walked slowly into the room, turning and closing the door behind her. Very deliberately she reached up and locked the latch, then turned and approached him, holding his gaze

with her own. As she came close she allowed her eyes to roam boldly down his bare torso and up again, and she licked her lips as she smiled in approval.

Simon stared at Katherine as if seeing her for the first time. What had inspired this unexpected transformation from shy waif to bold tigress? But he had lived long enough to not question a good thing when he had it. He reached up and touched her face, gently tracing the line of her jaw before burying his fingers in her soft hair. She closed her eyes and sighed, leaning her head into his hand.

He pulled her slowly to him, and her eyes opened but she didn't resist. She lifted her mouth to meet his and he kissed her long and deeply. As their tongues danced, he felt her arms wrap around him and the heat of her body pressing against his through the thin fabric. He luxuriated in the feel of her lithe form, running his hands down her back to cup her slender waist.

Abruptly she pulled back, her breath coming fast and ragged, and she held his gaze as she said intensely, "I'm not worried about myself, Simon. Just promise me one thing. Whatever happens, please don't ever do anything that would hurt Jessie. If you do, we're through."

Simon smiled as he met her eyes without flinching. "I wouldn't have it any other way," he said.

He had just enough time to register the gratitude in her smile before she pressed against him once more, her mouth and hands eagerly exploring. He grinned and returned the favor, and that effectively ended any conversation for some time to come.

That first time was intense and raw, a release of pent-up passion and longing grown out of years of abstinence, plus weeks of resisting the attraction they had both felt almost from their first meeting. Desire quickly overcame their initial awkwardness, and they lost themselves in the sheer animal pleasure of their coupling. Katherine was generous and hungry at the same time, alternating between slow seduction and urgent need, and Simon matched her energy move for move, losing himself in the primal rhythm, riding her as he built to his peak, reveling in

the sight and feel of her nude form arched beneath him, and the naked emotion in her eyes as she climaxed. He followed her a moment later, giving in to the release as she wrapped him tight with arms and legs, and he tried with all his strength to make them one.

Later that night they lay entwined in his bed, Katherine's head on his chest as he held her close. He couldn't stop drinking her in, the delicate lines of her face, the curve of her bare shoulder as his fingers slowly traced it, and most of all that look of happiness in her eyes. He had waited a long time to experience that, and he didn't want to let it go ever again.

She stirred against him and murmured dreamily, "I love your touch."

Simon smiled and replied, "That's a good thing, because I love touching you."

Her arms tightened around his torso and she remained silent for a few moments. Eventually she looked up at him, saying softly, "I really want this to last, Simon. What's going to happen to us?"

"We're going to survive, that's what," he said firmly, stroking her hair as he did his best to sound confident. "You, me, Jessie, all of us, we're going to make it. That's why we're planning ahead. Your father has a great head for strategy, and we've done well against superior numbers. We may have to leave this place, but we'll endure."

"For how long?" Katherine replied, and though she was putting on a brave face, he could see the fear lurking in her eyes. It killed him that she had to feel that, in a moment that should be filled only with the joy of discovery.

He did his best to reassure her, saying, "We won't have to hold out forever. SpaceForce will regroup and come to liberate this planet; I'm certain of it. Eden is a priority to the Federation, not some half-developed planet with a marginal habitat. As soon as they can muster the forces, the space fleet will return. The aliens have greater numbers, but they're spread all over this sector. If we focus on one planet at a time, and concentrate our

forces there, then we have a fighting chance."

"When do you think they'll come to our aid?" Katherine asked him, propping herself on her elbows to watch his face.

"I suspect it will be soon," Simon replied, and he was being honest. "The Federation will want to act before the Crabs have time to strip Eden's population. We've got some new weapons that look like they can do real damage, if we can deploy them properly with the right support. We'll take the offensive soon."

"I hope you're right," she told him, snuggling her head onto his chest once more. Her fingers lightly traced circles on his skin as she murmured, "I want a future with both you and Jessie in it." Then she looked up again as a thought occurred to her. "Oh, my," she exclaimed, giggling even as she frowned. "What are we going to tell Jess?"

"I expect we won't have to say too much," he laughed. "Do you really think she'll protest?"

"I suppose not," she agreed, chuckling. "She's just a little taken with you, I think."

"And how about her mother?" Simon replied teasingly, reaching to pull her to him.

"Oh, definitely taken," she purred, and for a precious little while the world outside their room receded as they lost themselves once more in each other.

CHAPTER EIGHT

The next day Simon and Katherine came downstairs together for breakfast. They had overslept, and everyone else was already in the dining room, halfway through their meals. Multiple pairs of eyes looked up as they entered, and Simon could feel the unspoken questions filling the sudden silence in the room. He and Katherine smiled self consciously, and they approached the table to find that two adjacent seats had been left open for them. Blushing, Katherine took her seat as Simon pulled it out for her, and he quietly sat down beside her.

Amanda was the first to speak, saying, "You look cheerful this morning, Katherine! Did you have a good sleep?" The brothers chuckled, and she turned and shushed them.

"I feel great this morning, thank you," Katherine replied demurely, pouring herself some juice from the pitcher. She glanced over at Simon, and no one at the table could miss the warmth in the look they exchanged.

Simon focused on his food, chancing a few glances around the table as conversation slowly resumed. Sarah was staring at the two of them, smiling broadly as she nibbled on a breakfast cake. Tyrus looked a bit surprised but pleased. Amanda had a knowing twinkle in her eye, and the three brothers kept exchanging comments in low voices, with an occasional audible snicker that was quickly quelled by a disapproving glance from their mother.

Jessie sat across the table from Simon today, and she was grinning from ear to ear, looking from Simon to Katherine and

back again, as if she could not believe what she was seeing. She was practically bouncing in her seat, and she shoveled in her food so fast that her mother had to chide her to slow down lest she choke. Simon glanced at Kate, and she gave him a knowing grin. He winked and nodded; things were going to be all right with her daughter.

After breakfast Tyrus approached Simon alone and said quietly, "I must say, it gives me great pleasure to see Katherine smiling again. It's been a long time since I've seen her so full of life."

"She deserves to be happy. Kate's a woman of rare qualities," Simon said, and he meant every word.

"Well, this probably goes without saying," the older man told him, "but I expect you to treat her well. I do not want to see her get hurt again."

"We're on the same page there," Simon reassured him. "I don't plan on letting anyone, or anything, hurt her or Jessie."

Tyrus smiled and laid his hand on Simon's shoulder. "You're a good man," he said. "I'm glad that fate dropped you into our lives."

Simon grinned broadly back at him. "So am I, Tyrus. So am I."

The days following were spent patching the damage to the house and their defenses, preparing for another Knacker assault should it prove small enough to be repelled. The breaches in the front wall of the home were patched with mortar and stones, and the fire ditches were prepared for reuse. The men struggled to repair and re-hang the heavy driveway gate, and eventually hammered and welded it back into a reasonable facsimile of its former self. After the pitfall trap was set and covered, and land-mines checked and replaced, they were essentially as prepared as they could be.

During these hectic days the work occupied most of their waking hours, but at night Simon and Katherine took time to explore their growing love for each other, and with each passing day the bonds between them grew stronger.

After the home defenses were solidified, it came time to address the other contingency, that of life on the run. What to take with them, and where to run to, were the primary concerns that needed addressing immediately.

"I don't know of any other homesteads that are set up well to defend themselves," Tyrus began as he addressed the gathered family one evening. "Nor could they take in a group our size for long. Resources will be limited, now that overland travel for supplies is so risky."

"How about finding an abandoned farm or building somewhere remote?" T. J. asked. "It would be hard to find us there, wouldn't it?"

"I suppose," Simon answered. "Do you have a place in mind?"

"Well, no," the young man admitted. "Nothing specific."

"That is our problem," Tyrus concluded. "I should have thought of this before the Crabs came a-calling. It's too late now to worry over what should have been. The simple fact is, we have no good destination in mind. Where do we go from here?"

Sarah spoke up, "We could stay on our own land; we've got a lot of property, and some of it borders heavy woods. Papa, you've often said the Knackers hate forested terrain, right?"

Tyrus looked thoughtful. "Ay, that I did. I must admit, the thought of staying close to home, near our own property, has appeal. I've taught everyone basic survival skills in case we had to live off the land." He glanced over at Simon, who shrugged noncommittally. Turning back to his daughter, he said, "You've done the most exploring these last few years, Sarah. How well do you know the hill country out west?"

She grinned. "Like the back of my hand."

He nodded. "Are there good water sources other than Byre's Creek? More remote ones where we can hole up?"

"Yes, there are other creeks, some of which persist year around, up in the hills."

"What about food?" Simon asked. "How would all of us subsist in the woods?"

"There are a number of edible animals living there," Sarah replied. "Some are small, but a few would yield quite a bit of meat, like the Dire Bucks."

"We'd need plant sources too, for a balanced diet," Simon countered.

"I know some wild plants which are nutritious," Sarah replied. "And I can get on the computer and look up information on Eden's outdoor resources; years ago I bought a digital book with pictures of edible plant and animal life."

"Load that onto a portable reader, then, and pack it in our travel supplies," her father told her. "That may just save our lives."

"What about shelter?" the eldest son, Keith, asked. "If we don't take refuge in a building, how will we deal with the elements? Especially if we're out there for more than a short time? It won't be summer forever."

"True," Tyrus replied. "I'm thinking heavy all-weather tents should do the trick; we've got those in our outdoor gear, along with portable stoves, coolers, bedding, and the like."

"I've got a couple of thoughts," Simon answered. "The Knackers are probably using the human road system to move around on the ground. Is there any way to monitor how much alien traffic is traveling on the highway that runs past your property? It could give us some idea of the activity in our area, and we might see an attack force coming."

"Hmmm. We could put a sensor-camera up on one of the trees near the highway, and it would tell us what is passing by. I should get back to monitoring the Crab transmissions more regularly, too. We have more than one translator now, and we really need to know what they're up to."

Simon nodded. "Good idea."

"Okay, Sarah," her father said. "You know the territory. Head out in the smaller floater and see if you can find a possible site for us to retreat to, should the need arise. We want something that's fairly deep in the woods and defensible, preferably approach-able from only one or two directions. Thick forest would be

ideal, as the Crabs won't easily spot us from the air, and their larger floaters and shuttles can't penetrate the deep woods."

"And don't forget a potable water source nearby," Simon added.

Sarah nodded. "Got it. I'll start scouting tomorrow."

"Take a partner, and go armed," Tyrus cautioned. "Keith, why don't you ride with her."

Sarah's brother nodded. "We'll handle it," he said.

"Simon and Samuel, I'll leave it to you to set up the highway sensor," Tyrus continued. "Meanwhile I'll work on converting some additional Knacker weapons for human use. Those plasma rifles and grenade launchers would be really helpful out there." He stood, rubbing his hands together briskly. "Let's get some rest, and we'll start work first thing in the morning."

With that the family disbanded, its members heading off to their rooms. Simon held Katherine's hand as they headed upstairs together, and he helped her get Jessie tucked into bed. Then he accompanied her to their room at the end of the hall. They had decided to share Katherine's bedroom, as it was larger and better appointed than the guestroom that Simon had been occupying. Once alone they made love with an urgency borne of the uncertainty ahead, drawing strength from their shared warmth, and finally falling into a peaceful sleep cradled in each other's arms.

* * * * * * *

The following morning Simon and Samuel headed out to set a sensor-camera device near the highway, while Sarah took Keith into the west hills to explore the forest. By noon the men had returned, but the sun was sinking low in the western sky by the time the front door opened and Sarah walked in. Keith followed soon after, his feet dragging.

Amanda heard them entering and walked into the front room to meet them. "Well, there you two are! We were beginning to worry!" Once she saw that they were unharmed, her tone

turned teasing. "Keith, darling, you look worn out. Did little Sarah run you ragged?"

He waved a dismissive hand, saying, "Yeah, yeah, she's used to climbing all over the hills. I've had better things to do with my life until now."

Sarah and Amanda exchanged amused grins, and then Sarah's expression turned serious as she said, "We'd better gather the others so I can brief them on what we found."

Her mother nodded and told her, "You'll find most everyone in the greatroom, dear. They're checking out the new road camera and listening to the enemy airwaves. Go on in; they've been waiting for your return. Keith, you come with me and we'll fix up some food for the both of you. I imagine you must be hungry." She headed off toward the kitchen with her son in tow, and Sarah went to find the others.

When all the family had assembled, they reviewed the day's activities. "Sam and I found a tree near the highway where we could mount the camera," Simon began. "It's well hidden and can be aimed down the road in either direction, giving us a good view of what's coming and going. The camera has a sensor array that will alert us if it detects motion. We ran the controls through the main video console." Sarah glanced toward the screen, which currently showed a still image of the highway that ran along the east border of their property. Simon punched a button, and the view panned to the right, showing a long stretch of road that shrank into the distance.

"Nice work," Sarah said, grinning as she took in the images. "No action there yet?"

"Nothing so far," Tyrus answered. "This area has not been a hotbed of activity for the Knackers. I wouldn't expect more than an occasional floater, until they mount another attack."

"How about their airwave communications?" she asked Tyrus.

"Mostly just routine ops chat, nothing specific to us. Much of it originates from more than one hundred klicks away."

Simon interjected, "What about your findings, Sarah? You

look like you're bursting with news."

She grinned. "Well, we followed Byre's Creek into Dark Hollow for a bit, then turned west and went up over the hill into the next valley. Another small stream runs there, and when we got to looking around, I remembered that I had explored that area years ago. That's when I also recalled something else."

"Tell them, already!" Keith said from the doorway, grinning. He held a plate with a sandwich and a piece of fruit on it, and he came over and handed the food to Sarah where she sat. "Eat up, sis," he said. "You need your strength."

"Look who's talking," she retorted around a mouthful of sandwich. "Okay, where was I? Oh, yes, we were on the valley floor between the hills, and I thought I recognized the place. On a hunch we turned and headed upstream along the creek. As we proceeded the land began to rise, at first a little, then more steeply. The tree cover was still dense overhead, but rock outcrops showed up here and there, which grew as we climbed, until they were narrow spires reaching ten or twenty meters high."

"Sounds like columnar basalt," Tyrus commented. "The erosion of the stream and winds must have exposed them over time. Those hills are supposedly ancient remnants of volcanic peaks, so that would fit."

"Well, they were a pain to navigate through, I can tell you that," Sarah declared, and Keith chuckled as he seconded her opinion. "Then we squeezed between two particularly large formations, and just beyond, we found it."

"What?" Simon and Tyrus asked together.

She grinned like a Groon eating a Blue Hare. "The hideout."

Her father looked at Simon with a puzzled expression, then back at Sarah. "You mean a good place to hide, I assume. But what makes it so right for our needs?"

She shook her head and replied, "No, I mean it's a hideout already! Or it was, for poachers most likely." She laughed at the confused expression on the men's faces and explained, "There's a log cabin already built there, nestled in a little sheltered area.

It has tree cover shielding it from the sky, and limited ground access due to the dense woods and rock formations. The stream flows close by, so water is ready at hand. The structure is in some need of repair, as it looks as if it's been abandoned for a long time. But it's sturdy, and it can provide shelter from weather and wildlife. Nine people would find it a tight fit, but there's room to sleep all of us at night in roll-up beds."

Simon looked at Tyrus, and his expression was excited. "If this place is defensible...."

"It is," Sarah avowed. "Anyone approaching would likely be coming up the valley as we did; the terrain above and behind is very rough, with rocks and thick forest and steep slopes. Also, there is nothing beyond the cabin but more wilderness; anyone coming from populated areas would hit the valley first. From that approach, attackers would be at a disadvantage. We'd have the high ground, and they'd have to wind almost single-file through the rock pillars and tree trunks. Defenders could hide behind those features and fire away."

"I like it," Tyrus grinned, nodding. "You've outdone your-selves, kids. We'll still need a large tent or two, for housing our supplies and for extra living space. But as a base home and sleeping shelter, it sounds perfect. Being made of wood, and nestled among rocks, it won't show as easily on scanners as synthetic materials. We should go check it out tomorrow, and get to work fixing it up. Simon, want to join me on a little ride?"

"Sounds like fun," Simon said with a broad smile. "I'd love to get out in the air again."

They discussed their plans a bit more, playing with the camera monitor on the highway as they did so, before calling it a day and retiring for the evening. Tomorrow would require an early start.

* * * * * * *

Just after dawn the bed alarm woke Simon from a deep sleep. He groaned as he fumbled to punch the button that would silence

the intrusive noise, finally succeeding. His Darter emitted an annoyed chirp from its cage next to the bed as it too protested the disturbance. As he lay on his back in a fog, a warm shape next to him pressed against his side, and a delicate hand slid across his chest. He smiled as he felt soft hair tickling his bare shoulder and even softer lips caressed his ear. It was hard not to start the day at peace when he had this amazing woman in his life.

He turned and met her lips with his, and after a few moments of bliss he reluctantly pulled away, saying, "I've got to go, milady. Tyrus and the others will be waiting."

She pouted cutely, her face shadowed in the dim light. "Can't I come with you?" she asked him, batting her eyes.

"I'd love nothing better," he told her, sighing. "But the small floater only carries four, and Tyrus, Sarah and T. J. will be coming along. We'll scout out the site, and bring a few tools to begin repairs on the cabin. After we all know the route to the hideout, we'll start sending the floaters back and forth with supplies, and you can hitch a ride on one of those trips. We'll need most of the family working on this to get things ready quickly."

"All right, but promise to be careful!" she told him, planting a last kiss before pulling away. "Now, if you're going to leave me here, I'm getting some more sleep!" She winked as he growled something about lazy people, and he left her wrapped in the warm blankets as he stumbled toward the bathroom.

A short time later he was gulping breakfast in the floater as it headed toward the west hills. Sarah was piloting, with her father by her side, and Simon and T. J. sitting in the back of the vehicle. They zipped across the fields and grasslands with the rising sun at their backs, approaching Byre's Creek and entering Dark Hollow within fifteen minutes. From there the trip slowed to a relative crawl as Sarah deftly maneuvered their craft through tree falls, boulders, and massive old growth trunks that towered around them on all sides. The creek ran along a gulch between two slopes that angled upward to their left and right. At times

the gradient of the hills was moderate, but in other places the land rose steeply away from the water.

In a short while they came to a bend in the creek where a rockslide had once tumbled down the western slope. The ground to their right was littered with half-buried rocks and boulders, ranging in bulk from the size of a man's head to half the length of their floater. Here the hillside was only moderately steep, and the trees grew a bit more widely spaced than in most areas of the hollow. A visible animal path meandered over the groundcover vegetation, tracking its way upslope around trees and rocks.

Sarah turned the floater to follow the path's direction, weaving over fallen logs and around obstacles as they gained elevation. The hill was sizable and the going slow, and it took a handful of minutes to reach the crest of the rise. When the floater topped the ridge, Sarah took it straight down the other side. In awhile the land leveled out again into a small valley, wherein coursed a creek slightly smaller than Byre's. Turning left to head upstream, they followed the water through a green meadow dotted with yellow and purple flowers. Post-dawn mists still clung to the ground here and there, and large insect-toid life resembling iridescent butterflies fluttered in the early morning light.

As they proceeded up the valley, the ground became gradually more rocky and broken, and they reentered the woods. Eventually the land began to hump and buckle, and the way steepened. Even here the forest remained thick and pristine, with Ironwood trees vying for space with many other species of plant life, both large and small. The undergrowth was a solid thicket in places; it would have been tough going had they needed to hack through at ground level.

The creek now splashed and tumbled in a series of small waterfalls, as it fell over shelves and outcrops on its descent through the rough terrain. The valley narrowed until they were hemmed in by forested slopes on either side, the sky shut out by the looming hills and a solid canopy of green overhead. The rock around them began to sprout vertical black pillars with odd

hexagonal shapes. These reached skyward, some many meters tall, like fingers of buried titans grasping for air. Between the rock columns and the ranks of trees it was becoming increasingly difficult for the floater to navigate the terrain. Just as Simon was starting to think that they would have to continue on foot, Sarah squeezed their ride through a narrow gap in the stones and he saw their destination.

A small area of flat ground maybe twenty meters on a side lay directly ahead. It too was thickly forested and dotted with the ubiquitous stone columns, and was backed by a high bluff. At some point in the past most of the undergrowth had been cleared away, making the site feel open and airy compared to what they had been traveling through.

Toward the rear of the area, amidst a cluster of old growth Ironwoods, sat a square, one-story cabin. The age-darkened logs comprising its sturdy walls and roof were covered with mossy saprophytes, making it seem as if it had stood there as long as the forest itself. Its simple design spoke of durability and functionality rather than style. Small windows and a single front door were the only visible adornments. A stone chimney ran up the outside of one wall, ending a meter above the sloped roof. Despite being the only artificial construct for kilometers, the cabin felt like it belonged there, as if the woods and the rocks had somehow given rise to the structure when it was needed.

Sarah gently set the floater down on level ground between the trees, about thirty meters from the building. "Well, guys, here we are," she said, grinning. "Quite a sight, isn't it?"

Simon asked, "Have you been inside?"

She shook her head. "No, the door is locked. We figured we'd wait until we brought someone back before breaking it open."

"Let's go have a look," Tyrus declared, raising the floater door.

They got out and approached the structure slowly, alert for signs of danger. Sarah and Tyrus headed the group, guns drawn. They moved almost soundlessly as the soft loam beneath their feet cushioned their steps. The burble of the creek sounded close

to their right, just out of view. Seeing nothing out of place, they walked up close to the cabin, examining its exterior.

Tyrus grunted in appreciation, pointing to the corners where the wall timbers came together. "Would you look at this," he commented approvingly. "Whoever built this place knew something about old-time construction. Mortise and tenon joints, no nails...this thing will stand until the rain and bugs rot the wood away."

As he talked, Simon walked up to one of the small windows, rubbing it to clear off the dirt. He shaded his eyes and stepped close to peek inside. It took a moment to adjust to the dim interior, and then he saw what appeared to be a table in the middle of the room, and boxes stacked against one wall. A fireplace, and maybe a counter with a sink along one wall...suddenly he was staring into a pair of large round eyes pressed against the glass, and he let out a yelp and fell backwards. The afterimage of slitted pupils surrounded by vivid red irises burned in his mind's eye, and he pointed at the window as the others turned to him with weapons raised. "In there, something big!" he gasped, stumbling to his feet and pulling his Service pistol.

"Large enough to be dangerous?" Tyrus asked, sidling up to the wall next to the window.

"Easily," Simon answered. "From what I saw, it's at least as large as an adult human, maybe bigger."

Sarah and Tyrus exchanged glances, and her father said, "Well, whatever's in there, it's occupying our space, so we need to get it out. Simon and Sarah, flank the door with your weapons. T. J., stand about fifteen paces back, facing the entry head on. I'll get the lock open, and swing the door wide when you're ready."

They nodded and took their positions. When they were set, Tyrus approached to examine the portal. The mechanism was simple, a single round knob that could be grabbed and turned to work the latch, and lacking any visible locking device. A metal hasp was attached to the frame, securing the door with a portable lock that looked sturdy but was badly corroded. Even

had he possessed the key, Tyrus was doubtful the thing would open.

He said over his shoulder, "You brought the zip blade, right?"

"Yes," T. J. answered.

"Then run and get it," Tyrus said. "I don't want to damage the door too much by forcing it."

In a minute T. J. returned with the saw, and when it was tuned, he deftly cut the lock in half without touching the door hasp. "Nice work," his father complimented, and T. J. grinned as he backed off, resuming his ready stance with his sidearm. Tyrus used his gun barrel to jiggle the smoking lock, and it fell in pieces on the ground. "Ready, people," he said. "Here we go!" With that he turned the knob and kicked the door in.

Dust flew outward as the hinges squealed in protest, the dark opening yawning like the maw of a beast. For a few seconds nothing happened. The group stood frozen with guns leveled, Tyrus backing off to the side as he watched the open door. Then a scraping sound issued from the interior, followed by a rustling as of dried skin and bones sliding together. They tensed as something moved within the shadows, and then it came toward the door.

"I see it!" T. J. shouted, and he aimed at the shape, which came forward into the light, and resolved—into a large bird.

The flyer shot out of the cabin in a flurry of golden wings. Simon glimpsed a broad head comprised almost entirely of two huge eyes, which it squinted at them before arching upward toward the canopy above with powerful down strokes. Diminishing into the distance, it emitted a long mournful cry that echoed back through the woods. As the sound reached their ears, Sarah lowered her weapon and snorted in disbelief. "A Glimmer Owl!" she exclaimed, chuckling. "*That's* what we were afraid of?"

T. J. turned toward Simon with a smirk. "As big as a grown man?" he asked, eyebrow raised.

Tyrus grinned. "Maybe larger," he added.

They all had a good laugh at Simon's expense, and then they

got to the business of investigating the cabin. "Window's busted in the back wall," T. J. said as they poked around the interior. "That's how it got in. Looks like it may have been nesting here, based on how much flyer poop is on the floor."

"The boxes are mostly empty, a few have old clothing and some dried-out food packages," Sarah said. "Nothing really useful."

Tyrus nodded and said, "Let's get to cleaning out this place. I'll set up a work light in here so it's easier to see. I need to check the structural integrity of the roof and walls, but overall this looks good. Sarah, once we get the floater unloaded, you can head back to the house and pick up more supplies and your other two brothers. We'll put them to work out here, doing reconnaissance and setting up a sensor grid. Make sure to bring back a folding table and chairs; this one's so rickety a breeze could knock it over. We'll dig a fire pit out there in front of the cabin; it can be used for cooking at least some of the time, and a bonfire will help keep forest critters at bay."

"Including owls," T. J. added with a goofy grin.

Simon shook his head, chuckling sheepishly. "You're never gonna let me live that down, are you?"

"Nope," was all Tyrus Junior said.

CHAPTER NINE

Over the next several days the family worked feverishly to set up camp at the remote cabin. Floaters shuttled back and forth nonstop, ferrying people and goods between the main house and their forest getaway.

Soon they had a defensive perimeter established in the woods around the camp, with motion and life sensors, and some carefully placed mines which were harmless until activated by a remote signal. Two heavy tents stood on either side of the cabin, with a large firepit out front. Tyrus had installed a modern door latch which could be locked from inside or out. Sarah and her brothers had scrubbed the place as clean as was practical for a wilderness setting, and they were pretty much set to go. The only thing remaining was to stock a sizable food supply in case they needed to stay awhile.

Tyrus nodded in satisfaction as he checked off another item on his digital pad. "That's got most of the essentials nailed down," he said.

"Don't forget a long-range airwave monitor," Simon reminded him. "If we're out there alone, we'll have no other way to know what's happening in the world, other than by recon sorties, which I'm not too keen on."

"Got it covered," the older man said. "There is one other thing, though."

"What?"

"If we're forced to abandon our home, I'll be damned if I'm going to hand it to the Crabs. If it's going to be wiped out, which

is likely, then I'd prefer it to be in a manner of our choosing."

"Ah-ha. What exactly do you propose?" Simon asked, intrigued.

"That's what I want to talk to you about. It's not entirely legal, but in these times, I'm not sure anyone's gonna care...." He went on to describe what he had in mind, and as he continued, Simon's grin grew wider and wider.

* * * * * * *

A few days later Simon was talking to Katherine in the kitchen of the main house. It was late morning, and they were preparing to load another shipment of foodstuffs into the floaters. "Tyrus and Amanda think we'll be stocked for six months in the wild by the end of this week," she commented as she checked her list of goods. "Longer if we supplement our stored supplies with hunting and gathering. Sarah and Samuel finished harvesting our live crops yesterday, so we've got fresh vegetables for awhile."

"Excellent," Simon said, peeking over her shoulder at the digi-pad. "Just a few more days' work—.

His comment was cut short as Tyrus ran into the room puffing, and barked at them, "Our work is done. We've got to leave—*now*!" Seeing the unspoken question in Simon's eyes, he nodded and said curtly, "Yes, they're coming. We have no time. Gather everyone, quickly!"

Simon and Katherine rushed through the house, alerting the family members to grab essential belongings and get to the floaters. Everyone knew what to do, as they had practiced and planned for this eventuality. After seeing Jessie into the larger shuttle, Katherine turned back to head into the house. "Where are you going?" Simon called. "We've got to get out now!"

"I'm not leaving the Darters!" she said. "I'll just be a moment!"

Simon cursed under his breath and dashed after her. "I'll help you capture them," he said as he caught up. They ran together

into the nursery, and spent a frenzied minute rounding up the flighty little animals from their cage, popping them into spare pouches, before heading back to the floaters. On the way out they passed through the greatroom, and Simon chanced a glance at the vidscreen. What he saw there made him stop in his tracks and stare.

The monitor showed a view of the highway facing south toward Altonia. In the distance, still a kilometer or more away, advanced an alien armada of a magnitude beyond Simon's worst expectations. A score of floaters and tracked vehicles filled the highway from shoulder to shoulder, with massed foot soldiers too numerous to count scuttling around the vehicles. Flying high over the ground troops were two assault craft of the typical ovoid Knacker design, plus a third disc-shaped craft which looked massive enough to wipe out the house by simply sitting on it. This was definitely the time to run.

"Simon! Come on!" Kate called from the doorway, and he tore his eyes away from that image of approaching death. They ran toward the front of the house and out the door, and Simon had the presence of mind to slam it closed behind them. No reason to give the Crabs a clue that they had abandoned their stronghold. One floater was already skimming across the fields, the other waiting for them with open doors. Simon dived in, pulling Katherine after him. "Go!" he told the driver, which turned out to be Keith. He nodded and gunned the engine, and they all held on as the vehicle banked sharply and went straight over the wall, skimming it by less than a meter. Then they were clear and accelerating over the crop fields toward the untilled grasslands beyond.

Katherine turned to look somberly behind them, and Simon knew what she was thinking. Following her gaze, he took in the receding house and surrounding lands, sitting proudly in the open countryside. This family had made their livelihoods there, had found a home which they had filled with laughter and love and memories. Now they were leaving, and probably they would never see this place in its present form again. Simon

reached for Katherine's hand, and she gripped his tightly as they fled toward the unknown.

Keith kept the floater low and pushed the acceleration to maximum. They flew over the ground at breathtaking speed, landscape features blurring by them as they strove to put distance between themselves and the house. Simon kept looking back, but could see nothing approaching over the flatlands as yet. It looked as if they had gotten out in time.

Within minutes they approached the forested slopes of the western hills, and they turned to find the outflow of Byre's Creek. The deep woods of Dark Hollow beckoned invitingly as they drew near, but Tyrus spoke up from the front passenger seat. "Halt just outside the trees for a moment."

Simon and Katherine looked at each other in surprise. "Why stop here?" she asked. "We're in the open and could be spotted when the Crabs come. We've got to get under cover!"

"I want to see this happen," Tyrus gritted. "No Knacker is going to take our homestead without paying the price." With that he held up a little remote device, and Simon began to smile as he realized what the other man had in mind. He assured Kate that it was all right, as Tyrus broke out a farscope and began scanning the far distance for signs of movement.

They waited about fifteen minutes before the retired captain said, "Ah, there they are! Come on in, you slime. Come get what papa has for you."

Katherine looked quizzically at Simon, and he just held his hand up in a "be patient" gesture, then pointed for her to watch out the window.

Tyrus dialed the farscope up to maximum gain, and it clearly showed the mass of troops and support vehicles advancing slowly toward the house across the flat ground in front. At this distance they looked like little spiders creeping. It appeared that some of the force was breaking off to surround the building, preventing any escape attempt. He grinned fiercely. *Too late, little Crabs, your prey has already left. All you have is an empty nest, with a little something extra to remember us by.*

Prepared though he was, he flinched as he saw puffs of smoke shooting up from the massed forces, and a series of explosions rocked the house. They were hitting it with heavy grenade salvos. Apparently they had been instructed to wipe out this human threat, and live captives were not a priority. He saw a corner of his home crumble and fall, leaving a gaping wound about where his bedroom had been. *Damn them! They will pay, and pay dearly.*

The bombardment continued for a number of minutes, pecking away at the building and its surrounding yard, before the aliens ceased fire. Possibly the lack of a response had them puzzled, or maybe they thought that they had destroyed any defensive capabilities the humans might have had. But they were being cautious, Tyrus noted, holding the troops at a safe distance while they observed the house for signs of life.

After an indeterminate time, he saw movement at the top of his field of view, and he raised the farscope slightly to focus on the newcomer. It was the largest of the alien assault craft, and it was now gliding forward high over the ground forces, slowly closing distance with the house. The ship was massive, nearly as large as the entire building, and it hovered maybe a hundred meters above ground as it took up position directly over the family's home. Even without the farscope, the other passengers in the floater could see the alien craft in the distance, and they knew from the location what its target had to be.

Tyrus cursed as the alien ship spat a beam of brilliant energy down at his home. Just a split second flash in his farscope, and the house exploded outward in an expanding ball of smoke and fire that instantly enveloped the surrounding landscape. He held the scope steady, his heart numb as he watched the product of years of sweat and devotion wiped away by an implacable foe. A few seconds later a low rumble resembling thunder reached their ears. The humans in the floater sat frozen, watching the rising cloud in the distance.

The haze obscured the overhead attacker momentarily, but as Tyrus watched through the scope, the air cleared, revealing the

silver shape still hovering undamaged over the scattered remains of what had been a two-story building. "You like explosions, do you?" he muttered to himself. "Try this one on for size." He raised his left hand, the one holding the remote trigger, and depressed the single button in its center.

The device he had planted in the cellar below the house, the one he had confided to Simon about, was a little piece of hardware no larger than a dinner plate. It was something he had found during his time in the ground forces bomb squad. His last years in the service had included time spent decommissioning explosives, charges that had been planted by humans in anticipation of an alien invasion. The military had at one time mined key installations, both military and civilian, with devices that could be triggered remotely. The thinking was that if the Crabs occupied a facility, one flick of a switch would wipe out considerable numbers of the enemy, including possibly some of their command structure. Calmer minds had later concluded that having highly volatile explosives distributed throughout densely populated areas may not have been the wisest tactic. The military was then ordered to remove these "contingency bombs" from all civilian sites.

Tyrus had found and deactivated numerous explosives during his time in the ground forces. Most he had turned in for disposal as was mandated. But he hadn't been able to resist the temptation to keep one or two for himself, knowing what was likely coming in Eden's future.

The little beauty planted under his home was an antimatter bomb, a small one, rated at only about 0.3 kilotons. But size is relative, and the device generated a destructive energy equivalent to the detonation of three hundred tons of conventional high explosives. The blast that resulted when the bomb went off was over ten times what the alien weapon had produced. It also had completely different consequences.

When Tyrus hit the trigger, the entire area in his viewer went white, as a huge fireball hundreds of meters in diameter materialized in a wink. The Knackers' ground forces were wiped

out instantly, swept away in a conflagration that no light armor could withstand. The expanding mass of energy engulfed the disc of the assault craft directly overhead, throwing it up into the air as the shock wave smashed into its underside, flames clawing at its metallic skin. The ship was built of heat resistant materials and did not burn, but the force of the impact damaged its propulsion systems and stunned the crew inside. It rose for a moment, buoyed by the expanding pillar of heat from below. Then it listed to one side and fell, diving edge first toward the ground.

The ship's weight drove it deep into the soil on impact, and the hull compressed as the metal succumbed to stresses far exceeding its design parameters. The slender disc suddenly became short and fat, rupturing open along its margins and spewing thick black smoke. The two smaller ovoid craft were out of the direct blast zone and survived the explosion. They pulled back rapidly as their larger comrade began to burn on the ground. Tyrus clenched his fist around the detonator and hissed, *"Swallow that, you hungry bastards."*

The sound of the second explosion came to them clearly now, a prolonged growl of vengeance carried on the wind. Even as the distant rumble began to subside, Tyrus drew a sharp breath and said, "I think we'd better get moving." He lowered the farscope and added, "The remaining ships are heading this way."

Simon asked, "How do they know to come here?" even as Keith punched the vehicle forward into the woods.

"They may have tracked the signal from my detonator," Tyrus said, tossing the device aside. "Maybe they just saw us. However they know, we don't want to be caught in the open."

Keith piloted the floater as fast as he dared through the hollow, pushing the limits of safety in the cluttered corridor. Several times they were jarred by impacts as he cut corners and bounced the vehicle off logs and trees. Even so, the pace seemed like a crawl to the anxious passengers. They looked behind them repeatedly, waiting for the inevitable image of the Crab vessels in pursuit. If the enemy got within firing distance,

it would be over very quickly.

Nothing appeared to be following them, however, and with great relief they spotted the slope where they would leave the hollow for the deeper woods.

Keith turned the floater up the hill, and for a few minutes they wound their way through the forest as they gained elevation. Simon had just begun to breathe easier when a bolt of plasma ripped into a tree trunk in front of them. They veered sharply as shreds of bark rained across the window. Simon yelled, "Where the hell did that come from?"

"Get up the hill fast!" Tyrus directed. He didn't have to ask twice. Keith hit the accelerator, and they were thrown back into their seats as the floater leapt forward. More glowing bolts ripped the landscape around them, and they appeared to be coming from above.

"They're flying over the forest canopy!" Simon said, and Tyrus nodded.

"How are they firing if they can't see us?" Katherine asked, holding on to Simon as they rounded a boulder. A plasma impact chipped fragments off the rock, narrowly missing them.

"Their sensors are probably tracking the floater's energy emissions," Tyrus said. "We need to find a sheltered spot and kill the power."

"You mean stop and sit?" Keith asked incredulously, glancing over at his father.

"Yes, that's our best option," Simon said. "We need to do it soon, somewhere that's shielded from direct hits, like maybe against a large rock or tree."

"If you say so," Keith replied, wrenching the controls as he maneuvered the craft around the base of an Ironwood. He gunned the engine again and the floater shot toward the hilltop. They crested it a few moments later, going so fast that they shot out into space as the ground abruptly dropped away on the other side. "Hold on!" he told them as the nose of the floater came down. "This may be a rough landing."

The vehicle was not designed to maintain elevation of

more than a few meters above ground, and their momentum had carried them considerably higher. The repulser fields had nothing to push against as they dived back to earth, free falling over the crest of the ridge as plasma bolts sizzled the air above them. The ground rushed to meet them, and as they were about to impact, the floater's energy field engaged once more. The repulsers whined as they strained to keep them from bottoming out, but the speed of their descent was too great. Overloaded, the generator blew, and the floater plowed hard into the dirt, sliding down the slope for a hundred meters before coming to rest against a downed tree.

Everyone sat in their seats, stunned, for several seconds after the vehicle stopped moving. Tyrus's voice spoke first, "And that's why we wear harnesses. Is everyone all right?"

No one was seriously hurt. Simon looked out through the windows, and saw plasma bolts ripping up the ground a good distance up slope behind them. Tyrus said, "Ay, they're shooting at the last place we had energy emissions. After we hit, the floater went dead. We slid most of the way without power."

"So we're safe, for now," Simon said. "We'll have to walk it from here, though."

"We're not all that far from the cabin, just five or six klicks," Keith said. "We can easily make it before dark."

"Let's get moving," Tyrus answered. "I do not want to be wandering in the woods at night."

They grabbed their weapons, and the few supplies they had brought in the floater, and carefully eased the doors open. The barrage behind them had tapered off, and an uneasy quiet reigned. Hefting their baggage, the four moved away from the wrecked vehicle and slowly began the trek down the slope.

Over three hours later they finally limped into camp, tired and sore. Although the distance hadn't been great, they had had to toil through rough terrain, heavy undergrowth, and a steady uphill climb on the final leg. Add in the stress of being on constant alert for a surprise attack, and they were exhausted.

The rest of the family were anxiously awaiting them, and

everyone had to hear about their flight from the Knackers, the loss of the floater, and most of all the final fate of their home. Jessie could hardly be pried from her mother's side, as she had obviously feared the worst when they had failed to arrive on time.

Eventually Amanda intervened, saying, "All right, everyone, they've been through a lot today; we all have. Let's let them get cleaned up and rest a bit, then we'll get dinner started." She beckoned to Simon and Katherine, saying, "I've heated some water for bathing; it's in a big pot on the counter. You can take it into the right-hand tent and wash up; conserve as much water as you can." They thanked her and went off to lose the trail dirt.

That evening the family had their first supper in their new abode, eating around a pair of tables in the middle of the cabin. Tyrus had rigged lights powered by a fuel cell that would last for years. Later, as twilight gave way to the starless black of night in the forest, they gathered around the firepit to warm their bones and share companionship. A roaring fire was a calculated risk, but one they felt worthwhile, both for its warmth and protection, as well as for the peace of mind it brought. There was something primal about flame, at once energizing and relaxing to the spirit. Simon could feel the remnants of the day's tension ebbing as he sat on a folding chair next to Katherine, watching the red and yellow tendrils flicker and dance.

When it came time to sleep, the three shelters were divided up by mutual agreement, with the two couples each having a tent, and the other five young people sharing the cabin. Simon was worried that Sarah and the brothers would resent being crammed under one roof, but they seemed relieved to have the more protective walls of the cabin around them.

He and Katherine bid the others good night and retired to their tent. They fell asleep in each other's arms, wrapped in a warm bedroll, to the background sounds of small creatures chirping and the faint crackle of the fire outside.

* * * * * * *

Tyrus called a meeting in the cabin the following afternoon, to discuss recent events and the Knackers' likely response. They sat around the two tables and looked at a large topographic chart of the homestead property and surrounding region. "I'm worried," Tyrus said, hands clasped in front of him. "The Crabs know the region we've headed into." He tapped the area in question on the map. "They followed us further than I had hoped for, and they know the spot where our shuttle died. If I were them, I'd send soldiers to investigate that locale on foot or in small floaters."

"Then they'll find our vehicle," Simon concluded.

"Yes. From that, they'll be able to surmise that we've not gone very far. Our path on foot may also be traced, either via physical signs or chemical signatures we left behind."

"So we have to expect that they may find us here," Keith said.

"How long until they come, do you think?" Amanda asked, a frown creasing her brow as she scanned the map.

Tyrus shrugged. "It's hard to say. They could be here soon, if they've got the resources and motivation to seek us out. Or it could be delayed for weeks, as the attacks at the house were."

"Any information on the airwaves?" Simon asked him.

"Nothing specific. There's still a surprising amount of human transmissions coming through; I'd have thought those would have been silenced by now. But nothing I've heard, either human or Knacker, relates directly to us."

"So we'll have to wait it out," Katherine said, snatching a stray bug that had crawled across the table. She opened the pouch at her neck and dropped the treat to her Darter who grabbed it hungrily.

"I'm afraid there's not much else we can do," Tyrus replied. "It would be best to devise a defensive plan now, figuring out where each of us should be if an attack comes, how to get into position quickly if awakened during the night, and so forth.

"We should also scout a possible escape route to use if things turn ugly. Sarah, why don't you and Samuel check out the land behind the cabin, see what's over the bluff and how easy it will

be to retreat under fire. Later today we'll go through some field drills."

With Simon and Tyrus overseeing the exercises, the family learned the features of the terrain around the cabin over the next two days. They plotted out ideal firing positions, fields of coverage for each defender's weapon, and the most likely avenues to be used by an attacking force. Tyrus and Keith set up additional land mines along the primary approaches, and triggered them to be activated by a single remote signal. Sarah found a negotiable path over the bluff behind the cabin, but as she put it, "It's rough going, and I'd not want to have to climb up there while under fire."

Tyrus glanced at Simon when she gave them the news. His expression was neutral, but they could tell he didn't like what he heard. "Well," he answered after a moment's reflection, "We'd better make sure we hold them off. I'm not keen on leaving anyway. If we're pushed out of here, we'll truly be fugitives on the run with no resources and no refuge."

"Do you think we can keep them at bay?" Simon asked, eyes narrowed.

"I believe so," Tyrus nodded. "The Crabs don't like the woods, and the density of vegetation in here will prevent them from bringing heavy equipment to bear. We know the terrain, and we've had a chance to dig in. I've modified enough alien plasma guns for each family member to have one. We've also got several of the Knacker grenade launchers. All the advantages fall to us. I'm not even sure the Crabs will make more than a token effort to find us, now that we've gone underground."

On that last account he was dead wrong. Two days later, just as noon approached, the perimeter alarms abruptly went off on their wrist units. Tyrus leapt up from the table in the cabin, where he had been going over supply lists with Amanda. "Everyone to their stations!" he yelled as he ran for the door, grabbing his weapons and gas mask as he went.

Once outside, he whistled and shouted, "Take defensive positions, people! Weapons at the ready! Don your masks now, and

be sure they're tight! Get tucked into your spots, we don't want anyone hit by sniper fire! Boys, grab your grenade launchers. The rest of you, be sure you've got your hand grenade belts."

Tyrus hustled to the near tent and retrieved his remote control unit. As he exited through the door flap, he bent low and scurried across the encampment to his designated defensive position. Upon reaching cover he held his wrist com to his mouth and said quietly, "Is everyone accounted for?"

One by one they reported in. Simon was across the way behind a large boulder. The three brothers each had a tree trunk they stood behind, guns in hand. They also had alien grenade launchers leaning against their trees. Katherine and Jessie had taken up positions in the cabin windows, with weapons propped in the openings. Amanda and Sarah were off to his right behind a large fallen log.

When all the family had sounded off, he nodded, satisfied that no one was caught out in the forest. Glancing at the control box in his hand, he punched the switch that activated the defensive mine grid.

As he did so, a detonation rocked the woods a short distance down the slope, followed by the shrill screech of an alien vocalization. Tyrus grinned; one mine had found its mark. As the echoes died away, the forest went deathly still, all the normal animal sounds absent. Peeking around the trunk of the Ironwood that was his shelter, he scanned the area beyond the camp intently, searching for the enemy. Nothing moved among the trees; even the air was motionless. Minute after minute ticked by, time stretching interminably as the defenders waited in taut anticipation.

Abruptly the crack of a second explosion, and then a third, reverberated through the stillness, one coming from a point straight ahead of him, the other off to the left. Tyrus welcomed each report as the likely death of a Knacker, but he worried about what size force might be advancing up the hill toward them. He suspected they would find out all too soon.

Staying tight against the smooth bark of his tree, he glanced

over at Simon. The other man crouched behind his boulder, cradling his heavy automatic rifle. Catching Tyrus's look, Simon nodded back, his masked face inscrutable. Tyrus flashed him a thumbs-up sign. It was time to get down and dirty.

As Tyrus turned back to view the woods in front of him, a flicker of motion jerked his gaze to the right. For an instant he could see nothing in the jumble of vegetation, then his brain sorted the chaos and he spotted a long jointed leg protruding from behind a thick shrub. He reacted without thinking, yanking the muzzle of his gun around, and clawing at the trigger as it came to bear on the target. A plasma bolt erupted from his weapon and blew a smoking hold through the shrub. The branches shook violently and a Crab burst out of the greenery, sporting severed stumps where three of its right-sided legs should have been. An intact limb raised a weapon and fired in a blur of speed, and Tyrus barely had time to squeeze off a round before he had to duck behind his tree.

When he did so, Sarah and Amanda opened up with their weapons, plasma bolts flashing in tandem as they lit up the alien. Tyrus chanced a look and saw the Crab jerk and spin as the lances of energy impaled it, and the alien went down in a smoking heap within seconds.

As the body hit the ground, the forest erupted with a fusillade of plasma fire that seemingly came from everywhere. Blue-white energy hits ripped the cabin, blowing deep chunks out of the walls. The beams came fast and hot, impacting tree trunks, rocks, and vegetation with equal abandon. There was nothing the humans could do except hunker down and hope that they stayed alive. The two tents went down instantly, collapsing in burning heaps as the alien weapons riddled them. Smoke filled the air as vegetation ignited and small fires flared all around the camp.

Stray plasma charges shattered the cabin windows and glanced off the frames of the open portals wherein Jessie and Katherine resided. Simon hissed into his wrist com, "Stay down, everyone! Kate and Jess, do *not* try to rise up and use

your weapons! We've got to reduce the weight of fire we're receiving. Those of you with grenade launchers, use them! Stay in cover while firing!"

So saying, Simon pulled an incendiary hand grenade from his belt, and squeezed both sides simultaneously, arming it. Working from memory, he reached around the trunk of the tree and threw the weapon as far as he could muscle it, toward what he hoped was a gap in the forest ahead of him. His aim was true, and the grenade flew in an arc down the slope into a thicket of trees. It detonated on impact, its explosive core igniting dozens of pellets which flew outward at hundreds of meters per second. The compound used in the flammable projectiles burned at a temperature of nearly 3100^0 C. Whatever it touched caught fire.

By dint of sheer luck, the grenade Simon had thrown hit quite a lot. Three Knackers were hiding in the brush adjacent to the impact point, and the vegetation—and the aliens within—were instantly engulfed in flames. The plasma guns that the aliens had been using to lay down suppressing fire now discharged spasmodically into the surrounding forest. The random bolts in turn ignited other bushes and struck several of their comrades, maiming two and killing another outright.

Other fireballs erupted as the brothers let loose with their launchers, and grenades cascaded down on the attackers. Here and there they hit live targets, and burning Crab bodies careened through the woods spreading flame through the dry late summer foliage.

The resulting gaps in the attacking force lowered the incoming fire to the left side of the encampment. As the pressure eased, Simon barked into his wrist unit, "Samuel, Keith and T. J., fire your energy weapons at will! Protect yourselves at all costs!"

The young men to his left immediately dropped the grenade launchers and whipped around their protective tree trunks, opening up with their plasma rifles. Simon added his heavy automatic to their fire, the gun growling out a staccato counterpoint to the snap and sizzle of the energy weapons. Tyrus and

the women joined in from his right. Together they laid down a deadly barrage along the primary approach routes to the camp.

Simon cursed as he swept his gun across the woods and back again. The forest was alive with scuttling shapes, too many for him to count. They came up the slope and into view beyond the edge of the camp, and as fast as he could mow them down, more arrived to take their place. He saw Crabs scurrying up the far side of the larger trees, their clawed limbs the only parts visible as they wrapped around the trunks. When they had achieved a height advantage, the aliens peeked around and began firing down upon the defenders. The incoming fire was mounting once again, forcing the humans to take cover. Just as Simon thought it couldn't get any worse, it did.

A droning sound overhead penetrated his awareness over the noise of the combat. Glancing up into the forest canopy he saw nothing. He was about to look away when suddenly a brilliant flash seared his retinas. A plasma beam hundreds of times more powerful than a rifle bolt ripped down from the sky, hitting the far corner of the cabin. Heavy logs flew apart like twigs, and the roof caved in along that entire side.

"Katherine!" Simon screamed, his heart in his throat when he saw the structure collapsing. He cringed as more strikes rained down from above. Explosions rocked the camp and dust choked his lungs as the ground was pockmarked with impact craters. He could barely see through the smoke and debris.

"We're all right," came the faint reply over his com link. "Jessie and I are all right."

With a snarl Simon rose up from behind his boulder and unleashed a volley of armor piercing rounds at a Knacker high on a tree. Bark chips flew as the bullets walked across the trunk. He adjusted his aim and the Crab spasmed, the rounds blowing a hole into its body and out the other side. Yellow and red fluid cascaded outward like a fountain. The creature loosed its hold and fell in slow motion, trailing multicolored streamers as it crashed to the ground far below.

"That's the spirit, Simon!" he heard Tyrus's voice roaring

through the pandemonium around him. "Get the bastards!"

As one the humans resumed firing, unleashing their weapons in a last stand against the doom closing in upon them. Sarah and Amanda plied their energy guns on the camp's right flanks, peeking up from behind their fallen log to raze the woods beyond, then ducking down when return fire sought them out. Tyrus's three sons stood behind their protecting trees, firing bolt after bolt as fast as their guns would discharge. Tyrus and Simon caught Knacker after Knacker in their deadly crossfire, and the forest soil was soaked with the spillage of alien body fluids.

For a glorious moment the tide was turned, and the Crabs wilted under the onslaught, pushed back by the unexpected resolve of the humans. Then the unseen ship overhead unleashed a second volley of energy bolts. Violent explosions ripped the ground around them, blowing the humans off their feet and leaving them stunned. Simon fell to his knees, his ears ringing. He looked up as more Crabs crawled into view between trees, behind rock pillars, everywhere he could see. Their numbers were simply too great, and the odds had finally caught up with the defenders. The only thing the humans could do now was decide how they wanted to die.

The others knew it as well. Through the dust and smoke Simon saw Tyrus on hands and knees behind his tree, and their gazes momentarily met. Over the top of the gas mask Simon could see the hopelessness in the man's eyes. He had done all he could to save himself and his family, and it would not be enough.

The three brothers struggled to their feet and looked at one another. They had often spoken of what they would do if the end came, and no words were needed as they exchanged knowing looks. Almost as one they raised their guns, stepped from behind their cover and opened fire on the advancing aliens. A part of Simon's mind screamed that it was suicide, but he knew there was no alternative. He stood and added his fire to theirs, burning ammunition with no thought to the future. Dimly he

heard Tyrus and the others joining in around him. The aliens maintained their attack, and incoming energy rounds zipped through the air seemingly from every direction. Twice he felt his skin burn as a bolt narrowly missed him, and he knew it was only a matter of time before he went down for good.

Another explosion rocked the forest, loud enough to penetrate his awareness through the battle fog. A heavy cracking and popping sound dragged his gaze upward, and as he did so, the green canopy hiding the sky parted. A flaming ovoid came crashing through the tree branches, gathering speed as it dropped like a rock into the midst of the Knacker ground force. It blew apart on impact, spreading metal fragments and flame in all directions. The Crabs on the ground scattered as they tried to avoid being crushed or incinerated.

Simon just stared for a moment, uncertain what to make of this development. A few seconds later he heard the rumble of flyers overhead, and a series of flashes lit the forest beyond the encampment. Muffled concussions echoed through the trees. The Knackers within view ceased their fire and froze, turning toward the sound. A second volley of explosions followed, and the aliens suddenly began withdrawing, melting into the woods as quickly as they had come. Within a few moments the dazed humans were alone in the battle-scarred landscape, holding their smoking weapons with no targets left to shoot at.

Tyrus was the first to react, tearing off his mask and raising his arms to the sky. "They've come back!" he shouted, turning to the other defenders with a jubilant look on his face. "SpaceForce has returned to Eden! They're kicking Knacker butt!" Even as he spoke, further detonations could be heard as the unseen forces in the sky rained down destruction on the alien ground troops.

The family members stood staring numbly, too shell shocked to react at first. Slowly they began to realize what had happened, and a ragged cheer went up from multiple throats as despair gave way to relief, then exultation. Simon dropped his weapon and ran for the cabin, kicking in the door and franti-

cally searching for Kate and Jessie. He found them huddled in the corner, shaken but alive. Jessie sobbed and threw herself into his arms, wrapping him tight as he reached out a hand to pull Katherine to her feet. Her face was smudged with dirt and streaked with tears, but to his eyes she had never looked prettier. The three of them clung together in a close embrace as they stood motionless in the ruined dwelling, sharing the warmth of being alive for another day.

They eventually exited the cabin to find the family gathered on the left side of the campsite. To Simon's surprise the mood was somber, no one celebrating their last minute reprieve from certain death. Tyrus was staring at his boots, his weapon hanging limply from one hand. As they approached, he heard a woman sobbing, and he realized it was Amanda. She was kneeling on the ground, bent over something. His heart lurched when he saw that it was a prone body.

He and Katherine rushed toward the group, hoping to help, but Tyrus looked up and shook his head, his jaw muscles clenching. One look in his eyes told them everything. Amanda glanced up at their approach, and when she shifted Simon could see that the person on the ground was T. J. He was not moving, and the smooth hole burned into the center of his forehead was testament that he would never rise again.

Katherine began crying, "Oh, no...no, no, no! Not T. J.! He was so young, he had his whole life...." Simon held her close as the sobs racked her, knowing there was nothing else that he could offer. He felt her pain, knew it all too well, and he knew how terribly long it would take for the family to heal. But heal they would, with the help of each and every one of those who were still living. He gathered Katherine and Jessie to him, stroking their hair as they clung to each other. They would draw strength from their closeness in the times ahead. This is what the Knackers didn't understand, what they always would underestimate. No matter the course of events, the human spirit would not easily be broken. Humankind might be wounded, but they would not stop fighting this menace from the stars. Not

until every last man, woman, and child was dust.

For now, it was time to rest and mourn, and that is what they did, huddled in the midst of the war-torn campsite in that lonely place in the forest.

* * * * * * *

They buried T. J. in a small grave near the cabin, in a place overlooking the stream where he had enjoyed sitting during quiet times. His two older brothers lowered his shrouded body gently into the earth, gazing silently at their sibling for the last time. No more silly jokes would they endure, no more pranks on unsuspecting family members. As they bid their brother goodbye, it was his sense of humor they remembered most, and they realized how much they would miss his laughter as they lived out the rest of their lives.

The family members took turns filling the grave, each adding a few shovels' worth of earth before passing the implement to the next person. Simon was last, and he tamped the dirt firmly down before backing away. They marked the spot with an Ironwood marker that bore his name. Amanda had engraved it using T. J.'s zip blade. Then they stood in a rough circle as they paid their final respects. A warm breeze wafted softly over them, carrying the sounds and smells of living things, a reminder of nature's steady strength amidst the turmoil that beset them. It was a peaceful setting, beautiful with the water and the rocks and trees all around. Simon thought that it was a fitting place to rest, when all one's work was done.

CHAPTER TEN

For two more months the family remained at the cabin. Tyrus monitored airwave transmissions from the radio set which somehow had survived the firefight. The news was encouraging; the Federation forces had set upon the Knackers in a surprise attack, and were slowly retaking the planet. After wiping out the alien fleet still in orbit, the humans had used space-based rail guns and mass launchers to destroy the alien landers where they sat on the ground. The mass launchers threw small meteorites of nickel-iron composition, common space debris that could be harvested with ease. When shot from the launchers on an exact trajectory, these crude projectiles accelerated down the planet's gravity well to hit with devastating force on the surface. Precisely chosen for their size, so as to not burn up in the atmosphere, but also not to cause more than local destruction, the impacting rocks reduced the massive alien pyramids to piles of melted slag with stunning efficiency.

Each destroyed landing vessel took with it tens of thousands of Knacker soldiers. To overrun those structures with ground troops would have meant prolonged bloody battles and loss of countless human troops. On the down side, the ships were already loaded with thousands of human prisoners, all of whom were lost in those initial assaults. Such was the heavy price of war. Simon consoled himself with the knowledge that the people on board those harvest vessels at least died cleanly, saved from the nightmarish end the Crabs had planned for them.

The family stayed busy, in part because their survival

depended on it, and partly to avoid dwelling on the loss of their youngest boy. They repaired the damage to the cabin, making it weatherproof and livable once again. The tents were beyond hope, but they were able to salvage some goods that hadn't been consumed in the fires. Food and clothing were in shorter supply than had been planned, and Tyrus took his sons into the woods regularly to hunt and gather fresh foodstuffs. Living under one roof was crowded, but they were beyond any embarrassment or awkwardness at this point, and everyone pitched in to make it work.

It was late autumn, with days becoming short and a chill in the air, by the time Simon and the McKinleys left the cabin for good. They slowly made the trek on foot through the deep forest, over the hills and out into the grasslands of the homestead. As they exited Dark Hollow at last, they stopped and looked around, squinting in the unaccustomed light of the open sky as they took in the outside world for the first time in months.

Tyrus spoke for them all when he said, "It's damned good to see the sun again."

Simon nodded, smiling at Katherine as she stood by his side. She had lost some weight, and her hair hung long and unstyled, but she still was the most beautiful thing on Eden. He turned to Tyrus and asked, "Where will they meet us?"

The older man shrugged uncertainly. "Somewhere out on the flats; I gave them our approximate location and homestead designation. We'll just have to head toward the house and see what happens."

Everyone nodded stoically; living in the wilderness had hardened each of them, and the thought of an additional overland trek didn't elicit the slightest protest. They picked up their belongings and began the long hike across the fields, moving at a relaxed pace. Everyone still carried weapons, as much from habit now as from need, but there was no anxiety, no searching the sky for the enemy. It was safe to walk Eden once again.

They actually traversed nearly the entire five kilometers to the homesite before anyone found them. A distant growl turned

into a rumble, and a speck in the southern sky materialized into a Federation transport ship heading their way. It saw them and altered course, slowing and setting down gently a few hundred meters from where they stood waiting. Ironically it was only a short distance from where the Knacker disc ship had crashed and burned during the assault on their home a lifetime before.

Captain Jake Mahoney jumped from the shuttle's landing platform to the ground, striding out to meet the survivors. He was young, in his mid-twenties, fit and trim, with blond hair that bristled in a regulation military cut. He had donned a freshly pressed uniform for the occasion, as he knew one of the personnel he was picking up was a SpaceForce major. He shook his head as he got his first good look at the ragtag group. They stood in a tight cluster holding a motley assortment of weapons, sporting tattered clothes, shaggy hair, and unshaven beards. To him they looked like a bunch of backwoods refugees. Still, they appeared to be in good health, albeit a bit thin.

He approached and hailed the group. "Greetings. I am Captain Mahoney of SpaceForce. Is one of you Major Simon Roy?"

"That's me," a dark-haired man to the left spoke up. He had his arm wrapped around a pretty woman who stood close at his side.

"Nice to see you're alive, sir," the officer said, coming to attention and saluting formally.

"At ease," Simon replied, returning the salute with his free hand. "What's the situation?"

"We've cleared this sector of enemy forces," the captain reported. "Now that we've got resources to spare, we're doing recon and picking up survivors where we can find them. We wouldn't have been this far out yet, except that we got your airwave communication a couple days ago."

"Well, we're certainly glad to see you," Simon said, grinning. "I could use a hot bath and haircut, not to mention a fresh uniform."

"We'll get right on that, Major," the captain told him with a

smile. The officer looked around the landing area, and whistled as he took in the blackened remains of the Crab ship and multiple armored transports that dotted the terrain. "What the hell happened here?" he asked in surprise. "It looks like a major skirmish was fought on this ground."

"There was one, and we kicked the Crabs' tails," Sarah spoke up, her chin thrust proudly forward.

"*You* did this?" the captain asked, eyebrows disappearing into his hairline. "Damn! I'm glad you're on our side. You've done yourself proud, Major." The captain sounded almost reverent as his gaze panned the field.

"I can't take the credit," Simon told the captain. "The rest of the family did their share; if it weren't for them, I wouldn't be here to tell the tale."

"Ah, I see," the ship's officer nodded. "These are your family, then?"

Simon hesitated, unsure of how to respond. Before he could reply, Amanda smiled and said, "Yes, he's part of our family." The others grinned and nodded, looking at Simon with open affection. He felt his face blushing, and simply nodded in return, not trusting himself to speak.

The captain smiled and gestured toward the waiting transport, and the family moved to the vessel where the waiting crew helped them on board. As the ship rose into the sky, Simon had a bird's-eye view of the receding homestead. The rubble of the ruined house was clearly visible in the center of a large scorched circle on the earth, surrounded by skeletons of Knacker assault vehicles. He, and his new family, had lived and fought and forged unbreakable bonds on that ground. Whether they ever came back to settle on it again, it would always hold a dear spot in his memories. Katherine held his hand tightly as the image dwindled to a speck, then the ship turned and flew southward toward civilization.

* * * * * * *

A few weeks later Simon stood on the spaceport landing field, next to the waiting shuttle that would take him to his carrier ship. His old commander, Colonel Hastings, had survived the initial defense of Eden along with his ship, the *Xerxes*. Simon's carrier had escaped annihilation via escape into hyperspace during the battle, and it now orbited the planet awaiting his arrival. It was being restocked with Avenger class fighters as fast as they became available.

Simon stood in his dress uniform, the lapel freshly adorned with a Gold Nova, the SpaceForce award for valor during combat. The family were all there to see him off. Tyrus was muted in his comments, his gaze half focused elsewhere as had been his tendency since that last stand in the forest. Simon took him aside when they had a moment, and spoke earnestly in his ear. "I know you don't want to hear any advice, but I'm going to give you some regardless," Simon began. Tyrus began to protest, but Simon held up his hand and said, "Just listen. I'll only say this once. I've watched you withdraw and become less a part of your family's life since T. J. passed. Believe me when I say that I know what it's like to lose those closest to you. My wife and daughter died in this war. They didn't get a chance to go down in a fair fight; they were taken, and I never knew their exact fate. I have to assume they were processed and became food for some alien dinner party."

Tyrus looked up at that, and Simon knew he had the man's attention. Pain was something the grieving father could relate to, and the fact that Simon had been there already was the only leverage he could use to get through to his friend. He continued, "I wasn't alive when I came to Eden. I was just a shell, something less than a man, and I lived only to exact vengeance on those who had injured me. Don't become that person, Tyrus. It's a lonely existence, and you still have those who need you. Whatever you're feeling, they are going through it as well. Your family needs your strength; give it to them. You'll find that you will heal yourself while you're helping the ones you love."

Tyrus nodded, his expression somber as he stared at the

ground. Finally he cleared his throat and said, "Those are wise words, Simon. I'll take them under advisement. It's just been hard to cope with the reality of him being gone. No father should have to outlive his son."

Simon smiled in sympathy and nodded. "Amen to that. But we can't change the past; we can only live in the present. Lean on your family, Tyrus; they'll be there for you. It's okay to grieve over your son's dying. Just don't let it keep you from celebrating those who are living."

He shook Tyrus's hand, and the other man returned his grip firmly. "Good luck out there," Tyrus said. "You make it back, you hear me? There's two ladies who will be missin' ya something fierce."

"I plan on it," Simon promised him. "Speaking of ladies, I've got to say goodbye to someone." He clapped Tyrus on the shoulder and moved off to where Katherine and Jessie stood together. They smiled as he approached, though little Jess seemed to be fighting back tears.

"Do you have to go, Uncle Simon?" she asked him, her lip trembling.

"Yes, my girl," he said gently. "I've got to help SpaceForce rid the galaxy of those darned Crabs. They'll keep pestering us if we don't get after them. But I'll return when I'm done, I promise."

"You'd better. I'll be really mad if you don't come see us again," Jessie pouted.

"And I'd be really sad if I didn't see you two again," Simon replied, kneeling down to face her. "You take care of your mom for me, okay? And watch over my Darter," he added, undoing the cord around his neck and handing her the small cloth pouch.

"I will," Jessie answered, her face serious. "I won't let the Crabs get us."

"Oh, I know you won't," Simon laughed. "Okay, give me a big hug." No sooner had the words left his mouth than he was wrapped in a steely grip. He held her tightly to him, feeling the warmth of her small body, so like that of his own little girl

in another place, another time. He closed his eyes and sighed. Although he would never forget his wife and child, Jessie and her mother had filled a void where those lost souls had once lived, and their love had allowed him to move on. From this point on, they would be his focus, his family, and he would care for them as his own.

He peeled himself from Jessie's embrace and turned to her mother. Katherine wiped her eyes as she stepped in close to him. The roar of a departing shuttle washed over them, and she waited to speak until the noise faded. "I'm going to miss you, Simon Roy," she said, wrapping her arms around his neck. "Think of me while you're out there, and know we're here for you whenever you return."

"You'll never leave my thoughts," Simon told her, looking into the depths of her dark eyes. "I don't want to go, but I have to."

"I know," she said, her voice unsteady. "Just come back to me. Promise me that."

"I promise," Simon said, and they sealed the deal with a kiss. Then he was walking away across the pavement, turning to wave to the family as he boarded the shuttle. They all waved back, Tyrus and Amanda standing together, their sons Keith and Samuel at their side, Sarah over to their left in a bright blue pantsuit, and Katherine and Jessie holding hands as they smiled at him. He climbed the metal steps into the main shuttle bay, and the doors closed behind him.

As the ship powered upwards, he looked out the small view port at the planet below, thinking of all that he was leaving behind. Chance had dropped him here, and he had found life again, in a place where he had least expected it. He not only had a reason to fight, but now also had something to survive for, and he meant to see the end of this conflict. Eden would always beckon to him, and he would return someday, even if he had to walk through hell to get there.

As his thoughts wandered, the planet's surface slowly receded, until the continents and oceans became visible as

swirls of color below him. Soon the curve of the planet's surface swam into view, and the ship went still further out, until Eden shrank to become a glowing blue orb hanging in the blackness of space. He settled back in his acceleration seat, feeling a tranquility that he hadn't experienced in years. Leaving wasn't so bad, when you knew that home awaited you in the end.

ABOUT THE AUTHOR

DR. MARK E. BURGESS is a veterinarian with a special interest in exotic pets. He has practiced in the Portland, Oregon area for nearly twenty-five years, and is a long-time reader of science fiction and fantasy. His first novel, *Dog Daze & Cat Naps: A Vet Student's Odyssey*, was loosely based on his own experiences, and provided a humorous look at four years in veterinary school. Dr. Burgess currently lives with his loving wife, Denise, and two beautiful daughters, Anna and Sarah.